ALL AT ONCE

All At Once

Emily Bunney

Published By: 4 Horsemen Publications, Inc.

4 Horsemen Publications, Inc.
PO Box 417
Sylva, NC 28779
4horsemenpublications.com
info@4horsemenpublications.com

Cover by Niki Tantillo
Typesetting by Valerie Willis
Edited by Jen Paquette

Library of Congress Control Number: 2023945814

Paperback ISBN-13: 979-8-8232-0320-3
Hardcover ISBN-13: 979-8-8232-0322-7
Audiobook ISBN-13: 979-8-8232-0319-7
Ebook ISBN-13: 979-8-8232-0321-0

Dedication

To you, the reader. Thank you for believing in me and my stories. I appreciate each and every one of you.

Table of Contents

Acknowledgements

I'd like to thank my wonderful friends and family for supporting me yet again, especially during this really difficult year.

Thanks to Jen, Val, Erika, Beau, and all the care bears for their undying support and understanding.

My reading team (Rachel and Sabine), you've embraced my crazy hockey family, and your love for them keeps me tapping away at my keyboard and weaving these stories for you.

And of course, everyone who takes the time to follow me on social media. You allow me to indulge my love of Tyler Seguin and all things hockey.

Thank you again for reading my stories. I never thought I'd be doing this, and it still amazes me every day.

If you enjoyed Trixie and Ford's story, please consider leaving a review. You have no idea how much it helps.

Lots of love

Emily xxx

PROLOGUE

Trixie

Ten years ago

Memphis, Tennessee

I feel ridiculous. The itchy black wig and the cheap sequin-encrusted basque are irritating the shit out of me. Why did I let my boss talk me into attending her annual costume party dressed as Cleopatra? Actually, I know why I let this happen; I'm ambitious and driven, and I want to be the best intern the sports agency has ever seen. I fully intend to get a permanent job at the end of the year, and nothing, not even an itchy, embarrassing costume, is going to stand in my way.

"Trixie! Looking sexy, sweet cheeks."

I turn at the sound of my name and openly roll my eyes. Bob is the other intern at the company, and he's sleazy with a capital S. His dad is a famous quarterback from the nineties, and he's an entitled, arrogant man child who thinks he knows everything about the business. He's constantly undermining me not only because I'm a woman, but because I'm from England. I'm always battling his stupid comments about the way I make my tea and the fact I call soccer football.

"Hello, Bob," I sigh, desperately scanning the room for someone I can talk to instead. But there's no one close, so I guess I'm stuck for the time being. "So, what's your costume supposed to be?"

I scan him from head to toe—he has a magnifying glass hanging around his neck and a black T-shirt with FBI written across the front. Other than those two details, he's just wearing jeans and a scruffy pair of sneakers. This is typical of Bob; his costume is a true reflection of his attitude to life and work—get by with as little effort as possible.

The smug, lecherous smirk that splits his face makes my skin crawl, and as he spins around to reveal the back of his shirt, I can see why he creeps me out so much. Written across his back are the words "Female Body Inspector."

Gross!

"You're very … creative," I say, trying not to visibly gag as he turns around and grabs the magnifying glass, scanning my body.

"And you're very sexy," Bob growls, licking his fleshy lips and openly gawping at my tits. Oh god, he's so disgusting.

"I think you'll find that magnifying glass will be inspecting your colon if you keep looking at my girl like that." The deep Southern drawl makes my bare arms break out in goosebumps, and I feel the large, muscular chest of my boyfriend press against my back.

I try not to smirk at the look of horror on Bob's sweaty face as he literally shrinks several inches before my very eyes.

"Hey Chris, I was just admiring Trixie's … costume," Bob blurts, backing away.

Chris chuckles deeply, close to my ear, and I swear to god my panties almost disintegrate. "Sure you were."

"Oh hey, there's the captain of the Memphis Jazz. I need to talk to that guy." And with that, Bob scuttles away into the crowd.

"Thank you," I sigh, turning around to face the man who's been rocking my world for the last six months.

"Hey there, Sugar." God, his voice is the sexiest sound I've ever heard, but the rest of him isn't bad either. Chris Ford is tall, muscular with sandy blonde hair, moss green eyes that twinkle mischievously, and a sexy smile that lights up his entire face. His slightly crooked nose just manages to add to his good looks instead of detracting from them.

Even dressed as Julius Caesar, he's the most attractive man I've ever been with. He slides his big hands around my waist and slowly gives my bottom a firm squeeze, pulling me against his hard body.

"Your timing is impeccable," I sass before his lips press firmly against mine, and all thoughts of sleazy Bob and my stupid costume fly out of my head. As always, when I'm in Chris's strong arms, I'm completely lost in the moment. It actually scares the shit out of me how quickly I've fallen. I promised myself when I came to the States for college that I wouldn't be distracted by boys, and I managed to keep that promise for most of my time at the University of Memphis.

But then one night, my roommate made me go to a Memphis Jazz hockey game, and my life changed forever. Of course, doing a degree in Sports Management, I'm a fan of most sports, but ice hockey was my least favorite.

Until that night.

I was spellbound by the fast-paced aggressive play from the first period, and in particular, the handsome winger I couldn't stop watching. When he incurred a penalty in the second period for high sticking, he slammed into the Sin Bin right in front of our seats. As he threw his stick down, our eyes locked, and he smiled at me around his mouth guard. I was a goner from that moment on.

At the end of the game, I watched as he spoke animatedly to one of his coaches, his eyes constantly flicking over to me as if he was afraid I was going to leave. He then grabbed a pen from his coach's hand, whipped his jersey off, scribbled something on it, and skated over to us. My roommate squealed with delight as he threw the sweaty jersey over the glass, and I snagged it out of the air before anyone else could grab it. Scrawled across the front were the words, *"Hey Sugar, fancy a date? Call me"* followed by his phone number.

That was the beginning of six months of the hottest, sweetest, most mind-blowing sex of my entire life. I now understand why women follow hockey players around like love-sick puppies.

Talk about stamina!

Now, I've graduated and landed an internship at SPC, and Chris has started his third season with the Jazz. We've lived in a happy little bubble, and we both believe nothing can destroy our perfect world.

"Mmmmm, if I keep kissing you like this, we'll have to find a quiet corner so I can make you come for the second time today," Chris growls as he lets his lips trail down my neck, causing my entire body to vibrate with anticipation.

"You can't talk like that," I gasp, wriggling in his arms. "My boss is right over there."

He chuckles wickedly, and it sends a shiver down my spine. "I love how proper you are. I thought I'd managed to fuck all that English propriety out of you."

Bloody hell—that man's dirty mouth just about sets my knickers on fire.

Suddenly, Chris pulls back and straightens his Roman chest plate. "But you're right. I can't do what I want to do to you in front of your boss and sleazy Bob. Let's get the fuck outta here." He grabs my hand and tries to pull me toward the front door, but his ringing cell phone interrupts our tug of war, and he releases me. "This isn't over. As soon as I'm done with this call, I'm taking you to my place, and I'm gonna make you come all night long."

I feel my cheeks heat up at his naughty words and grab a flute of champagne from a passing waiter to try and calm down. He has a ridiculous effect on me whenever he talks like that, and I just can't help myself. I chug the fizz as I watch Chris take the call, and I can immediately tell it's something important by the way he's waving his hands around and pacing back and forth, gripping his hair. Shit, I hope it's nothing serious. I know he has no living family so it can't be anything like that. Therefore, it must be something to do with his place with the Memphis Jazz. That's the only thing that would make him so agitated.

My stomach starts to twist into nervous knots as I watch him end the call and look over at me, his eyes dark and stormy. Oh shit, this looks bad. I begin to twirl the fabric of my skirt around my fingers nervously as he approaches, his bottom lip clamped firmly between his perfect white teeth.

"Is everything okay?" I ask, reaching out to touch his arm.

"I'm not sure," he mumbles, barely able to look me in the eyes. "I've been traded to the Titans. I have to be in Toronto by Wednesday for a game."

It's as if the floor disappears from beneath my feet, and I can't seem to catch my breath. Did he really say he has to move to Canada in the next few days? I'm not an idiot. I work in Sports Management, so I understand that trades happen, and they happen fast. But this is our life, and it's suddenly imploded.

"Trixie? Are you okay?" Chris's voice sounds like it's coming from the other side of the room. I feel him usher me into a quieter part of the party, and things come back into sharp focus.

"But they can't just trade you like that," I cry, my voice high pitched and squeaky, tears stinging my nose. "What about us?"

The look of anguish in his eyes is almost too much for me to bear, but I can't look away. "Trixie, you know how this works. If I wanna play hockey, I've gotta go where they tell me, at a moment's notice. You know that." He sighs, running his calloused hands up and down my arms. I usually love the rough feeling of his hands on me, but right now I need to think clearly, and I never do when he's touching me.

"That doesn't answer my questions," I snap, taking a step back. "What about us? Are we going to do the long distance thing? Because I can't move to Canada right now. I'm this close to getting a job at SPC, and I can't jeopardize that…"

"For us?" Chris snaps back. "I fucking knew it. I knew your career was more important to you than I am."

It's like his words have punched me in the stomach, and I feel like I'm going to throw up. He's always been so supportive of my career ambitions to be a sports agent. We used to talk long into the night about how I want to set up my own agency one day and represent my clients with integrity and respect. But it seems like he was just saying what I wanted to hear because his real feelings have just slapped me in the face.

"You expect *me* to give up *my* dream and follow you while you pursue yours." It's a statement, not a question, because I already know the answer. He doesn't want a partner; he wants a hockey wife who'll look pretty and churn out babies.

Well, fuck that!

"Trixie, that's not what I'm saying," Chris implores as he steps toward me again, grasping my arms as if I might vanish. "You can be a sports agent anywhere. There are four professional sports teams in Toronto alone…"

"That's not the point!" I cry. "I want to work for SPC. Gloria was the first professional female sports agent, and I have so much to learn from her. I won't give that up. I have six months of my internship left, and if she offers me a job, I fully intend to take it."

"Well, I guess your mind's made up." Chris shrugs, and I see the moment he closes off his heart to me. "It's been fun, but I've gotta pack my shit up and try and find somewhere to stay in Toronto. I'll call you."

I try to keep the quiver out of my voice, but I can still hear it. "Don't bother. If you're walking away from us because I won't follow you, then we're done. Good luck in Toronto."

I spin on my heel and march back into the party, desperately trying to find a bathroom before the tears overflow and ruin my thick Egyptian eye makeup.

Once I'm safely behind a closed door, I slide to the floor and allow the heartbreak of the last ten minutes to consume me. I cry for the loss of the man I thought was the one and the fact he turned out to be just like the rest. He talked a lot about me having a career, but when it came down to it, he expected me to give up my dream. Well, that's not a partnership in my eyes, so I guess it would never work out. I'd always play second fiddle to his career, and that's not what I'm about. I came to America to change my life, leaving the grubby council flat in the East End of London far behind me, wanting every part of the American dream. I guess there's one part I'll never have now—the love of my life has just destroyed my heart, so I'm taking it off the table.

As I drag myself up off the bathroom floor and fix my ruined makeup, I'm determined to show that Beatrix Cavendish from Bethnal Green will be a success above all else.

1

Chris

God damn it, Ford! Stop crowding the goal!" Matt growls as we both fight for possession of the puck. I'm defending Thor's doorstep like my life depends on it, not giving my Assistant Captain any wiggle room to slip it past me into the goal.

"Not a fucking chance, man," I chuckle, coiling my body like a spring, shoving Matt's large frame backward. He loses his balance for a second, and I take the opportunity to sweep the puck clear, looking up long enough to see Bugs, our captain, ready to receive it.

"Motherfu…" I don't hear the rest of what Matt says because I sprint away toward the other end of the rink, where Bugs passes me the puck and I flick it over the shoulder of our second string goalie for a sweet top shelf goal.

As I drop to my knee and fist bump the air in my signature celebration, I hear the string of curses coming from the other team. Bugs pats my shoulder and looks very pleased that we're beating Matt and Nate in this preseason two on two.

We're all back from our summer breaks, tanned, rested, and ready to kick ass this season. I spent some time in Memphis working with the foundation I set up to help kids from disadvantaged backgrounds get college scholarships, and then I headed to Maui where I surfed, hiked a volcano, and had a brief but very satisfying fling with a professional surfer called Callie. As with all my trysts, we were hot and heavy, but my heart was definitely off the menu. It's been closed for the last decade. I love women, and I love spending time with them, laughing and having incredible sex. However, I make it clear from the beginning that that's all I'm offering, and as soon as I sense the woman is catching feelings, I split. This has ended in several different scenarios—sometimes they're great, and we end things amicably, and sometimes I end up with a drink in my face. That's never a great situation, but at least it's better than what happened in Memphis ten years ago when I broke the heart of the most incredible woman and left her behind to pursue my career. I was a young, arrogant asshole who thought my star would always shine brighter than hers, that her career goals paled into insignificance next to mine.

I've never been so wrong about anything in my entire life.

"Okay guys, I'm calling time," Bugs calls, skating slowly toward us, his hair plastered to his head.

"Can't keep up the pace, old man?" Knox laughs from the sidelines, bouncing a puck on the end of his stick.

Bugs pulls his mitt off and flips Knox off, but I must admit he looks exhausted. I suppose running around after an eighteen month old takes its toll. His daughter Sawyer is the cutest little thing, but she's definitely a handful. And even though he and his girlfriend Cameron have just hired a nanny in preparation for the start of the season, they're still very hands-on parents.

"I can keep up just fine, you little shit." Bugs laughs, good-naturedly. "It's this old man you need to keep an eye on. How old are you now, Ford? Thirty-five, thirty-six?"

He puts his arm around my shoulder, and I shrug him off. "I'm thirty-three in October, ass-wipe! Still very much in my prime. Just ask the surfer chick I spent the summer with!"

This elicits some whoops and nudges from the guys as we head down the tunnel toward the locker room, and despite their requests for all the gory details, I'm not that kind of guy. I was taught that manners cost nothing, and I definitely had some good ole Southern values instilled in me. We may have been dirt poor, but my momma was a proud woman, and she made sure I always said please and thank you and showed good manners at all times. She wouldn't stand for anyone commenting that her kid had bad manners or didn't know how to behave.

"You wanna carpool to Coach Casey's party tomorrow?" Knox asks as we change into our Whalers sweats, his light brown skin and black hair still damp from his shower.

I laugh and nod my head; out of the guys here, we're the only two that are single, so I guess it makes sense.

"You're all welcome to spend the night at my place," Matt says as he launches his sweaty jersey into the laundry bin. "Mila's already made up all the spare rooms. It'll save you coming back into the city."

"We'll have the baby so Cam will probably wanna go home, but thanks for the offer," Bugs replies, throwing his duffle over his shoulder. "We'll probably be the first ones to leave anyway."

"The joys of parenthood." Thor, our huge Swedish goalie, laughs.

"Don't laugh too soon, man." Bugs chuckles knowingly. "It'll catch up with you all eventually."

Thor visibly pales because he's in a very new relationship with Matt's little sister Lana. Despite being completely loved up, I'm sure they're not ready for kids yet.

"Don't you dare knock up my sister!" Matt growls, throwing Thor a shitty look. "I'm still getting used to the fact that you're … you know." He makes a gagging noise.

"Making sweet, sweet love every night!" Thor roars with laughter at the look of horror on Matt's face.

"For fuck's sake, man. I don't need to hear that shit!" he grumbles, picking up his duffel. "Just let me know if any of you wanna crash so Mila knows how much food to buy for breakfast. You guys eat like animals."

With that, Matt and Bugs leave, closely followed by Thor and Nate, leaving just me and Knox in the locker room.

"So, a surfer chick, huh?" Knox smirks, his light green eyes twinkling with mischief. "Bet she was hot."

I shrug nonchalantly and put my ball cap on. "She was cool, but it was definitely time to head home when I did. She started talking about meeting up when she comes back to California, so I made sure to make a clean break."

I remember the night I broke it off with her; it was the last day of my vacation so I don't know what she was expecting. But when she started making noises about meeting up when I was due to play in California, I could just sense that she was catching feelings. I'm not a heartless asshole, so I tried to let her down easily; however, I'm also not a liar, so I made no promises that it would happen.

Knox laughs and slaps me on the shoulder. "You're the fucking man!"

I let out a hollow laugh because after every fling I feel less and less like a man. They satisfy my need for sex, but that's about it. After what happened ten years ago, there's no way I'm getting in that deep again.

"C'mon, let's get a beer," I suggest because thinking about Trixie has made my chest ache, and I need a beer and a game of pool in a dark bar to make it go away.

"Fuck yeah!" Knox grabs his stuff and follows me out of the locker room, jabbering away about a pair of blonde twin models he can hook us up with. He's a good kid and the best damn player I've had the pleasure to be on a team with, but he's walking a fine line between having a good time and partying too hard. I've heard Coach and Bugs talking about his shenanigans, so I feel it's my duty as an OG of the team to keep an eye on him. Although thinking about it, the last time we went out for a quiet drink, we ended up at a strip club where Knox took to the pole and showed the girls on stage and some of the shocked patrons just how flexible hockey players need to be.

Jesus, maybe this isn't the best idea I've ever had.

The hangover throbs incessantly behind my eyes, and the Ray-Bans are doing very little to shield them from the bright summer sun. It also doesn't help that my partner in crime is snoring loudly in the passenger seat of my Tesla. At this moment, it's clear to me that I'm too old for the kind of fun Knox and I got up to last night. A beer and a game of pool quickly snowballed into a dark club with pulsing dance music, shots, and several willing female bodies pressed against me. Knox took full advantage of that situation; however, I reached my limit at about 4 am, so I put my drunk ass in an Uber and went home alone.

When I went to pick Knox up at noon, he was making out with a petite purple-haired chick with full sleeve tattoos on his doorstep. I vaguely recognized her from the club, but I couldn't be sure. Knowing Knox, he could have picked her up when he went out to get a latte.

Anyway, it must have been a good night judging by the deep, vibrating snore that interrupts my thoughts. As I turn off the road onto the bumpy track that leads to Coach Casey's waterfront home, I punch the brakes, and Knox jolts awake.

"What the fuck, man?" he grumbles, sliding his Prada shades down his nose to eyeball me over the top.

"We're here," I reply innocently, trying to hide my smirk.

"Thank god. I never thought we'd get here." He

sighs. "Could you drive any slower, Grandpa?"

As I pull my car up next to Matt's mustang, I punch the brakes again so Knox jolts against his seat belt before I kill the engine. "Next time, you can take an Uber all the way out here, you little shit."

I push open my door and climb out before I can hear his retort, popping the trunk to retrieve my bag. Coach Casey's Labor Day parties are legendary, and it's advisable to bring a change of clothes and towels because there's always a coaches vs players water volleyball game and other fun activities. Even though I'm looking forward to catching up with my teammates and their families, all I want to do right now is have a cold beer and find a sunbed in the shade so I can sleep off some of this hangover.

Knox and I make our way down the side of Coach Casey's impressive home, hearing the sound of loud hockey players and squealing kids before seeing them. We're slightly late so the huge backyard is already full of players, coaches, back office staff, and their families swimming in the pool, talking in groups on the large lawn, and walking down to the private beach. The smell of Coach's famous barbecue makes my stomach rumble, and I turn to speak to Knox, but he's already abandoned me, making a beeline for the bar.

I huff and shake my head, spotting the guys from my line sitting round a large table shaded by a striped umbrella. Mila, Coach Casey's assistant, is sitting on her boyfriend's lap. Matt is our starting center and one of our alternate captains, and he fell hard for Mila when she started working for the Whalers in his first season. Next to them are Nate, our big defenseman and his girlfriend Beth. As usual, the pair of them are making out like no one else is around, but we're all kind of used to it now and just let them get on with it. I can't see Thor, our goalie, but I catch sight of him throwing his girlfriend Lana about in the swimming pool.

Bugs catches my eye first because he's trying to slather sunscreen on a squirming baby Sawyer, but when he raises his hand in greeting, he loses his grip on her and she toddles off, squealing with delight when he gives chase. She comes in my direction but doesn't get too far before falling on her butt, her face scrunching up as she winds up into an ear piercing wail.

"Oh c'mon now, darlin'," I croon, managing to pick her up before Bugs makes it over to us. "No need for tears. Your daddy falls on his butt all the time, and you don't see him making such a fuss."

Sawyer stops crying and looks up at me with huge watery eyes, her little cupid bow lips spread onto a gummy grin, and she giggles at my joke. Quick as a rattlesnake, she reaches up and snatches my sunglasses off my face, waving them around in her chubby little fist.

"Thanks for the save, Ford," Bugs huffs when he joins us. "I was afraid we were gonna have a nuclear meltdown." He reaches out for me to hand over the baby, but she clings to me and begins to sob, shaking her head, saying no over and over again.

"Sorry, man, looks like you're the flavor of the day." Bugs laughs, holding his hands up in defeat. "Just like her momma, my little princess knows what she wants."

"Is that so?" Cam, Bugs' girlfriend and our General Manager's PA, appears by his side and puts her arm around him. "It looks like Sawyer certainly inherited my stubborn streak."

"And your love for hockey players, it seems." Bugs smirks, squeezing her butt. *Jesus, these two are so sweet they're giving me a toothache.*

"Well, I'm gonna take my date to the bar if that's okay with you guys." I laugh, dropping my bag by an empty chair at the table.

"That's fine. Just don't give her any brown liquor," Bugs calls as I carry the baby toward the bar to get a beer and some of the delicious looking nachos I spotted. Sawyer coos and babbles to herself as we wait in line to be served by the bartender, and I hardly notice when the person in front of us collects her drink and turns to leave.

Holy shit!

Trixie.

Her curvy hourglass figure is subtly accentuated by the sarong slung around her waist, and her generous tits are just about contained in a halter neck red bikini top. The pale, porcelain tone of her perfect skin is pink from the sun, and I can already see the smattering of freckles that come out on her shoulders and nose. She used to wear her blonde hair in carefree tresses, but when we've crossed paths, I noticed she now wears it in a choppy bob that skims her shoulders.

When she sees me, her navy blue eyes widen, and she takes a step back, bumping her plump ass against the bar. Even though we've worked in the same city for several years and run in similar circles, I've made it my mission to stay out of her way. And judging by the few times our paths have crossed, she's made it hers too.

"Oh, Chris," Trixie says in the husky British accent

of hers, "you're here."

I sense her internally wince at her words, and I try hard not to smile.

"Hey," I reply. "How are you, Sugar?" I drop her pet name as easily as I used to, and now it's my turn to wince.

Her cheeks pink up, and she drops her gaze from mine, intensely studying the floor. "I'm okay, thanks. Busy as a bee."

Jesus, she's still adorable.

"Yeah, I hear your business is really successful," I say, trying desperately to make this exchange less awkward.

But despite my best efforts, seeing her up close and personal makes me ache in every fiber of my being. Trixie is even more beautiful than she was ten years ago. She's grown into herself and become the success she always wanted to be. I know her agency is one of the best in the Pacific Northwest, and she represents athletes from most of the major teams in the area.

"Thanks," Trixie replies, lifting her almond shaped eyes and locking me with her tractor beam. "It's been bloody hard work, but I have zero regrets. I'm doing what I love, and I couldn't be happier." I can tell by the determined set of her chin that she means it.

But her words hit me like a puck to the heart—she's basically saying that our parting ten years ago was the right thing to do, and she has no regrets that we didn't fight harder to stay together. I know deep down that that's on me—I'm the one who made her choose between me and her career.

I self-consciously shift Sawyer onto my other hip because she's getting bored with this horribly awkward conversation. "Well, you seem happy. It was good to see you."

I nod, effectively ending the conversation and step toward the bar, asking the bartender for a shot of bourbon to steady my nerves. Trixie lingers for a few more seconds and then walks off toward the poolside. I don't let my gaze follow her in case I see her sit next to the date she's probably brought with her. That would make me lose my shit.

"Bugs said no brown liquor!" Cam's voice brings me back from my introspection, and I feel Sawyer being liberated from my arms.

"Huh?" I look across at her dumbly, and then I notice the shot glass of bourbon in my slightly shaky hand. I chuckle bitterly and knock the shot back, enjoying the comforting burn as it runs down my throat. "That was for me," I rasp.

"I came over because it looked like you needed rescuing," Cam says quietly, flicking her eyes over to Trixie, who is now sitting on a sunbed talking to one of the rookies. I know that Cam and Trixie are friends because she represents Bugs, so I'm sure she has at least some clue about our past.

"Nah, it's all good," I say, nonchalantly shrugging and plastering a grin on my face. "Just catching up with an old friend."

Cam cocks an eyebrow at me and pats my bicep. "Sure," she says. "Maybe just take it easy on the shots."

"Sure thing, mom." I laugh, grabbing a beer out of a bucket of ice and following her back to our table where I flop into a seat and try not to keep glancing over at Trixie.

2

Trixie

I can feel Chris's green eyes burning a hole in my back as I try to listen to the rookie witter on about how much he misses his girlfriend in Utah or some other place in the middle of this huge bloody country. I find myself nodding and pretending to listen, but instead I'm trying not to obsess about how much hotter Chris is now than he was ten years ago. Maturity certainly agrees with him—his body is toned to perfection and those board shorts do nothing to hide the delicious Adonis belt muscles at his hips. I remember what it feels like to run my tongue along them, heading down toward his huge…

"So what do you think I should do?" the rookie asks me, and I blink at him like an idiot.

"About what?" I ask, feeling all hot and bothered at being caught out in the middle of a sex replay.

"My girlfriend? She has two more years of college so can't move out here until then."

I huff out an impatient breath and stand up, adjusting my sarong. "Cut her loose, love," I say a little too harshly. "The long distance thing never works, and you have your career to think about. It's kinder in the long run."

The look of heartbreak and despair on his face makes me feel like a huge bitch, but he needs to hear some hard truths. Before his puppy dog eyes make me say something kind, I turn on my heel and head down to the beach to get some space and catch my breath.

I don't know why seeing Chris has affected me so much. We've been actively avoiding each other in Seattle for several years, and even when I've seen him before at Whalers events, he's usually had a date hanging off his arm, so I can just ignore him. But today, seeing him with Bugs and Cam's baby on his hip, looking all tanned and muscular, his damned crooked nose just making him look more attractive, I felt all those old feelings surge through me like a tidal wave.

When I get to the beach, I kick off my sandals and walk down to the shore, the frigid water of the Sound shocking some sense into me. I catch my breath and exhale loudly. I've managed to keep Chris's bright smile and sweet nature out of my mind for ten years, and I can't let him back in after one awkward exchange. *Keep him at a safe distance and keep your eye on the ball.* Still lost in thought, I make my way to a large driftwood log and carefully sit, replaying every second of the last decade in my head.

"Can I join you?"

I look up and shade my eyes from the sun, recognizing the familiar silhouette of Bugs standing over me. He holds a bottle of beer out toward me, which I accept, enjoying the feeling of the cold wet glass against my fingers.

"Take a seat." I nod toward the empty expanse of log next to me, and when Bugs lowers his large frame onto it, it creaks in protest but thankfully holds.

"How're you doing?" he asks as I take a long drink from the cool bottle of beer. It's not a frothy pint of my beloved Boddingtons bitter, but it'll do.

I think about how to answer his question as I wipe the moisture from my top lip.

"I have to say I've been better," I finally reply, flicking my eyes over to look at my friend.

I've known Bugs for years; he was one of my first clients when I came to Seattle, and he's been a loyal friend ever since. Even when I interfered in his relationship with Cam and gave him some shitty advice, he's had my back.

"Cam said you had a strained conversation with Ford earlier," he says quietly. "Did he upset you?"

I quickly look over at him and smile. He's such a sweetie. "No love, he didn't upset me." I give his knee a reassuring pat. "I knew he'd be here, but he just took me by surprise, that's all."

"Must be hard constantly avoiding someone. Have you ever thought about clearing the air properly so you can both get on with your lives?"

"Bloody hell, Bugs. You don't pull your punches, do you?" I laugh, taking another big swig of my beer. "If I'm honest, I've thought about it a lot, but I always chicken out. Anyway, he ended things, so if anyone should make the first move to clear the air, it should be him."

Bugs laughs loudly. "You're both as bad as each other. You know how stubborn he is. He's like it on the ice. He'll never back down, so I think you're gonna

14

have to be the grownup and initiate the conversation."

I shake my head as I'm bombarded with memories of all the times Chris and I butted heads over things. "He is a stubborn wanker, but I always did like arguing with him."

Smiling sadly, I drain the last of my beer and stand up. "Thanks for the chat, love. I think I will try and clear the air before the season starts. I'm representing a few more guys on the team, so I'll be around a lot more. I don't want to keep avoiding him."

Bugs stands up as well, towering over me, pulling me into a warm hug. "Sounds like the right thing to do, Trix."

I look up at Bugs and smile. "How are you so wise?"

"It's all part of my Captain's super powers," Bugs replies, trying to keep a straight, serious expression on his face. "Giving sage advice to those in need."

I cock my eyebrow and give him my best "cut the shit" expression, and we both burst out laughing, walking back up the beach to rejoin the party which is now in full swing because the food has been served. And if there's one thing hockey players love more than the game, it's good food and plenty of it.

"I'm never eating again," Beth moans, leaning back in her chair, rubbing her bare stomach, which to me still looks perfectly flat, adorned with a diamond belly button ring. "Will you rub my belly, cowboy?" She looks over at Nate with big puppy dog eyes and a pouty expression. He immediately drops the rib he's working on, wipes his hands, and pulls Beth's tiny body onto his lap so he can carry out his task.

I'm sitting at a table with most of the Whalers' first line and their girlfriends but only because Chris has chosen to sit with Coach Casey.

"Whipped!" Knox coughs into his fist, making everyone around the table laugh and begin pelting the love birds with potato chips and napkins.

"Hey, I love my princess, and I'm not ashamed to show it!" Nate protests, defending them from the deluge of missiles with his cat-like reflexes.

"You tell 'em, baby," Beth coos, kissing Nate's neck, which immediately diverts his attention, and the two of them start making out.

Watching their adorable yet sexy exchange makes me reflect on the pathetic state of my own love life. Other than a short rebound relationship after Chris dumped me, I've only had a few brief flings that fizzled out as soon as the guy knew how career focused I was. I still find it amazing how many men are emasculated by a woman's need to have a successful career. I always thought Chris was different. He'd said all the right things when we first got together, but when push came to shove, he didn't mean a word of it.

"You hanging in there, Champ?" Bugs whispers as the conversation turns to talk of the upcoming training camp and exhibition games.

I turn and offer him a tight smile, feeling like I'm on borrowed time before Chris comes back to join his linemates at the table.

Bugs cocks his head in the direction of the table Chris and Coach Casey are sitting at, and I quickly look over to see him gathering his plate and empty beer bottle, standing up, preparing to leave.

"Looks like this is your moment," Bugs whispers, patting my shoulder. "Go get him."

I huff out a breath and mentally pull up my big girl pants, my stomach filling with snakes that squirm and churn. Suddenly I'm regretting that extra chicken drumstick I ate.

"If it looks like it's going tits up, please come and rescue me." I sigh, standing up and gathering my own empty plate and a few others that look like they need clearing.

I follow Chris up to the table where people seem to be leaving their dirty dishes and deposit my own plate next to his.

"Hey," I say quietly so as not to surprise him again. Standing this close to him, I can see the eagle tattoo on his bicep and the dent in his nose that gives him that rough edge I used to love so much. I always thought that if his nose was perfect, he'd be too good looking.

But that's beside the point. Right now his stupid handsome face is looking right at me with a quizzical expression.

"Trixie? You okay?" he asks, reaching over and gently squeezing my bare shoulder. My skin immediately breaks out into goosebumps at the contact, and I take a step back in a vain hope he hasn't noticed.

"Yeah, I'm fine. Just saying hey," I reply, laughing a little too loudly.

"You sure because you seem a little nuts," Chris replies, smiling kindly.

Jesus, I can't fool him for a second. He could always

tell when I was wired and trying to say something difficult. So I exhale and try to relax a little bit before I speak.

"Sorry, I didn't mean to come over here like a nutter. I've just been thinking about the upcoming season and how it's stupid that we keep trying to avoid each other when inevitably we end up at the same games and social events. Bugs and Cam are my good friends, and I hate having to ask them every time they invite me somewhere whether you're going to be there or not. So, in short, I want to clear the air." I take a huge intake of air and realize I've said all of that on one breath so now I'm panting like a racehorse.

Chris just stares at me with wide green eyes, looking a little shell shocked.

"Fucking hell! Say something, will you?" I hiss, feeling completely vulnerable and out on a limb. Is he really going to leave me hanging like this? Is he really that cruel?

Suddenly, he's by my side, his big hand on the small of my back, and he's urging me forward. "Let's get outta here, Sugar. If we're gonna do this, I don't wanna do it in front of all my teammates. Get your stuff and meet me at my car."

With that, he disappears to collect his things, and I head back to the team table to find my purse and beach bag.

As I gather everything as covertly as I can, Bugs approaches. "Everything okay? Do you need that rescue?"

I laugh nervously and shake my head. "No, it's fine. We're going to head off somewhere to talk a bit more privately. So can you tell Cam thanks for the lift out here? I'll head back to the city with Chris."

Looking up, I see a brief look of concern cross Bugs' face. "Are you sure?"

"Yes, I'm sure. I feel safe with him. It might just be awkward, but he'd never do anything to hurt me. Don't worry." I give his large bicep a comforting pat and make a quick round of goodbyes to everyone, leaving before they can start with the questions as to why I'm leaving before the water volleyball tournament.

As I approach the front of the house, my breath catches in my throat. Chris is leaning against his sleek white Tesla, his arms folded across his broad chest. Thankfully, he's put a t-shirt on, but its tight fit does nothing to hide the dips and valleys of his pecs and abs. His board shorts hang low on his hips, clinging to his thick muscular thighs, and I can't help the tingle of arousal in my lady garden. Even after ten years, he can still turn me on like no one before or since.

"What's the plan?" he asks when I'm within earshot, a sexy, cocky grin splitting his face.

"Well, I'm not exactly dressed for a bar," I say, holding my arms out to emphasize the fact I'm in my beach wear. "Shall we go to my house?" I feel like I need to have home ice advantage for the conversation we're going to have, and I'm thankful when Chris gives a short nod of agreement and opens the door for me.

As I slide past him into the passenger seat, I get a face full of his fresh scent. Yet again I get all sorts of confusing feelings downstairs.

God damn it, Beatrix! Get a grip! You're not that hard up that you have to lust after the man who broke your heart. That's why god invented vibrators!

"Can I have your address?" Chris's deep voice shakes me out of my self-admonishment, and I turn to look at him dumbly.

"Huh?" I ask, confused at what he's asking me.

"I need your address for the GPS." He chuckles. "I don't know where you live."

I suddenly feel like a complete idiot. Why does he have the ability to turn me into a brain dead moron whenever I'm in his presence? This is one of the reasons I later decided we wouldn't work—I become consumed by him and lose myself, and that's not something I'll let happen again.

Clearing my throat, I give him the details he needs, and we head back toward the city in an awkward silence. It's so strange that you can have the most intimate connection with a person and then find yourself stuck for small talk.

Thankfully, the journey to my Montlake home doesn't take too long, and I breathe a quiet sigh of relief when Chris pulls up outside my Spanish style bungalow and kills the engine. I love my house. I fell for its understated charm as soon as the realtor showed it to me. It's quirky, with vaulted ceilings, exposed beams, and a fireplace. But the thing I love the most is accessing the loft bedroom via a ladder—I've had a few scary climbs after too many glasses of wine, but it just adds to the charm.

"I like your house. It's very … you," Chris says as he follows me inside, and I can hear the smile in his voice.

I throw my beach bag on the floor by the door and turn to face my ex. It's so strange having him in my personal space, and suddenly, I'm regretting this location. But before I can spiral, he says, "Why don't you go and change into something more comfortable, and I'll fix us some drinks? I feel like this conversation will have a two drink minimum." He smiles kindly and heads off toward my open floor plan kitchen area, easily finding the small bar. Once he's busy, I clamber up the ladder and quickly change into yoga pants and my favorite slouchy sweater. Usually I'd find my cutest outfit and dress it up with some killer heels, but with Chris, I don't need to. I'm not trying to impress him. I just want to be comfortable.

When I return downstairs, I find him looking at my photo wall, a bottle of beer in his hand. I feel my cheeks pink up at the intense way he's inspecting the pictures: my granddad in his World War Two Air Force uniform, me and Gloria on the day I became an agent at SPC, me and Bugs at his first game for the Whalers, and so many other memories that I've accumulated over the last decade.

As I approach, Chris turns around and hands me the beer he's been holding in his other hand.

"You've made quite a life for yourself, Sugar," he says quietly, a touch of sadness in his voice even though he's smiling.

"I've done okay," I reply nonchalantly, shrugging. I indicate for him to follow me to the couch where I seat myself safely at one end, tucking my legs underneath me and taking a long swallow from my beer. He sits at a respectful distance at the other end and takes an equally long draw from his bottle. It's weird that we're so nervous in each other's presence—I mean, the man has kissed and licked every inch of my body, yet I feel shy around him.

"So what do you wanna say, Trix?"

I take a deep breath. "I think it's time to clear the air so we don't spend the rest of the season avoiding each other. But I'll need something stronger than beer because I'm nervous as hell." I laugh self-consciously, getting up to retrieve the bottle of Patron and two shot glasses from the bar. This is definitely a tequila conversation.

3

Chris

There's a tiny, evil mouse with a drill and it's attacking my temple with an insistence that makes me want to scream. Why does this mouse want to kill me?

As I flick my sticky eyelids open to locate the demonic rodent, I realize two things–firstly it's my phone vibrating on the nightstand that's making that noise, and secondly, I'm not in my bed, and I'm not alone.

I slap my hand out to stop my phone buzzing and try to unstick my tongue from the roof of my mouth. God damn it, I've not been this hungover ever. My stomach is doing somersaults, and my mouth feels like an ape took a dump right in there. But as I look to my left and see the messy blonde mop of hair spread out next to me, I feel like I'm going to puke.

Oh shit! The events of the previous night come screaming back to me—the tequila, the reminiscing, the truce, and then the hot as fuck making out on the couch. After that, everything is blurry, but I'm pretty sure that we didn't have sex. I quickly lift the bedsheets and am relieved to see that I still have my board shorts on, and Trixie is wearing her yoga pants and bra. I don't have time to admire her luscious curves; if Trixie wakes up and finds me in her bed, we'll be right back at square one—her hating my guts and avoiding me. Hopefully if I can get out of here before she wakes up, she'll be too hungover to remember what happened.

As stealthily as I can considering my size, I slide out of bed and search for the rest of my clothes. When I can't find them, I remember Trixie pulling my shirt off on the couch, so I grab my phone from the nightstand and maneuver down the fucking ladder that almost ended my career when I carried Trixie up it firefighter style.

I'm just fixing myself a huge glass of water when my phone starts to vibrate again. This time instead of ignoring the call, I look at the display and immediately recognize the Memphis area code. Who the fuck is calling me at 6 am? But that means it's 8 am in Memphis.

Before I miss the call, I hit the green answer button and quietly say hello.

"Mr. Ford? Is this Mr. Christopher Bartlett Ford?" The woman at the other end of the call surprises me by using my middle name.

"Yeah, who's this?" I growl. It's not unusual for enthusiastic fans to get hold of my cell phone number so I'm ready to hang up.

"My name is Martine Hill, and I'm a family attorney in Memphis. I wonder if you have a moment to talk."

My heartrate suddenly kicks up a notch as I wonder what this lawyer wants with me. Shit, perhaps an ex has filed some kind of lawsuit against me, or maybe it's to do with my charitable foundation. Whatever it is, I don't want to have a whispered conversation while Trixie is snoring lightly upstairs.

"Now isn't a great time. Can I call you back when I'm able to talk freely?"

"Of course, Mr. Ford. Please call me on this number as soon as you can; it is a matter of some urgency," she replies a little sharply before ending the call.

I'm left a little stunned, and the sick feeling I had when I woke up seems to be getting worse, so I chug the water, put the glass in the dishwasher, and scribble Trixie a quick note on a chalkboard she has on the wall.

I feel like absolute shit for running out on her while she's still sleeping, and I'm pretty sure this action will undo all the good ground we made up last night, but I have a midday session with my trainer on the other side of the city, and I now have this lawyer to call back.

Thankfully there's a Starbucks a block over from Trixie's place, so I get the biggest coffee I can and drive across town to my apartment. I live in the same building as a few of the other players, and I'm relieved when I don't bump into Thor or Nate on my way up to my apartment. After dumping my bag in the laundry room, I make myself some whole-wheat toast with peanut butter and finish my coffee, the tequila fog finally beginning to clear.

Memories of Trixie's soft kisses and silky skin start to flash through my brain. We were like horny teenagers making out on the couch. I can't deny it was hot as fuck. She always had the ability to make me hard with just a look, and if my memory serves, it was a hot and needy look that got us attacking each other last night. We'd gotten into such a good place, putting all the shit from the breakup to rest and reminiscing about those good times back in Memphis.

Shit! Memphis.

Thinking about my hometown reminds me that I have to deal with the lawyer who called earlier. I pull my cell phone from my pocket and bring up my recent calls, clicking on the last number, waiting for it to connect.

"Hill and Frost, how may I direct your call?" a professional sounding receptionist answers after three rings.

Shit, what was that lawyer's name again?

"Hi, yeah, I'm Chris Ford," I mumble awkwardly. "I had a call from one of your lawyers this morning…"

"Certainly, Mr. Ford. Ms. Hill is expecting your call," the receptionist replies. "I'll connect you now."

I hear the internal line ring once, and then I'm connected. "Mr. Ford, thank you for calling me back so quickly."

"No problem," I reply, standing up and moving from my kitchen counter to the large sectional couch and flopping into the deep cushions. "How can I help you, Ms. Hill?"

"I'm afraid I'm calling with some difficult news."

I sit up a little straighter, my interest piqued. I have no living family in Memphis; my parents are both dead, and I was an only child. I think I may have some very distant relatives somewhere, but no one that's ever got in touch.

Ms. Hill continues, "Were you aware your father had another relationship following the one with your mother?"

At the mention of my father, my hackles rise, and I clench my fist tightly around my cell phone. "It wouldn't surprise me," I hiss, the anger and hatred I feel for that poor excuse for a man rising like bile in my throat. He walked out on me and my mom when I was barely out of diapers, and even though he would reappear every few years and she would stupidly take him back, he'd always fuck off again once money ran short or my mom would get at him to find a job.

"Well, your father was married to a woman in 1992 who resided in Clarkedale, and they had a daughter called Andrea in 1993. Obviously, I know your father passed away in 2012, and his wife in this relationship passed away in 2016…"

"I have a half-sister?" I ask in a quiet voice that sounds like it's coming from another room. I knew my father had another wife, but I had no idea they had a kid together.

"Yes, Mr. Ford…"

"Jesus Christ, I don't need this shit," I snap, immediately feeling like crap. This woman is just doing her job. "Look, I'm sorry. This is just a lot of information to take in."

"Can I ask what my father's second family has to do with me?" I feel my frustration reach boiling point, so I stand up and pace in front of my couch, gripping handfuls of my hair. I only found out that my mom and dad weren't actually married when I went through her papers after she died. I'm not surprised to find out he had a second family; it just cemented him in my head as the lowest form of dirtbag, and I put him to the back of mind.

But as this lawyer rambles on and on about his cheating ways, I feel all those memories and pain come flooding back.

"…so that makes you his sole living relative. Are you there, Mr. Ford?"

The lawyer's voice brings me out of my rage, and I feel a cold chill run down my spine.

"I'm sorry. Can you repeat that?" I splutter, unable to tell whether I heard her correctly.

"I said that you are the sole living relative of your half-sister's son; therefore, I was hoping to talk to you about legal guardianship," Ms. Hill says in a matter-of-fact way that makes my head spin. "As I was saying, your half-sister Andrea passed away a few days ago, and as per her instructions, she has asked that you take on legal guardianship of her son."

"She knew about me?" I ask, wondering why she never made contact with me before this.

"Yes, she knew about you and made it very clear to me in the last months of her life that she wanted you to be Danny's legal guardian."

I feel that chill up my spine again. "She knew she was going to die." I phrase it as a statement and not a question because I already know the answer.

"Yes, Chris, she did," the lawyer replies sadly. "She had ovarian cancer that was too far advanced by the time they found it, so she made arrangements for Danny as best she could. Obviously, she knew that you had the financial security to look after him. The question is, are you willing to take on this responsibility?"

Fuck! That's a question that's just too big for me to deal with over the phone.

"I think I should come to Memphis and meet with you in person. I need to speak to my agent and my coach before I make any decisions," I say quickly.

"Of course, I completely understand. This is a life changing decision to make, and with your position in the public eye, I appreciate your need to consult with your team. I will ask my assistant to email you all the relevant paperwork so your people can look it over, and I'll see you when you get to Memphis."

"Thank you," I mutter, still completely shell-shocked by this news. "Can I ask one thing?"

"Certainly."

"How old is he? Danny, I mean." For some reason, I have a picture of a tiny helpless baby in my head.

"Danny turned six just last month," the lawyer says, and I don't know if it's my imagination or not, but I'm sure I hear a thickness in her voice as she holds back tears.

"Thank you, Ms. Hill. I'll let you know my flight details so you know when to expect me in Memphis."

I hang up the call and flop back onto the couch, dragging my hands through my hair.

Jesus, I thought waking up next to Trixie was going to be the biggest thing I had to deal with today.

And as if she can sense me thinking about her, my phone vibrates again, and her name flashes on the display. I stare at it numbly for a few seconds and then cancel the call. I can't get into that drama before I sort out the other bombshell that's just dropped on my world.

A kid. What the fuck am I supposed to do with a six year old kid who has no idea who I am? I need to talk to Blake and see what my options are.

I quickly grab my phone and call my agent, checking the time to make sure the lazy asshole will be awake. He answers on the third ring.

"Chris, you know it's my golf day. I'm about to tee off. Can it wait?" he answers in an irritated tone that pisses me off and makes me wonder why I pay this prick nine percent.

"Well, I've just been told I've inherited a six-year-old kid from a sister I didn't know I had, so yeah, if that can wait, then have at it," I yell into the handset. "Get your ass to my apartment, Blake! Now!"

I end the call and launch my cell phone into the couch cushions, feeling the bile rise again. How can my life just turn on a dime like this? A few hours ago, I was making out with the love of my life. And now what? I'm a father? How am I supposed to fill that role in the kid's life when I've never even met him? Where is his own father? Shouldn't he be taking care of the kid?

But then I think about my own father and realize that some men just don't take that role seriously, and some take no responsibility for their kids at all.

I must get lost in my thoughts because the next thing I know, my intercom is buzzing to announce Blake's arrival. I push up off the couch and buzz him in, opening the door and leaving it so I can fix us a drink. I get the bourbon from the bar and pour two shots while I wait for Blake to come up.

"What the fuck, man?" he asks as he breezes in wearing his ridiculously bright golfing gear. "Hell of a way to start a Tuesday morning." He takes the shot I offer him and knocks it back, hissing as the bourbon travels down his throat.

I take my shot and begin to pour us more, but Blake covers his glass with his palm. "No more for me and I suggest no more for you. You need a clear head for this." He snatches the bottle from my hand and returns it to the bar.

As he takes a seat, an email pings onto my phone, and when I open the app, I see it's from Hill & Frost Family Attorney. I quickly forward it to Blake.

"Okay," he sighs, steepling his fingers under his chin. "Tell me everything."

I relay all the information I was given and that I can remember in a dead, robotic voice that I hardly recognize. I feel completely overwhelmed, and I hope Blake will tell me what to do. Then we both open the email sent by the lawyer, and I watch Blake read through the information.

All I seem to be able to do is look at the picture of the kid. He's smiling at the camera with a big goofy grin. A few of his front teeth are missing, but he's as happy and carefree as a little kid should be. His light-brown skin and curly black hair make him completely different from anyone in my family, but then I see those moss-green eyes that me and my dad share. The closer I look, the more I realize he has the exact same eyes as us, and it hits me like a sledgehammer to the heart. This kid is my blood, and I can't abandon him, no matter how I feel about my own father.

"Excellent!" Blake suddenly pipes up, and I realize my eyes are shiny with unshed tears.

"What's up?" I ask, quickly swiping the back of my hand over my eyes so he can't see the emotion that seems to be leaking out of them. Blake is as cold and predatory as a great white shark, and as an agent, I love that about him. As a human being, he's a dick, but I don't pay him to be my friend.

"You have a get out clause. As part of the guardianship process, you will also need to prove to the court that you are physically and emotionally fit to care for the child as well as that you have the financial resources necessary to provide for the child's maintenance. The court may order a home study to ensure that you have a safe home and that the home environment is the best place for the child." Blake looks up and smiles, looking very smug.

"How is that a get out clause?" I ask, raking my hands through my hair again, wishing I had another shot of bourbon. "I have the financial resources; that's not a problem."

"Yes, but with your travel schedule, they'll never agree that your home life is a safe and stable environment for a little kid," Blake says smugly, sitting back on his stool and linking his fingers behind his head, that shit-eating grin firmly in place.

"But lots of players have kids. Bugs and Cam cope just fine when they both have to travel with the team. They have a nanny."

"You think a court will allow a child who has just lost their mother to be taken to a strange city and left with a nanny?" Blake scoffs, rolling his eyes. "Dude, the best thing you can do for everyone concerned is to cut the kid loose. He's still little. Someone will adopt him."

"And in the meantime he just lives in some foster home?" I ask, shocked by Blake's flippant attitude to another human being's welfare.

"For fuck's sake, Ford, he's not little orphan Annie, and you're not Daddy Warbucks. Get a fucking grip! You're coming into the last years of your career, and you need to concentrate fully on having your name engraved on the Stanley Cup and not getting put out to pasture on the farm team. You have to work hard to keep your place on the first line at your age, and having a little kid distracting you, nanny or no nanny, will end all that."

Blake gets up and grips my shoulder. "Go to Memphis, sign the paperwork, and move on with your life," he whispers in my ear, and I feel a ripple of disgust roll through me. I always knew Blake was a heartless son of a bitch, but this is too much. I know that if I don't agree with him, he'll be on me until I do.

So in order to get some breathing space, I say, "Sure thing. I'll book the first flight to Memphis I can get on."

"Good man. You know it's for the best." Blake slaps my back and grabs his cell phone and keys from the countertop. "Okay, I've got a rescheduled tee time in an hour, so I'm heading out. Call me from Memphis if you need me. Later, man."

I grunt a goodbye as Blake shows himself out of my apartment, and I'm left wondering what the hell to do next.

4

Trixie

I scrub the shampoo into my hair with so much rage I feel like I might have bald patches when I'm through. How dare Chris Ford creep out of my bed in the middle of the night, leave me a bullshit note, and then refuse to answer my call? I thought after our reconciliation and hot make-out session last night that we were at least on the road to being friends again. But he's ruined all of that by being a shady wanker.

I rinse my hair and allow the shampoo to run into my eyes so I can pretend it's that and not my furious tears that are stinging them. Climbing out of the shower, I wrap a towel around my body and one around my head, sitting at my vanity table, rubbing my hair dry and combing it out. As I look at my reflection in the mirror, I see my chin begin to wobble and my eyes fill with tears.

How could I have been so stupid? I've worked really hard to get over Chris, and just like that, I let him back in, and I'm back where I started. This is one of the busiest years of my career, and I can't afford to let this derail it.

I won't.

I quickly swipe at my eyes and get dressed in a black pencil skirt and my favorite green sleeveless blouse that I cover with a fitted jacket. I know which pumps I'm going to wear, but I keep all my shoes downstairs because trying to negotiate the ladder in heels is impossible.

I'm just pouring my coffee into my traveling cup when someone starts hammering on the door like there's a bloody fire! It scares the shit out of me, and I end up spilling most of my coffee onto the counter instead of in the cup.

"Bloody, bollocks, shit!" I curse to myself. "Hold your horses, I'm coming!" I yell at the person trying to bust my door down. I leave the flood of coffee dripping off my countertop and stomp toward the door.

"WHAT?" I yell as I fling the door open and see Chris standing in front of me, looking like he's about to cry and have a heart attack at the same time. I should be pissed off at him for what happened last night, but he looks so forlorn and lost I can't be mad.

"Look, I know shit's suddenly got even weirder between us, but I need your help. I don't know where else to go." His green eyes are shining, and my heart just breaks for him, so I grab his arm and pull him inside, pushing him down onto the couch and pouring what's left of my coffee into a cup for him.

"What the hell happened?" I ask, sitting next to him. I can see his hands shaking as they try to hold the cup, so in order to avoid more spillages and protect my rug, I take it from him and put it on the table in front of us.

"I got a call from a lawyer in Memphis this morning,

and it seems I had a half-sister I didn't know about, and she died," he mumbles, not looking up at me.

"Oh I'm so sorry, love." I put my hand on his shoulder and squeeze it. I know Chris always had a turbulent relationship with his dad, but this must be a real shock for him. "How did she die?"

"Ovarian cancer." He looks up at me, and I can tell there's more to come. "She had a six-year-old kid."

Oh god, my heart just breaks. My own mum left me with my granddad when I was about that age, so I know what it's like growing up without one. Although that selfish cow chose to leave me, this poor little soul had his mum taken from him in the cruelest way imaginable.

"So what do they need from you?" I ask, wondering why the lawyer is contacting him.

He fixes me with his most serious face. He doesn't show it very often, but I know he means business. "Apparently I'm the kid's only living relative, and his mom wants me to be his legal guardian."

"Oh wow!" I say on a breath. "That's huge news."

"No shit!" He laughs bitterly. "What the fuck am I supposed to do with a little kid who has no idea who I am?"

"Did they say what your options are?" I ask, trying to keep my business head on and not let his intense vulnerability and fear cloud my judgment.

"I have an email from the lawyer."

"May I read it?" I ask gently.

"Sure." He unlocks his cell phone and hands it to me, the email open on the screen.

"Let me read this. Drink your coffee." I pick up the

cup and place it in his hands, then I get up and pace while I read the information on the email. I do my best thinking when I pace. I'm no lawyer, but I've read my share of legal documents, and this one seems fairly straight forward—Chris can take legal guardianship of Daniel Sebastian Ford, or he can sign that away and he'll become a ward of the state where he'll be placed into the foster care system while he awaits adoption.

The last thing I open is a JPEG that makes my breath catch in my throat. The gorgeous smiling boy who looks at me with the goofy toothless grin and Chris's eyes just breaks my heart, and I feel the tears slip down my cheeks.

"Oh Chris." I sit next to him on the couch and pull him into my arms, feeling the tension in every one of his perfectly formed muscles. "What are you gonna do, love?"

He pulls away, and I see how vulnerable he is, and all I want to do is make it better for him. "I need to go to Memphis." He looks down at where his hands are clinging to mine. "Will you come with me? Please."

"Shouldn't you go with Blake? It's bad form to step on another agent's territory," I reply, feeling a bit awkward. Blake is notorious for being a pitbull, and I've had enough run-ins with him to last me a lifetime.

Chris scoffs and shakes his head. "Blake knows. Obviously I went to him first, and I'm sure you can imagine what he told me to do."

The sick feeling in my stomach tells me exactly what he said. "Blake told you to sign him over to the state, didn't he?"

"Yep. And I'm sure that's the sensible thing to do.

But I can't. I just couldn't live with myself. You hear all these horror stories of kids growing up in a string of foster homes and then aging out with nowhere to go. It would make me the most selfish asshole in the world if I let that happen to him."

God damn it, I need to hold myself together because right now it feels like my ovaries are about to explode. He's speaking the truth—it could so easily have been my story if my granddad hadn't stepped up when my mum abandoned me. I've never heard Chris even talk about having children before. We were way too young when we were together to have that discussion. But seeing him now, talking about becoming a father, it makes me have all sorts of feelings I shouldn't be having.

"You're a good man, Chris Ford. And of course I'll come to Memphis with you." I cup his scruffy cheek in my hand and gently stroke my thumb over it.

"Thank you." He tilts his head and kisses my palm, sending shockwaves up my arm, making the hair on the back of my neck stand on end.

I quickly take my hand away as if he's scalded me and stand up—I need to put some distance between us. "Right, you go home and pack a bag. I'll rearrange my week and get some flights and a hotel booked." Suddenly, I need to be all business because that's my safe space. And if I'm not careful, I'll let my feelings for him overwhelm me, and I can't let that happen.

Chris stands up as well, towering over me. "Okay, I have a few team things to rearrange, and of course I need to speak to Coach Casey and Bugs. Just let me know when the flight is, and I'll come and pick you up."

"I'll get us a car service. I don't think either of us

are in the right frame of mind to drive to the airport." I laugh, bending to pick up my cell phone from the coffee table.

"And Trixie?" He wraps his fingers around the tops of my arms and holds me steady. "About last night…"

"Oh hush," I scoff, wriggling free. "Now is not the time to talk about that. Forget it ever happened. We're all good, I promise." And as the lie falls off my tongue, I know we'll have to talk about it eventually, but now is definitely not the time.

Chris is unusually quiet on the drive to the airport. He speaks only to answer my direct questions, telling me that he's spoken to Coach Casey and Bugs about the situation, and they were both really understanding.

At the airport, I make a quick call to Bugs while I wait for Chris to get a coffee, and he confirms that Chris has the support of the team behind him, and Coach Casey will give him whatever time he needs to make arrangements and adjustments once Danny comes to Seattle.

With Chris's permission, I forward the paperwork to my lawyer, and she agrees that this is a straight-forward situation, and as long as the court agrees that Chris will be a suitable guardian, then Danny will be released into his custody.

"Are you okay, love?" I ask for what feels like the millionth time once we settle into our cramped coach seats. Chris seems to have shut down, and he's not showing the emotion from earlier today.

"Yeah, I'm fine." He flicks his eyes at me, and I notice his fingers are gripping the armrest so hard his knuckles are turning white. I slide my hand over his, and even though he flinches briefly at the contact, he doesn't move it.

We sit like this for the rest of the flight, and I'm thankful that he ignores the air stewardess when she comes past with the drinks trolley. The last thing I need is having to maneuver nearly two hundred pounds of drunk hockey player through an airport.

When we land in Memphis, we disembark quickly, and as we only have carry-on luggage, it's not long before we're in the SUV I booked, heading to the hotel. Chris is still silent and thoughtful, and even though I want to fill him in on the plans for tomorrow's meeting, I don't want to interrupt his introspection. He always was a deep thinker; despite his carefree exterior, I know that his waters run very deep indeed.

It's early evening by the time we check into the hotel, and when I hand Chris his keycard, our fingers touch, and it's as if that shocks him back to life. His green eyes flare and flick up to meet mine, and I can feel the electricity from last night crackle between us.

Jesus, was that only last night?

"I got you a suite. I know how much you like to spread out," I say, swallowing hard to dislodge the lump in my throat. Why the fuck is my mouth so dry all of a sudden? I'm dehydrated from the flight, that's all.

"And what about you, Sugar?" Chris asks in an equally raspy voice, the sexual tension crackling between us like static.

"I have a room a few floors down. You need your rest.

Tomorrow's going to be a difficult day." I look down and realize our fingers are still touching around his key card, and I quickly snatch mine away and smooth my skirt down. "Let's settle in and then I'll meet you back down here for dinner at 8. We have some things we need to discuss before tomorrow. Okay? Umm, bye."

I grab the handle of my carry-on bag and stride toward the bank of elevators, determined to put a little distance between us so I don't end up doing something stupid. Thankfully, an elevator has just arrived, so I quickly enter it and turn to face the foyer, Chris disappearing from view as the doors close. I release a shaky breath and lean back against the wall, my heart hammering against my chest.

Perhaps I was stupid to think Chris and I could be friends and that I could help him through this emotional time. Maybe there's too much history for us to get out of this situation without getting hurt all over again. I open my eyes and look at my reflection in the mirrored wall—everyone else would see a composed, confident businesswoman, but all I can see is the young girl I was when Chris broke my heart into a million pieces. I see doubt and fear. Who the fuck do I think I am? I'm still just little Beatrix whose mum didn't love her.

As the elevator doors open to my floor, my imposter syndrome is in full force, so I race toward my room, press my key card to the lock and burst inside, slamming the door behind me. I lean back against it with my eyes closed until my breathing regulates, and I can compose myself.

This is not the time or the place to have a breakdown.

So I take a deep cleansing breath, straighten my shoulders, and throw my bag onto the bed. I need to wash the plane smell off me before dinner with Chris; therefore, a hot shower is the next thing I do. But not before checking out the mini bar and cracking open a Grey Goose which I down in one gulp. I'm definitely in need of some Dutch courage before dinner.

5

I've been sitting in the bar for an hour when Trixie finally makes an appearance. I don't know if it's the four shots of bourbon I've drunk or the fact that she just gets more beautiful every time I see her, but I can't tear my eyes away as she sashays across the foyer toward me.

She's changed into a tight fitting navy blue dress that clings to every one of her luscious curves, that damn heart-shaped ass swishing from side to side, hypnotizing every guy in the bar. I have the sudden urge to rip out all of their eyes. None of them are man enough to look upon her beauty. Even I'm not man enough, but I still stare at her like a lovesick idiot as she speaks briefly to the bartender, pointing to my table before walking over and sliding onto the bench seat next to me.

"I see you've made a start without me," she says, flashing her eyes toward the half-empty tumbler of amber liquid in my hand, cocking a disapproving eyebrow. "How many have you had?"

"Not nearly enough," I scoff, draining the rest of

the liquor, holding up the glass to the bartender so he knows I want another one.

"Okay, this is your last one," Trixie says sternly. "I need you focused so we can talk about what's going to happen tomorrow."

I huff out a breath and slouch back against the padded backrest. "Do we have to talk about it? Can't I just enjoy my last night of freedom?" I look up at her with my best puppy dog eyes, and I see the corner of her mouth tip up as she tries to hide a smile. She never could resist my puppy eyes.

"But I want you to be fully prepared..." Trixie protests, trying her best to remain professional. Even though she's here more as a friend, she can't help always having her business head on.

"Look, the meeting isn't until 11. We can have breakfast in my suite and talk about it then," I suggest hopefully. "Please, just for tonight, can we pretend you're just you, and I'm just me, and we're just two people sharing some drinks and having a good time?"

With a swelling sense of victory, I see Trixie give in just as the bartender brings her glass of red wine and my next shot of bourbon.

"Fine, but we're going to have dinner because after all that tequila last night, I should probably line my stomach." Trixie laughs and clinks her glass against mine.

When our table is ready, we move through to the restaurant and order a couple of steaks and a bottle of good red wine. I'm pleased that even with everything going on and the awkwardness of what happened last night, the conversation still flows, and the attraction between us is undeniable. We spend more time catching up on what's happened to us over the last ten years, and I'm so proud of what Trixie has achieved. I remember the conversations we used to have laying in bed after making love, talking about our hopes and ambitions. From what I recall, Trixie has achieved almost everything she set out to do.

"So now that we've covered work and careers, tell me about your love life." She knocks the wind out of my sails with that, and I'm suddenly lost for words.

She must notice the look of horror on my face because she bursts out laughing and takes a big gulp of wine.

"Oh calm down, Romeo." She laughs. "I don't want all the horny details. I just wanna know if you've had any meaningful relationships since…" She waves her empty wine glass between us.

While I organize my thoughts, I pour the rest of the red wine into our glasses and wave to the waiter to bring us another.

"Put it this way," I say carefully, "I've had my fair share of meaningless relationships." I shrug and take a long drink from my glass, enjoying the warm buzz it creates in my chest.

Trixie laughs and shakes her head. "I must say I kept expecting to see you settle down with some spokesmodel or Instagram influencer, but you've managed to keep your love life out of the public eye. Well done for that." She clinks her glass against mine, and I can't help but notice the twinkle in her dark blue eyes.

"So what about you, Ms. Cavendish? How much 'D'

have you had since we split up?"

I bark out a laugh as Trixie almost spits her wine in my face, but she manages to clap her hand over her mouth in time to prevent me from having a merlot shower.

"Fucking 'ell," she coughs, dabbing her lips, chin and cleavage with a napkin. I love how her brash London accent comes out more when she's a bit drunk. But what I love even more than that is the way a droplet of red wine is slowly rolling down the curve of her breast and disappearing between the generous mounds.

Shit, is it hot in here, or is it just me?

She must notice me gawping and quickly wipes the rest of the wine away. "My eyes are up here." She chuckles, raising a sharp eyebrow, her voice taking on a sexy rasp that tells me she's enjoying my appreciation of her assets.

"C'mon Trix, dish the dirt. I bet you're beating them away with a stick." I push the point because I need to know every guy who's touched her so that I can add them to my list of people I need to track down and hurt.

Trixie's cheeks glow a very pretty pink, and I think only half of it is due to the wine. "I had a very short relationship soon after you left Memphis," she replies, keeping her eyes fixed firmly on her glass. "But other than a few short flings, I haven't had anything meaningful either."

I can't help the small seed of hope and excitement that plants itself in my heart. Could now be the right time for us to rekindle our relationship.? I think back to all the amazing things about our time together and wonder for the millionth time whether we'd have stayed together if I hadn't been transferred out of Memphis.

"What are you thinking about?" Her question brings me back to the moment, and I see the confused look in her eyes. *Can she tell that I'm yet again questioning my decision to walk away all those years ago?*

"I'm thinking about whether…" I begin, but Trixie holds up her hand to silence me and suddenly pushes her chair back, standing up.

"Don't say it. Please," she whispers. "This is an emotionally charged situation, and I don't want us to make a mistake just as your life is about to change forever."

"But…" I say, also standing up, tossing my napkin onto the table.

"No!" Trixie says a little too loudly, causing some of the other diners to look over at us. "I'm not doing this with you now. It's time for me to go to bed. Alone."

She grabs her phone and keycard from the table and storms out of the restaurant.

What the fuck just happened?

I quickly sign the check and dash after her, finding her waiting at the bank of elevators, tapping her foot impatiently. I can feel my heart hammering a thousand beats a minute as the doors open, and she steps inside, turning around just in time to see me slide through the quickly closing doors.

"What are you doing?" she gasps, backing away into the corner of the elevator.

I know what I'm about to do is crazy, especially with what my life is about to turn into, but every fiber of my being is telling me I need to show this incredible woman how I feel about her.

How I've always felt about her.

So, instead of using words, I show Trixie the depth of my feelings for her. As the elevator ascends, I step forward and crowd her into the corner, my hand reaching up to cup her cheek, sliding it down the smooth column of her neck, gripping it lightly, just how she likes. Trixie releases a moan as I draw her so close to me that I can smell the red wine on her breath and see the gold flecks in her navy blue eyes.

"Chris…" she whispers in her sexy voice, but her next words are muffled when our lips crash together, devouring whatever she was going to say next. It obviously wasn't a protest because her tongue strokes against mine in a way that always makes my cock feel like it's going to punch through my zipper. I tighten the grip on her throat, and she moans into my mouth, pressing her hips against mine which causes a growl to rumble through my chest.

Just as I think we might end up fucking in the elevator, the bell rings, and the doors slide open at her floor. To my shock, Trixie pulls her lips away from mine, grabs my hand, and marches down the corridor toward her room.

I think about asking what she wants to happen, but I get the picture when we get to her room. She presses her key card to the door, opens it, and literally drags me inside by my lapels. Next thing I know, Trixie pushes me against the inside of the door, causing it to slam shut, and then her mouth is on mine again. I crave the feeling of her soft pillowy lips, insistent and searching, her arms sliding up around my shoulders, fisting the hair at the back of my head.

I always did love how confident Trixie was in bed, but I want to take control of this, so I spin us around, running my hands down her sides. I grab the hem of her dress and slide the material up around her hips and then palm her ass so I can press her against the door. Trixie gasps, and I feel her lips stretch into a smile under mine as my steely thickness finds the sensitive needy place between her thighs.

"Oh fuck, Sugar," I moan, tracing the angle of her jaw with my lips. "How is it possible that you're hotter now than before?"

Trixie chuckles, deep and throaty, squeezing her thighs around my hips. "I don't think I'm hotter. I just think we're both hornier."

"Not true, baby. You're a fucking knockout." I keep her body pressed against the door with the weight of mine and use my hands to cup her generous tits, testing the weight of them and feeling her nipples harden against my palms.

Jesus, I'm going to need to slow this runaway train down before I make a mess in my pants.

But before I can suggest we take a minute, I feel Trixie's thighs loosen around me, and she slides to the floor, shimmying her dress back down. I can tell she's having doubts, so I take a small step back and covertly reach down to rearrange my hard dick so it's not so obvious.

"As hot as this is, I think we should stop." She sighs breathlessly, closing her eyes and letting her head drop back against the door with a thud.

I laugh and shake my head, reaching up to cup her cheek, running my thumb over it, feeling the heat of her satin soft skin.

"Trixie, open your eyes," I command, and she does as I ask, her pupils huge with arousal. "It's okay. I know this probably isn't the smartest move."

"It's not, but fuck me, it feels so good." She wraps her fingers around my wrist and gently moves my hand away from her face. She steps to the side so she's no longer between me and the door and sits on the edge of the bed, running her hands through her messed up hair.

As I stand there and look at this sexy woman, her lips swollen from kissing, I realize that if we make love tonight, I'll never be able to let her go again. So in the interest of self-preservation, I put my hand on the door handle and turn it.

"I'll order breakfast in my suite for 8:30," I say, looking back over my shoulder, offering her a half smile.

Thankfully, Trixie smiles back at me, and I feel the huge wave of relief wash over me. I have a feeling I'll need all the friends I can get in the coming months, and I know Trixie will always tell it to me straight.

"I'll see you in the morning, love." She winks at me, kicking off her shoes and disappearing into the bathroom.

"Good night," I say, quietly leaving her room so I can return to mine and take a very cold shower.

6

Trixie

I feel like I'm waiting outside the Headmaster's office. My stomach is in nervous knots, and I can't stop my knee from bouncing and my heel from clicking on the floor.

"Trixie, please stop," Chris growls from his seat beside me, his large hand sliding onto my knee to stop it bouncing.

I glance over at him and notice he's pale and looks absolutely terrified. For all the nerves I'm feeling, he must be feeling it a hundred times more. At breakfast, he was his cocky, confident self, making all the jokes and seeming carefree about the whole situation. But as we took the car through Memphis toward the lawyer's office, he got quieter and quieter. By the time we reached our destination, he looked like he was about to walk up to the gallows for execution.

Thankfully, Martine Hill was waiting for us, and she took us straight through to her office where she offered Chris her condolences and then began to talk through the process of him becoming Danny's legal guardian. We'd agreed at breakfast that he would ask about Danny's father, just to make sure that he wouldn't suddenly reappear some time in the future. Martine reassured him that the father had never been in the picture and isn't even named on Danny's birth certificate. I could tell by his body language that he felt a sense of relief and disappointment. After he had that piece of information, I could tell he wasn't really listening to her, so I made notes on my iPhone of the important legal stuff.

Once she finished with the legalities, Martine suggested we head over to Danny's foster home to meet him before signing any paperwork. It was so sweet how insistent Chris was that he was taking on guardianship and that he didn't need to meet the kid, but Martine was clear that it was as much about Danny's reaction to Chris as his reaction to Danny.

So now we're waiting outside the office at the foster home while the head social worker collects Danny from the art room. When I heard the words "foster home," I imagined a dirty, old, ramshackle building full of thin, pale boys dressed in rags. Obviously, this place is the complete opposite to what I imagined, and from the look of relief on Chris's face, he had the same misconceptions that I had.

But even though it's bright and warm and all the staff look kind and smiley, it's not a place I'd want to grow up. And it sure as hell isn't a home.

"Is it bad that I'm shitting my shorts right now?" Chris whispers.

I turn in my chair and put my hand over his—it's cold despite it being in the mid-80s and humid as hell. I have to admit, the Tennessee climate was always difficult for me—Seattle is more similar to England, and I find the drizzle quite comforting.

"You have every right to be nervous. But perhaps less swearing in front of the kids," I joke to try to relax him, but he just looks at me like he's dropped an F-bomb in church. "Seriously, just relax. He's gonna love you."

"Mr. Ford." A voice causes us both to look down the corridor where the social worker is standing alone. "I'm Madeline Connors, Danny's social worker. He's ready for you now. He seems more comfortable in the art room, so we've moved the other children outside to play, and you have some privacy. If you'd like to follow me." She smiles kindly and indicates for us to follow.

Chris takes a deep, shaky breath and stands up, his hand gripping mine as we follow Madeline through a maze of corridors until we reach a door covered in kids' artwork and pictures.

"Just relax and follow Danny's lead," she suggests before we go in. "He's not spoken much while he's been here, so don't expect to get much conversation. But keep talking to him, tell him things about you and ask him questions. You never know, he might talk to you."

With that last piece of advice, Madeline opens the door, and we enter a bright sunny room with a huge rainbow mural on the wall and large windows looking out onto the garden. There are easels and tables of different sizes and shelves full of art supplies and a bank of iPads and laptops. It's a lovely space, and I can understand why Danny enjoys it here. It would've been heaven for me as a child.

As my eyes scan the room, they fall upon a small

table in the far corner surrounded by tiny red plastic chairs. And sitting on one of the chairs, hunched over a large piece of paper with a red crayon in his hand is Danny. He's wearing little basketball shorts, high-top sneakers, and a t-shirt from the Memphis NBA team. His loose black curls are long on top but shaved at the back and sides, and as he concentrates on his drawing, his little tongue peeks out the corner of his mouth.

I glance over at Chris, and he's as frozen in place as I am, mesmerized by the little boy in front of us. His eyes are wide, and if I'm not mistaken, they're slightly shiny with emotion.

"You can go and say hi," Madeline whispers, sensing that both of us have no idea what to do.

I don't want to encroach on this moment between Chris and his nephew, so I gently push him forward, and he starts to walk toward the table. When he's standing next to Danny, I realize how enormous he looks in comparison, so when he looks at me with pleading eyes, I make a motion for him to sit down so he's not so intimidating.

As Chris maneuvers his huge frame onto the tiny plastic chair, I fear it might collapse, but even though the legs bow in protest, it holds.

I realize I'm holding my breath, and when Chris finally speaks, I let it out in a quiet gust.

"Whatcha drawing there, buddy?" he asks in a gentle voice that I've never heard him use before.

Danny looks up slowly and stares at Chris for a minute, and then looks back at his picture, swapping the red crayon for the blue one. Chris looks at me, seeming completely lost, so I make a "keep going" motion with my hand.

"I see you like basketball," Chris tries again to engage Danny. "I played in high school, but I was better at hockey. Do you like hockey?"

Danny shakes his head and keeps coloring, not lifting his head to even look at Chris, and my heart just breaks for both of them. I hate to see Chris looking so out of his depth, so I decide to see if I can help. I have little to no experience with children, not since I was one, but it can't hurt.

I walk over and sit on the small chair across from Danny and lean forward. "Hello Danny, my name's Trixie. That's a great car you've drawn. Do you like cars?"

I look over at Chris when he doesn't reply and grimace, shrugging my shoulders.

"You talk funny." The quiet voice shocks us both, and Chris physically jumps in his seat, making the legs crack loudly.

I laugh and nod slowly. "Yes, I suppose I do. Do you know what country I'm from?"

Danny finally lifts his head and looks at me with the green eyes he shares with his uncle. It feels like he's looking directly into my soul, and I have to admit it unnerves me quite a bit. As he examines me, he bites his bottom lip and squints, like he's really running through all the possibilities.

"You talk like my favorite soccer player, and he's from England," Danny finally says and, without waiting for my reaction, goes back to his drawing.

"That's right." I laugh, thrilled that he's so smart. "But if we're being accurate, you should really call it football. Who's your favorite player?"

But to that question, I get no response. He goes back to his drawing. It seems that small exchange is all we're getting today.

"Hey Danny, you wanna go out and play with the other kids?" Madeline has come over and probably senses everyone has reached their limit.

Danny nods and gets up, putting his crayons away in the right box. Before he leaves, he stops next to me and hands me his drawing.

"Is this for me?" I ask, feeling my throat close up with emotion as he nods sincerely. I hold the picture up and look at what he's drawn. It's a red car with a little boy and a woman in the driver's seat. "Who's this?" I point to the woman, but instead of replying, Danny runs out of the back door into the garden and disappears round the corner.

Chris and I both stand up and look out into the garden after him and then back to Madeline who looks over at the drawing Danny has just given me.

"That's his mom," she says sadly. "She's been in every picture he's drawn since he came here. No matter what he draws, his mom is always in the picture."

I bite down on my bottom lip to stop it wobbling as I think about Danny's situation. *Poor little poppet just misses his mum.* No wonder he doesn't want to talk to a couple of strangers.

"He liked you." Chris's voice makes me jump a little, and when I look at him, I can see the hurt in his eyes.

"I'm sorry. I didn't mean to interfere," I say, feeling like shit for stepping on his toes.

"Don't be sorry, honey," Madeline says. "That's the most he's spoken since he came here."

I feel Chris tense up even more next to me at her confession, and I want to go back in time and stay out of their first interaction.

"And it's good that he'll speak to one of you when you get home and settle in together."

Both Chris and I snap our heads toward Madeline with our mouths hanging open—does she think we're a couple and are going to raise Danny together? I can see the hopeful look on her face. She just wants the best for this little boy, and it seems she'd feel more comfortable letting Danny go home with Chris if she thinks I'm part of the package too.

"Oh, no, we're not…" Chris begins, but I put my hand on his arm and interrupt him.

"We're not married," I blurt. "In fact, we haven't been dating very long. But we were a couple about ten years ago and have just rekindled things."

I almost laugh at the comical look of shock on Chris's face, but I try to keep calm. If this lady thinks we're a couple and that makes things run more smoothly for Chris, then I'll go along with it.

"Oh that's so romantic," she gushes, blushing a little. "I'm just going to check a few things with my manager and then we can move things along for you."

She turns to leave, and I can tell that Chris is about to explode with questions once the door closes.

"What the fuck, Trixie?" he whisper-yells, pacing back and forth, raking his fingers through his hair. "We're not a couple. We're only just friends again. You can't go lying to social workers."

"It's not really a lie," I say, shrugging. "Look, Danny took a liking to me, and I think the whole process will go more smoothly if they think you have a woman in your life. Let's be honest: as progressive as the world has become, they'll still be happier signing him over to you if you're in a couple, rather than a single man with a job that means you're traveling every few weeks."

"But it's a lie," he hisses. "They'll find out as soon as they do the first home visit, and they realize you don't live with me."

"That's why I said we'd just started dating, but we have a long history. They won't expect us to be living together yet," I reply. "It's fine."

Chris huffs out a breath and nods his head. "He hates me."

The look of disappointment on his face is heartbreaking. "That's not true. He's a little kid who's just lost his mum, who I guess was the only person in his life. Then he's ripped out of his home, put here with strangers, and then more strangers show up. This has happened all at once, and he's probably just trying to keep up."

"But what am I gonna do if he won't talk to me?"

"You're going to have to be patient and let him do it in his own time," I reply, gripping his biceps. "And since when has Chris Ford shied away from a challenge? You've got this."

He slowly nods, but I'm not convinced he believes what I'm saying.

Then he surprises me by pulling me into a tight hug, burying his face in my neck so the scruff on his cheek scratches the sensitive skin slightly. I know it's not an appropriate moment, but that always turns me on, and I can't help but press my thighs together in an attempt to dull the ache.

"You guys are just adorable." Madeline's return causes the embrace to end, and I'm both relieved and disappointed to lose the warmth of his body against mine.

"So what happens now?" Chris asks, clasping my hand in his. I don't know if it's for her benefit, or he needs the comfort, but I let him hold my hand.

"We feel it would be best for Danny to have a gradual transition. You'll have some legal things to do with your lawyer, and they may insist on a home visit before they release Danny into your custody," she explains. "But if you're going to stay in Memphis during that time, then we'd love for you to come and spend as much time with him as you can. It'll help in the transition. Of course our counselors will be talking to him about what's going to happen so he should be prepared when the time comes."

Chris nods in agreement. "Okay, so we'll go back to the lawyer and start the paperwork. I'd really like to come back tomorrow and see Danny."

Madeline pats his arm and smiles kindly. "That would be wonderful. And just a little tip in case you want to bring him something to get the conversation started—he loves peanut butter cups."

Chris laughs for what feels like the first time in ages, and I know exactly what he's going to say. "I absolutely love peanut butter."

"Perfect! We'll see you tomorrow. The children go swimming between 1 and 3, so before or after that would be best."

Madeline starts to walk us out, and I feel Chris

beginning to relax, although he's still gripping my hand like his life depends on it.

I know that he's a good man, and he wants to step up for Danny; however, I'm under no illusions that it's going to be an easy ride. I just hope Chris allows his friends and the team to help him—he has a stubborn streak a mile wide, and he's going to have to compromise more than he's ever had to before.

The next few days are a blur of lawyers, papers, courts, and visits to the foster home. On Madeline's advice, Chris brings a bag of peanut butter cups on his next visit. While he watches Danny play a game on an iPad, he slowly pulls them out of his jacket pocket and puts them on the couch cushion between them. Danny still hasn't spoken to Chris, and as I watch the exchange from across the room, I pray the candy will at least get a reaction. But it seems Danny shares his uncle's stubborn streak because apart from a quick glance at the bag, he hasn't reacted.

Chris flicks his eyes to me, and I mime opening the bag and eating a peanut butter cup. So he does as I suggest, and it seems that as soon as the sweet smell of chocolate and peanuts hits Danny's nose, his interest is piqued. Chris puts his hand into the bag and pulls out a chocolate cup and pops it into his mouth, chewing and rolling his eyes in ecstasy.

"Oh boy, I love peanut butter cups," he says loudly and a little over-dramatically, but I like his commitment to the role. It makes me smile so hard my cheeks hurt.

Danny's eyes are now firmly on the bag of candy in Chris's hand, and the iPad is forgotten for now.

But he still hasn't spoken.

I told Chris in the car that he should push for Danny to ask for what he wants. This will help when they're living together. So I told him not to hand over any candy until Danny uses his words. The social worker agreed with this when we asked her if that was okay, and I hope Chris's willpower holds, and he doesn't give in.

"You like these too?" he finally asks, shaking the bag.

Danny nods his head but still doesn't say anything. His green eyes are fixed so hard on the candy, I feel like he's going to make one rise out of the bag through the power of his mind alone.

"Do you want one?" Chris presses. "I can't eat this whole bag on my own, and Trixie doesn't like them. She thinks peanut butter is gross."

As if to check what Chris is saying is true, Danny glances over at me, and I make a gagging sick noise which raises a little smile on his lips.

"So, do you want one, buddy?" Chris asks again and Danny nods, reaching out his little hand.

This is it—will Chris give in or make him ask for what he wants?

But he draws the bag away from Danny's approaching hand and shakes his head. "What do you say if you want something, buddy? I need to hear you say it."

Danny's lips press together in a hard line, and I think he's going to dig his heels in and give up his beloved peanut butter cups rather than speak.

However, to my joy and astonishment, his voice sounds loud and clear in the quiet room.

"Please may I have some candy?"

Chris looks like he's about to burst into tears as Danny looks up at him with pleading eyes, but he holds his shit together and nods. "Sure thing. Not too many, though. I don't wanna get into trouble." He looks over his shoulder as if he's expecting to see the social worker lurking and quickly lets Danny dip his hand into the bag and take a candy.

It's such a beautiful moment, and I'm struggling not to cry like a baby. As the pair of them enjoy way too many peanut butter cups and play on the iPad, I have a feeling things will be a little easier now they've made this connection. Not all of this can be solved with candy, but it's a good start.

7

Chris

"**I**s this too much basketball stuff?" I ask looking around my spare bedroom.

"No! Every kid wants a room that looks like their favorite team is using it as a merchandise storage room." Thor laughs, putting down the screwdriver he's just used to fix the little basketball hoop to the back of the door.

"Okay, so I may have gone a little nuts, but I want him to have things around him that he likes," I reply, looking at all the basketball themed stuff I bought— bedsheets, drapes, posters, toys.

"It's nice you did this, man," Bugs says, shaking out the bedsheets and doing a piss poor job of putting them onto the little racecar bed. "I mean we get SJ a shit ton of toys, and she still plays with this same smelly pink rabbit she's had since she was a newborn. Kids just want things around them that give them comfort."

I look at my captain, aghast. "You mean I shouldn't have bought all this stuff?" I throw my arms up in the air in exasperation. I wish I hadn't asked the guys around to help now. They've just made me more confused.

"No. That's not what he's saying," Nate says. "Perhaps what he means is give the kid your time and attention; it's not about stuff."

I sigh and know my friends are just trying to help. "Yeah, I get that. I'm just completely out of my depth, and if I'm honest, I'm fucking terrified I'm gonna break him or lose him or something."

"We've got you, Ford." Matt slaps my back and nods at all the other guys who show their agreement. "We may not know the first thing about kids, and I'm counting the captain in on that, but we'll do whatever we can to help you out."

"Despite the dissing of my parenting skills," Bugs says, flipping Matt off, "he's right. We'll do whatever we can to help, and I'm sure if Knox could be bothered to show up, he'd offer to interview nannies for you."

The guys laugh, and Nate helps Bugs finish making the bed while Thor clears away his tools. I'm so lucky to have such an amazing group of teammates, and not just that—I count these guys as my best friends.

"C'mon, we're done here. I promised you all beer and pizza, so let's order."

After I call in the order, we sit around the kitchen counter and drink some well-deserved beers. We're all very aware that training camp starts soon, so we're going to enjoy these treats while we can.

"So, Cam went out for coffee with Trixie, and I hear you two have made up," Bugs says, smirking around the neck of his beer bottle.

"Really? The cold war is over?" Thor chuckles, leaning his thick forearms on the marble countertop, raising his blonde eyebrow.

They all know about my history with Trixie and the fact we've been actively avoiding each other.

"Yeah, we've talked about what happened back in Memphis, and we've agreed to a fresh start," I explain, trying not to give away any details from our two extremely hot hookups.

"And…" Bugs pushes and I have a feeling Cam managed to dig some juicy details out of Trixie which she almost certainly passed on to Bugs.

"And nothing," I mutter, trying to protect Trixie's professional reputation. "She came to Memphis as a friend, and she's going to help with Danny when he arrives. The two of them hit it off, and I'll do anything to make this easy for him."

"Does that include faking a relationship with her?" Bugs finally drops the bomb he's been holding on to. Thor almost spits his beer out, and the rest of them just stare at me like I grew another head.

"That's not what's going on," I protest, just as the buzzer sounds to announce the arrival of the pizzas.

The guys at least have the decency to let me put the pizza boxes down before the Spanish Inquisition begins.

"You're faking a relationship with Trixie to what end?" Matt asks first, grabbing a slice of pizza.

"That's not what's happening," I protest again, suddenly losing my appetite.

"So explain…" Nate presses, dabbing his slice with a napkin.

"Okay, when we visited Danny in the foster home, the social worker made the assumption that Trixie and I are a couple. I was about to set her straight, but Trixie told her we'd just got back together after a ten-year break. She seems to think it'll make them less cautious about signing guardianship over to me if they think I'm part of a couple."

I take a big gulp of beer and look around at the astonished faces of my teammates. There's no judgment in their expressions, just concern and curiosity.

"For fuck's sake, say something," I groan. "Have I completely fucked this up?"

"Fucked up what?" Nate asks, swallowing his mouthful of pizza. "Your parenting of Danny or your relationship with Trixie?"

I think for a moment, remembering how great it felt to be with Trixie again and how naturally she interacted with Danny.

"I don't know," I finally confess. "I don't want Trixie to feel like I'm using her to help me with Danny, but it felt really great to reconnect with her."

"Do you want a relationship with her again?" Bugs asks, famously not pulling his punches.

"Jesus, that's a question I just can't answer yet." I huff out a breath, rest my elbows on the countertop, and cover my face with my hands.

"C'mon, man," Matt says, putting his hand on my back. "One thing at a time. Danny's arriving in a few days, right?"

I nod my head but keep my face covered with my hands, feeling completely out of my depth.

"Okay, so focus on getting him here and settled in. You have some time before training camp starts, so spend it getting to know each other. Hire a damn nanny, and things with Trixie can just stay on the back burner for now." Matt slaps my back, and I lift my head, taking a deep cleansing breath.

"You're right. Danny comes first. Trixie knows the deal. It was her suggestion in the first place so I shouldn't overthink things, right?" I ask, looking around the group.

Thankfully, I receive nods from everyone.

"Cam wants you and Danny to come for dinner sometime, so just let us know when you're ready," Bugs says, finishing his beer.

"Does that invitation extend to all of us?" Thor asks, a hopeful look on his face.

"Dude, you're dating a chef." Bugs laughs. "You don't need to come to my house and eat Cam's interesting food." He makes a face, but I can tell by the sparkle in his eyes, he wouldn't change his woman for anything.

Once the pizza and beer run out, my teammates begin to leave so they can get on with their Saturday nights, and suddenly my apartment feels too big and empty. I grab the last beer from the fridge and flop down onto the couch, looking around. Until now, I've never noticed that my apartment seems devoid of warmth and comfort. Sure, I've got the best high end furnishings, but there aren't any personal touches. The only thing that would show you this isn't an Airbnb is the picture of my mom and me at my high school graduation and my first Memphis Jazz jersey that hangs in a frame on the wall in my office.

As I wander around my place, I consider how Danny will fit in here. I think about how homely and child friendly the foster home is compared to the sterile design of my apartment. This place was just meant to be somewhere to rest my head between games and travel. I never stay here during Bye Week or the off season because I like to travel, so I've never really tried to make it a home.

But that's exactly what I need to turn it into now. Somewhere Danny can grow up and be happy and safe after the rough time he's been through. I've spent so long thinking about Danny's room, I forgot about the rest of my apartment.

I quickly pull my cell phone out of the back pocket of my jeans, and my finger hovers over Trixie's number. Should I call her and ask for advice? After what the guys said earlier, I'm worried I'm putting too much stress on our fragile new friendship.

But she did tell me to call if I need anything, and I really need some help making my place more child friendly. And from what I remember about Trixie's place, it's warm and inviting.

I'm about to hit her contact when a call from Blake fills my screen. Shit, I've been avoiding him since I got back from Memphis, but his persistent calls can only mean one thing—he's heard about Danny, and he's pissed that I didn't take his advice.

I take a deep breath and answer his call.

"Hey man, I…" I start, but Blake's angry voice cuts me off.

"What the actual fuck, Ford?" he shouts. I've very rarely heard Blake lose his cool, so I'm shocked by his outburst. "You fuck off to Memphis against my advice, and to make matters worse, you take that British ballbuster with you?"

Suddenly, I'm not pissed at him for yelling at me. My blood is boiling at his attitude toward Trixie.

"Now just wait one goddamn minute…" I yell back as I begin to pace angrily around my kitchen.

"No, you wait! Do you know how it looks when you take another agent with you?" Blake's voice is now low and dangerous. "It makes me look like a dick. I give you the best advice for your career, and you disregard it. Do you want me to be your agent or not?"

"C'mon, man. It wasn't about not taking your advice. Trixie and I have a history, and she came with me as a friend, not as my agent," I explain.

Blake's cold laugh makes my skin crawl. "Oh we all know about you and Trixie. You're a fucking fool if you think she'll give up her career to play house with you and the orphan. Isn't that why she dumped your ass ten years ago?"

The surge of anger that floods my system makes me grip my cell phone so tightly, I think I'm going to crack the screen.

"I think we should end this conversation now before either of us says something we can't take back," I growl. "If you want to continue being my agent, I suggest you adjust your fucking attitude toward this situation. It's happening, and I'll be doing it with or without you."

"Fine," Blake replies, and I can actually imagine the pouty look on his face.

"Oh and one more thing," I add. "If I ever hear you disrespect Trixie in a personal or professional way again, I'll rip your fucking head off. You hear me?"

Blake just grunts and hangs up. Jesus, that guy has a fucking nerve. I wonder again why the hell I put up with his shit.

But that's something to think about another day.

I've got enough going on right now.

So, before I can lose my nerve, I hit Trixie's number and prepare to ask for her help yet again.

8

Trixie

One thing I always appreciated about Chris was his punctuality—he's not one of those guys who keeps you hanging around. In fact, it's me running late today. I've been all the way across town at a meeting with my top football client, a meeting I couldn't reschedule when Chris called me last night asking for a favor.

He had a weird, tense tone to his voice, so of course I offered to help him. I promised before we left Memphis that I'll support him in any way I can, and if that means meeting him at my favorite furniture shop then so be it.

As I pull into the parking lot, I see him pacing next to his car, aviator shades covering his eyes. And damn he looks good—tight dark jeans show off his perfect hockey butt, and an Arctic Monkeys band tee clings to his broad shoulders and sculpted chest. I'd managed to get to a point where seeing Chris didn't cause a physical response, but now I'm back to that place where even seeing him at a game or on the TV causes my lady business to flutter and my nipples to harden against the lace of my bra. It's made worse now by the fact that I see him in real life—I get to inhale his scent and see the naughty glint in his green eyes.

Fuck my life! Why did I suggest this stupid arrangement? It's like I'm some kind of lovesick groupie, doing anything to be close to the object of my obsession.

So before I can chicken out, I doublecheck my face in my rear view mirror, look down to make sure my nipples aren't embarrassingly erect, and then hop out of the car. Chris notices me and the obvious look of relief on his face makes my heart ache. I know how stressful he's finding this life change, and I just can't let him flounder.

I heard from my assistant that his agent, Blake, has been bitching to anyone who will listen that Chris is being an idiot, and this will ruin what little career he has left. Some of the shit he's been saying about me doesn't even bear repeating. I've been dealing with misogynistic wankers my whole career, and Blake is nothing special—I'll deal with that little prick in my own time.

Right now, Chris and Danny are my focus.

"Thanks for coming, Sugar," he says on a breath, almost like he's been holding it since we spoke last night. "I know you're busy, but I'll just buy loads of crap that doesn't go together, and my place will look even worse."

I laugh kindly and pat his bicep. "It's no problem, love. This place is amazing, and Claire has the best eye for design. Did you take all the pictures of your place I asked for?"

"Yeah, they're all on my phone," he replies, waving his cell phone at me.

"Great, let's go."

Two hours later, we emerge into the Seattle drizzle. Chris is several thousand dollars poorer and a little bewildered, but his apartment will look much more homely once all his purchases are delivered tomorrow morning.

"Can I buy you lunch to say thank you?" Chris asks as he walks me back to my car.

"Oh that would be lovely, but I have another meeting in an hour," I reply, hating the crestfallen look on his face. "But I've made sure my diary is clear after tomorrow for a few days so I can help you settle Danny in."

Chris reaches out and opens my car door for me. He was always such a gentleman. "Okay, thanks. I know this is a busy time for you."

"It's fine. My assistant is worth her weight in gold, and she's taking a lot of the less high-profile meetings that I have booked in." I slide into the driver's seat, and before I let Chris shut the door, I remember something else. "Did you call those nanny agencies I sent you?"

Chris rolls his eyes and leans against the car. "Shit, I knew there was something else I had to do. I'll do it as soon as I get home."

"Make sure you do. You want the interviews lined up before Danny arrives so you can pre-interview each one before they actually spend any time with him. Go with the one who has the best connection with Danny. His happiness is most important." I sound like I'm being a nag, but I just want Chris to be as prepared as he can be for this huge life change. And with training camp starting just after Danny arrives, he's going to need a nanny in place.

"I'll also send you the numbers of those elementary schools. You should really get Danny a place as soon as you can. He's already missed the start of school, but the longer you leave it, the more difficult it'll be for him to settle in."

Chris smiles down at me. "You think of everything. I couldn't do this without you."

I feel my heart fill up to bursting at how vulnerable and open this experience is making him, but I can't let myself get seduced into falling for him. I'm here purely as a friend.

I just need to keep telling myself that, even if I know deep down it's a bloody lie.

"It's fine." I laugh as nonchalantly as I can manage. "I know you're no good with these sorts of things. I'm happy to help."

"Well, I really appreciate it." He reaches down and cups my cheek in his rough hand, smoothing my cheek with his thumb. "You're a very special woman."

I can't help closing my eyes, and a small moan escapes my lips at his touch. But as quickly as I give into the moment, I snap out of it and gently grip his wrist, moving his hand away from my face.

"I'll see you tomorrow to help with the furniture," I say in a raspy voice, reaching out to close my car door, causing Chris to step back. I'm thankful for the breathing space.

"See you later, Sugar." He gives me bone of his cheeky grins and offers me a mock salute as I slam the door and start the engine.

"You need to lock that shit down, Beatrix," I growl

through gritted teeth so Chris can't see that I'm talking to myself. "He only wants you to help with the boy. He's not interested in getting back together. Stop being such a delusional fool."

After the most pathetic pep talk in history, I shift the car into drive and head off to my next meeting, still trying to convince myself that there's nothing between Chris and me except a blossoming friendship.

My heart stutters at the thought of only being friends with him, and I rub the center of my chest where it's suddenly become very tight.

Shit, I never was a good liar.

"It looks great," I say, plumping the last throw cushion and standing back to admire Chris's new apartment look. "Claire did an amazing job picking out pieces that are stylish but comfy and definitely child friendly. No light colors just in case of spillages or chocolate smudges."

"Y'all did a superb job," Chris replies, looking around with a slightly bewildered but happy look on his face. "You know this place never felt very homey, and I was fine with that. But now I feel better about bringing Danny here. Thanks." He leans in and kisses my cheek, the scruff on his face scratching in a way that always made me shiver with pleasure. It takes every muscle in my body to suppress the urge to lean into his solid frame and allow him to hold me in the way he used to. We always seemed to fit together perfectly, my head resting on his shoulder in just the right place for me to press my face against his neck and breathe in his scent.

"Trixie? You okay?" Chris's voice brings me out of my daydream, and I look at him, his brow creased in curiosity. I must have looked totally zoned out while I was fantasizing about the smell of his neck.

"Yeah, I'm fine." I laugh self-consciously, my cheeks feeling a little too hot. "Let's take one more look in Danny's room and make sure you have everything he needs."

I quickly stride down the hall, needing a little distance from Chris so I can gather myself. I can't let him see that I'm starting to get feelings for him again. He has enough to deal with, and I don't want him to have the pressure of thinking about me on top of everything else.

When I push open the door to Danny's room, my breath catches in my throat, and my nose tingles with emotion. It's such a perfect room for him—all the basketball stuff and the little art table in the corner with every possible art supply imaginable. Chris even painted one of the walls with chalkboard paint so Danny can draw directly on the wall with a rainbow of colored chalks.

"You think he'll be okay in here?" Chris asks nervously, wringing his hands.

I turn and swallow down my emotion so he can't see how much his thoughtfulness has affected me. "It's perfect. You know exactly what he likes, but it's not going to be overwhelming."

Suddenly something catches my eye, and I walk over to the little table by the bed. I pick up the small wooden frame and look at the pretty woman with dark brown hair and a bright smile. She's holding up a laughing child, and they're looking at each other with so much love, I feel a tear slide down my cheek.

"I asked the lawyer to send me pictures of Danny and his mom so I could put them up around the apartment for him," Chris says as he moves to stand next to me, taking the frame from my hand and placing it back on the table. "I wanted him to have as many pictures as he wanted, but I wanted it to be something we did together when he arrives. You know, pick out the frames he wants, put them in places he chooses…" He shrugs like this gesture isn't the sweetest, most thoughtful thing he could have possibly done for this little boy.

Before I can stop myself, I wrap my arms around his neck, rise up on my tiptoes, and press my lips to his, my cheeks now soaked with tears. At first Chris's lips stay in a firm line, but then I feel his arms wrap around my back, and he returns my kiss, his tongue stroking mine as he deepens it. I moan slightly as his hands slide down my back and grab each of my generous ass cheeks, pulling me firmly against his body, the hard ridge of his dick pressing into my stomach. I can't help getting lost in the intoxicating mix of familiarity and excitement—Chris has certainly become a more skilled kisser since we were last together. The night in my house and in the hotel room in Memphis, we were both a little bit tipsy, but now we're both stone cold sober, and it feels even better than my fuzzy memories of those trysts.

But suddenly I realize we're standing in Danny's new room, making out like horny teenagers, and I get a major case of the icks. So I quickly pull away and put my fingers to my kiss-swollen lips.

"We can't do this here," I pant, trying to get my racing hormones under control.

Chris looks at me with those wild eyes, and I can tell he's as on the edge as I am.

"If we don't control this now, it'll make it so complicated," I say, trying to be the sensible one because I know that look, and if I give him the slightest indication that I'm feeling the same, he'll fling me over his shoulder and have me in his bed before I can blink. And as exciting as that sounds and as horny as I am, I can't let this run away from us.

Chris blinks a few times, and I see the fire die in eyes. He's getting control of himself, his senses coming back to him. "You're right." He sighs, stepping forward and giving me a hug. I take a deep breath, squeeze him back, and then end the contact. I know it was meant to be comforting, but in my heightened state of arousal, it was like pouring gas on a fire—catastrophe!

"Have you set up the nanny interviews?" I ask as we leave Danny's room and head back into the main room.

"Yeah, I'm seeing three tomorrow. Danny arrives the day after so at least I can bring the best ones in a few days later so he can meet them." Chris gets a couple of bottles of water from the fridge and hands one to me. "And we have some meetings at the two schools with spaces the week after training camp starts. Coach Casey has given me a day off to go and look around and set up registration."

"That's great. Well, it seems you're on top of everything." I take a gulp of water because I'm suddenly thinking about Chris on top of me, and my mouth has gone dry.

"Can I ask another favor?" he asks, picking at the label on his water bottle.

"Sure, what do you need?"

"Would you help me with the nanny interviews? I've never interviewed anyone before, and I have no idea what to look for." Chris looks down at his fingers nervously.

"Of course," I reply, patting his arm. "What time do you want me here?"

"The first interview is at 1. I don't even know what to ask them." He runs his hands through his hair and tugs it a little the way he does when he's stressed. "I'm so out of my element here. I've got no fucking idea what I'm doing."

My heart just breaks for him, but I know what a resourceful and capable man he is; he just needs reminding of that.

"Look, why don't you go online and search for interview questions to ask a nanny? You can find anything online these days." I stand in front of him and hold his arms, trying not to think about how hard and tight his biceps are. "You've got this, and I'll be here to back you up."

I see the relief wash over Chris's face and the determined set of his chin.

"Thanks, Trixie. You always know just what to say to make me feel better." He leans down and brushes a chaste kiss against my cheek, and despite the friendly nature of the kiss, it still sets my knickers on fire.

"Well, I'll see you tomorrow, love. About 12:30?" I

pull away and clutch my purse to my chest in a vain attempt to cover my hard nipples.

"Perfect. See you then." Chris offers me one of his crooked grins, and I turn on my heel because if I don't get out of here, I'll do something stupid.

Suddenly, I feel his strong fingers wrap around my arm, and I turn to look at him.

"Trixie, if this is too much, you need to say now. I can easily tell the social worker that we split up. The paperwork is all signed now so I just have to get through a couple of home visits, and it'll be done. I don't want you to get involved in this if it's too weird or uncomfortable."

I let out a deep sigh and put my hand on his firm chest. "It's fine, really. I said I'd help and I will. We just need to stop with all the kissing, and it'll be great."

He lets out a relieved laugh and shakes his head, leaning in to whisper in my ear. "I can't promise I won't kiss you again, Sugar. But I won't do it until you ask me."

My mouth drops open slightly, and I pull back, knocking into the bar stool behind me. I grab it and try not to fall over my feet, my head spinning as his words replay over and over.

"Okay then, I'm going. See you tomorrow." I untangle my purse straps from the back of the bar stool and steady it so it doesn't fall over. Chris has that sexy smirk on his face, and I stumble out of his apartment like an idiot. I speedwalk to the elevator and stab at the call button until the doors open and I literally fall into the safety of the car. As the doors slide shut, I lean back against the mirrored walls and exhale.

And right there I make myself a promise that I'll never ask Chris Ford to kiss me. Ever.

Chris

"**I** majored in Human Development with Early Childhood Education at Washington State," the pretty redhead gushes as she claps her hands in front of her. "I just love kids. I've been babysitting since I was thirteen, and I have four younger siblings. It's always been my dream to be a teacher, but I realized that I'd rather work one to one with a child to really help develop them into a well-rounded person."

"Wow." I swallow, a little overwhelmed by her qualifications and passion. She's the third candidate we've interviewed and so far she's the most qualified. The first woman was so old she walked with a cane, and I was worried she wouldn't be able to keep up with an energetic kid like Danny. And the second one was very experienced, but as soon as she set eyes on me, I could tell that she knew who I was. I mean, I am a well-known personality around Seattle so that had to be expected, so I didn't want to discount her because of that. I discounted her once she said her dream was to be a Whalers ice girl, and she asked me if I could get her an audition.

"So, Annie, tell me about your last position as a nanny. What did you learn from that role?" Thankfully, Trixie has the next question, so I have a minute to compose myself.

"Oh, they were a wonderful family. They had two children under four years old, and it had its challenges. But seeing the children grow and develop was so rewarding." Annie looks a little sad. "I was heartbroken when they moved to Tulsa, and I couldn't go with them." A fat tear rolls down her freckled cheek, and she quickly swipes it away. "I'm sorry. I must seem like a cry-baby."

Trixie hands her a tissue and looks over at me, smiling. "It's okay, Annie. Take your time. Do you have any questions for us?"

She dabs at her eyes and scrunches the tissue in her hand. "I understand Danny will be starting school soon, so would you want me here during the day, or am I free to run errands?"

"I'd need you to be here to help get him ready for school and take him when I have training or a game and for pick up at the end of day—you know, bring him home, feed him dinner, take him on play dates…" I look over at Trixie, seeking reassurance that I'm saying the right things.

"This is a very new situation for Chris, as we explained at the beginning of the interview," Trixie explains. "A lot of this will be trial and error and figuring out schedules as we go. One thing that will be expected is for you to stay overnight when he is away at games, and sometimes he could be away for several days at a time. Are you comfortable being in sole charge of Danny?"

"Oh yes, that's no problem," Annie replies, smiling confidently. "I used to live-in at my last position so I would often be in sole charge of the children when the parents traveled for work."

"Well, thank you for coming, Annie," Trixie says, standing up and stretching her hand out to Annie. She also stands and shakes Trixie's hand. "We have a few other people to see, so we'll be in touch in the next few days."

"Thank you so much for seeing me." Annie extends her hand to me as I stand, and we shake. "It was great to meet you, and I really can't wait to meet Danny if you take my application further."

Once Trixie has shown Annie out, I flop back on the couch and scrub my hands down my face. Who knew interviewing could be so exhausting?

"I really like her," Trixie says, kicking off her heels and sitting next to me, tucking her legs underneath her. I love how at home she feels in my place—I love that I can smell her perfume on all the things she's touched. But I also know that this thing has an expiration date; once Danny is settled, she'll go back to just being my friend, and I won't have an excuse to keep her close.

"She's definitely the best of the three," I reply. "She's the only one I'd be happy introducing to Danny."

"That's great. I'm pleased you found someone you're comfortable with." Trixie pats my thigh, and I can't help but flinch a little—her touch lights a fire in my groin, and I quickly sit forward so she can't see the bulge that's growing there.

"Yeah, I'll call the agency in a while and arrange for

her to do a trial day once Danny has settled in." I shift uncomfortably and order my dick to control itself—this is really becoming a problem when she's around. I seem to have a constant case of blue balls, and it's making me a little crazy.

"Are you still okay to come to the airport with me tomorrow?" I ask, trying to distract myself from thinking about the feeling of her lips around my cock.

"I certainly am. My assistant is all set to take my meetings so you have me for the day." Trixie claps her hands together and bounces excitedly on the couch. "I really can't wait to see Danny again."

I chuckle and shake my head, loving how excited she is. Trixie puts on this front as a hard, professional businesswoman, but I know all about her soft, squishy center. She's the woman who watches kitten videos on YouTube and cries at wildlife shows. She always gives money to charity and volunteers at animal shelters when she has some time off.

She's perfect in every way and that just makes this situation much harder to bear.

"So you want me to arrange a car service, or are you going to drive?"

Trixie's voice jolts me back to the moment. "Huh?"

"Do you want me to arrange a car service for tomorrow, or are you going to drive?" she repeats, scrunching her eyebrows together.

"Car service, I think. I still have to fit his booster seat in the back of the Tesla." I groan. "I guess I'm gonna have to buy a station wagon or some shit, aren't I?"

Trixie laughs loudly and slaps my arms. "You can keep your fancy car, love. Maybe just get something a little more practical as well."

I can feel the nerves rising in my chest, and I rub between my pecs. "I don't know if I can do this."

Trixie shuffles next to me and rubs my back. "You can absolutely do this. Look at everything you've achieved in your life—you have the skills to do this, love. You just need to relax and believe in yourself. And if you get freaked out, you have me and a whole team of big, burly men who have your back."

I chuckle and look over at Trixie, enchanted by her bright smile and navy blue eyes, memorizing every freckle across her nose because soon they will disappear once fall takes hold.

"Thank you. You always believed in me."

She smiles back at me, and the electricity crackles for just a second, firing up my libido again. Thankfully, she breaks the connection, getting up off the couch and slipping her heels back on.

"I'll get the car service booked," she says, smoothing her skirt down over her curvy hips.

I show Trixie out, and when I close the door, I lean back against it, closing my eyes. The sooner I can get into a routine with Danny and the new nanny, the sooner I can put her firmly back in the friend zone.

"That's his flight coming through now," I say to Trixie, looking around frantically as the swarm of people stream past us at the gate. I'm a tall guy, but I'm this close to climbing on a trash can so I can see over the people better.

But before I can completely lose my mind, Trixie places her hand on my forearm and nods. "There they are," she says, a sweet smile spreading across her face. Although I want nothing more than to gaze at her beauty, I look in the direction she's pointing and see Danny walking hand in hand with the social worker from Memphis. He's wearing his usual basketball jersey and jeans, little black sneakers on his feet, a backpack over his shoulders, and a ragged looking teddy in his hand. His eyes are huge and darting around like he's never seen an airport or that many people in his whole life.

Trixie nudges me in the ribs, and I look at her. "Hold up the sign you made," she whispers, and I remember the large piece of cardboard in my hand which I quickly hold up just as he looks at me. It's one of the signs the Whalers use when they're welcoming people at the airport, so it has the club logo on it and it says, "The Seattle Whalers welcome…" and there's a space to write the name in marker. Cam managed to snag me one from the GM's office when she heard I was collecting Danny from the airport. I thought it was a nice idea, especially if he's forgotten what I look like.

I watch as the social worker sees us, and she stops and drops down to Danny's level, pointing in my direction, saying something quietly to him. He looks over, and I remember to smile and wave, but he still looks very wary and scared. I mean, who can blame him? He's flown halfway across the country to a strange city to live with a person he's met less than a handful of times. If I was him, I'd be hot footing it back onto that plane.

But then I see something that gives me hope—he lifts his chin up in a determined way and covers the distance separating us without the social worker. Wow! What a brave little guy. I grit my teeth and clear my throat because suddenly I feel all kinds of emotions that I'm not used to.

"Well, hi there, Danny," I say when he's in front of me, squatting down to his level like the social worker did. "How was the journey? Was it your first time on a plane?"

Danny suddenly loses his nerve and reaches for the social worker's hand, stepping behind her a little.

"Mr. Ford, it's so good to see you again." She reaches out her free hand, and we shake awkwardly.

"Good to see you too, Madeline. I hope the flight was okay."

"Oh, it was wonderful, wasn't it, Danny?" She looks down to try and engage him in the conversation, but he retreats a little more behind her legs. "And it really wasn't necessary to upgrade us to First Class. But Danny sure did love meeting the pilot, didn't you?"

This time the question encourages him to come out from his hiding place and nod a little.

"Well, it was my pleasure to make that happen. Anything to make this easier for you." Suddenly, I remember Trixie standing patiently next to me. "Madeline, you remember my … girlfriend, Trixie Cavendish."

"Of course, great to see you again." Madeline looks down at Danny. "This little man has been looking at lots of maps of England, and he was wondering if he showed you one whether you could point out where you're from."

Trixie kneels down in front of Danny and smiles warmly at him. "I'd love to do that. I really like maps. Maybe if we go onto my laptop, we can look at some pictures of where I'm from too."

Danny nods enthusiastically, and even though I'm pleased to see them interacting, I can't help but feel a small twinge of jealousy that she has this connection with him. I know it's fucking childish to be jealous of that, so I push that useless emotion to the pit of my stomach and start escorting us out to the car.

On the drive to my apartment, Madeline talks about some of the processes we have to go through now Danny is here in Seattle. She's going to stay for a week to make sure he's settling in and that everything is in place such as a school and childcare. Then she'll return in a month for a final visit before the guardianship is completed.

As she talks, I keep leaning over the console, checking on Danny in his booster seat, looking out of the tinted windows as the city goes past. It's a typical rainy, gray Seattle day, so I bet he's missing the heat of Tennessee about now. He's still clutching that old teddy like his life depends on it, and I really feel for the poor little guy.

Once we arrive at my apartment building, he looks completely overwhelmed by the scale of the place, and he continues to hold his teddy as we ride the elevator up from the lobby. I think his eyes are going to pop right out of his skull when I open the door, and he walks inside.

"You have a beautiful home, Mr. Ford," Madeline

says, her eyes also on stalks as she looks around the open plan living area and kitchen. I'm so relieved I made the changes I did to the place because Danny heads straight to the couch and sits down, staring at the huge flat screen TV I have mounted on the wall.

"Thank you, but I owe it all to Trixie. She's definitely given this place the woman's touch." I put my arm around Trixie's shoulders and kiss the top of her head, the smell of her hair overwhelming my senses.

"Well, it's a beautiful home," Madeline continues. "My only concern is the lack of available outdoor space for Danny. He's used to a big yard where he can ride his bike and explore."

"There's an amazing park a few blocks over," I reply quickly, beginning to panic—I didn't even consider the fact I only have a small terrace, and I definitely wouldn't let Danny play out there on his own.

Madeline must sense my panic. "Please don't worry. I know this has all happened very quickly, and it won't all be perfect." She pats my arm and moves over to sit next to Danny on the couch. They speak quietly and then Danny looks up at me.

"Go ahead, honey," Madeline encourages. "Ask your question."

Danny blinks a few times, and it's almost like he's rehearsing his question in his head before he vocalizes it.

"Can I see my room, please?"

"Right this way, buddy," I say, tilting my head toward the hall that leads to the bedrooms. Danny gingerly stands up and then shocks the hell out of me when he slips his little hand into mine. I look over at Trixie with pleading eyes—what the hell do I do? She just smiles and nods at me, her eyes glistening slightly with emotion, and it gives me the strength to keep going even though I feel like crying like a baby.

"Well, let's go check out your room," I croak, smiling at Danny as I lead him down the hall. Trixie and Madeline don't follow. I guess they want us to have some bonding time alone, and I'm actually grateful for that. I need to see how we interact together, even though it's totally terrifying.

When we get to the end of the hall, I stop outside the room which has a basketball sign emblazoned with Danny's name. I push open the door and let him enter first, which he does a little cautiously. When he's a few steps inside, he turns and looks around, taking in the race car bed, the art supplies, the chalkboard wall where Trixie and I wrote welcome messages for him.

"Is this all for me?" Danny asks quietly.

"Sure is, buddy. But if there's anything you don't like, I can change it," I reply.

He looks around, and suddenly, his gaze lands upon the picture of his mom on the nightstand. He slowly walks over to it, and before I can tell him about my plan with the other pictures, he picks it up and puts it away in the top drawer.

"I like it just fine. Thank you, sir." He turns around and offers me a weak smile, but I can tell by the wetness of his green eyes that the picture idea has backfired, and I've upset him.

And what is with all that "sir" bullshit? I go over and squat down in front of Danny so we're face to face. "Buddy, you can call me Chris, okay?"

"Okay." He kicks his sneaker against the rug and

drops his eyes to look at it. "Can I have a snack, please?"

I let out a breath. "Sure you can. Let's go and see what we've got." I stand up and mentally thank Trixie for arranging a grocery service to deliver enough food to survive a zombie apocalypse. I get all my pre-made meals delivered from the team's nutritionist, and it didn't even occur to me that Danny probably doesn't follow a hockey player's meal plan.

"How'd you like your room, Danny?" Madeline asks when we go back to the kitchen, and I start to look through the cupboards for the goldfish crackers and juice boxes.

"It's good," he replies, sitting back on the couch next to his teddy. "I like the wall. Can I draw on it?"

"Of course you can." Trixie laughs. "You have lots of chalks so you can draw lovely pictures and then just wipe them off and start again."

I hand Danny the crackers and juice box. "Hey, do you wanna watch some TV with Trixie while Madeline and me have a quick talk?"

Danny accepts the food and nods, looking to Trixie who picks up the remote and finds a cartoon on Netflix that he said he likes.

"I think I messed up," I whisper once Madeline and I are out of earshot in the kitchen. "I put one of the pictures of his mom on the nightstand, and when he saw it, he just put it away in the drawer."

Madeline smiles kindly. "You haven't messed up. He has a picture of his mom in his suitcase, so maybe once he's settled, he'll put that one out. But it was a really nice touch. And I love your idea about letting him put up the pictures. You're doing great."

I exhale loudly and scrub my hand down my face. "It's just all so real, now he's actually here."

"Just take it a day at a time. Don't be afraid to ask questions or ask for help. There's no shame in that. You're a new dad and just because Danny isn't a newborn doesn't mean you're not on a steep learning curve"

I nod in agreement, but as I look over at Trixie and Danny watching the cartoon in what appears to be a comfortable silence, I worry that I won't get that kind of connection with him.

"I'll be here for the week, and even though I want to give you guys the space to bond, I'm only a phone call away if you have any questions or you need help." Madeline hands me her card with all her contact details on.

"I really appreciate that." I take the card and attach it to the fridge underneath a magnet. "I've arranged the car service to take you to your hotel. And if you need to get around the city, just call the number I gave you, and the car service will take you wherever you need to go."

"I really appreciate your generosity, but I have an expense account, so I'd be more comfortable taking an Uber." Madeline smiles. "So I'll be back tomorrow at 3 to see how you guys are getting along."

She goes over to Danny and says goodbye to him, accepting a big hug from the little boy who seems reluctant to let her go.

As I close the front door and the lock clicks into place, I feel the weight of responsibility press down on my shoulders. I look over at Danny and watch him popping goldfish crackers into his mouth, knowing that it's now my job to keep this little human safe and alive. My heartrate suddenly kicks up a gear, and I find it hard to catch my breath, sweat breaking out on my temples.

"I'm just hitting the bathroom. Be right back," I croak, rushing down the hall to the bathroom, slamming the door and leaning over the sink, pressing my forehead against the cool mirror.

"Stop panicking, you pussy," I whisper to myself, squeezing my eyes closed.

"Chris, are you okay?" Trixie's quiet voice accompanies a light tap on the door.

I huff out a breath and unlock the door, allowing Trixie to step inside.

"What's going on?" she asks, her eyes scanning my face. I'm sure she's noticed how pale and sweaty I am.

"I can't do this." I shake my head and look at my feet, ashamed to admit my weakness in front of Trixie. "Blake was right. This is a huge mistake, and it's gonna ruin everything."

"Bloody hell." Trixie punches me lightly in the chest, causing me to lift my gaze to meet hers. "I say this with all the support in the world, but you need to get your shit together. You can do this. But I'm not gonna pretend it'll be an easy ride. It's going to be difficult and frustrating, and you'll want to give up every day. But that little boy out there is relying on you, so put your fears aside and do this for him. And fuck Blake! He's a soulless prick."

I can't help but snort out a laugh at the venom Trixie spits when she talks about my agent.

"Okay, I know you're right," I reply quietly, lifting my chin. "I never thought I'd play hockey for a living, but I managed to make that dream come true. I can do this."

"There you go!" Trixie slaps my chest again and smiles. "Now let's get back out there before the kid manages to stick his finger in an outlet or something." She laughs, but I see the realization of that happening cross her face, and we both hustle out of the bathroom to check Danny is still in one piece.

10

Trixie

"**H**e's asleep," Chris whispers as he flops down on the couch next to me. I've seen this guy come off the ice after a brutally long shift, and he didn't look as beat down as he does right now.

After Madeline left, we ordered pizza for dinner, and Danny ate a slice and then asked if he could go to his room. Chris looked a little conflicted, but he let Danny go and spend some time alone, checking on him occasionally to make sure he wasn't crying or upset.

"He'd fallen asleep on top of the comforter so I took his sneakers off and covered him up. Is that okay?" Chris asks, glancing over at me.

"Of course it is." I reach over and pat his thigh. "You're doing a great job."

He lets out a huge breath and scrubs his hands down his face. "How is it possible to be this exhausted? I feel like I've been running on nervous energy since I found out about him."

I laugh. "I think exhaustion is something you'll need to get used to. Just look at how knackered Cam and Bugs are all the time."

"I don't know how they do it," I reply in awe.

I place my hand on top of his and squeeze it. "They do it out of love."

Chris looks over at me, and I see the fear and doubt in his eyes. "Love? That's great, but Danny and I are strangers. How are we gonna get there?"

"Time." I shrug and smile. "When I moved in with my granddad after my mum left, we were virtual strangers. He wasn't looking to take care of a little girl, but he stepped up and was a wonderful parent … eventually. I'm not going to pretend he didn't make mistakes. He fucked up plenty, and I wasn't the easiest kid to live with. But we got through it, and after every mistake, we were a little bit stronger, a little bit closer."

"It's day one, I guess. And he's still in one piece, so I'll take the win." Chris chuckles and shifts a little closer to me, the warmth of his muscular body awakening my arousal. He rests his head on my shoulder, and the smell of his hair does nothing to put out the fire. "Are you gonna stay tonight?" he asks quietly.

Oh god, there's nothing I want more than to spend the night with Chris, but it'll just be so complicated.

"I can make up the pull-out in my office if you do want to stay. I know Danny would like you to be here when he wakes up."

Chris's words are like a bucket of ice water to my libido, and I remember that I'm here for Danny and not to rekindle our relationship.

I swallow the lump of disappointment in my throat and nod. "Sure, that sounds good. I'm quite tired so I think I'll turn in now."

Suddenly, it feels really awkward between us—I

use the bathroom while Chris makes up the pull-out and leaves one of his T-shirts for me to wear in bed. I hold the soft material to my nose and breathe in his familiar scent, hating myself for being so sentimental.

"Do you need a glass of water or anything?" His voice makes me jump, and I spin around, hiding the shirt behind my back, my cheeks burning with embarrassment.

"Were you sniffing my T-shirt?" he asks with an amused grin on his face.

I laugh a little too loudly and then remember Danny is asleep next door, so I clap my hand over my mouth. "No! Don't be gross," I scoff in a loud whisper, holding the shirt out at arm's length. "I was just checking it was clean, that's all."

Chris raises his eyebrow. "Sure thing, Sugar." Then he leans over and brushes a sweet kiss on my cheek. "Good night. And thanks for everything."

"Good night," I whisper, desperate to ask him to stay, but I know it's not the right thing to do. We can't complicate this situation with sex.

So I get undressed down to my panties, and then slip Chris's soft gray T-shirt over my head, engulfing me in his fresh linen scent. As I pull it down over my breasts, my hard nipples brush against the fabric, and I let out a soft moan, imagining his lips there.

I flop down onto the pull-out, and all the sexual tension and frustration that's been building up in me bubbles to the surface, and I can't hold back. I close my eyes and slide my hand over my breast, tweaking my already pert nipple, my back arching with desire. In my head, I picture all the times Chris and I made love—the hard, urgent fucks we had in the early days when we just couldn't keep our hands off each other. Then later, the gentle, romantic times when I felt the tears of joy and contentment slide down my cheeks during our mutual climax.

With all these memories swirling around my head, I'm almost ready to explode by the time my fingers slip inside my panties, past the small patch of soft blonde curls and between my slick folds.

As my fingers slip over my tight bundle of nerves, I let out a soft moan and spread my legs a little wider, dipping my fingers into my wet channel then back up to my clit. I gently rub myself in a steadily increasing rhythm, getting closer and closer until I have to bite down on my fist to muffle the groans of pleasure. I ride the wave of my orgasm until the muscles in my thighs begin to seize up, and I have to whip my fingers away, breathing heavily.

Suddenly, I hear a noise outside the room, and I sit up, the euphoria of my orgasm disappearing in a flash. Oh god, what if it's Danny getting up to use the bathroom? What if he heard me coming? I cover my face with my hands, completely mortified.

I keep listening for a while longer and don't hear anything more, so when my heartrate calms, I lie down and cover myself with the comforter, bringing it up to my chin. It takes a while, because the pull-out isn't very comfortable, but eventually I begin to drift off to sleep.

The next morning the smell of bacon draws me from my sleep. I roll over, groaning at the pain in my back and neck from an uncomfortable night on the pull-out. I quickly use the bathroom, rubbing some toothpaste over my teeth with my finger and getting dressed in my creased clothes. I make a mental note to keep an overnight bag in my car in case this ever happens again.

"Good morning," Chris says brightly when I make an appearance in the kitchen. "There's coffee in the pot and juice on the counter. You like your eggs scrambled, right?"

"Ummm, yeah, scrambled is great. Just make sure they're not runny." I laugh, sitting on one of the high stools at the counter.

Chris laughs as well and flips rashers of crispy bacon onto some paper napkins. "I remember how you like your eggs." He smiles softly, and I think about how much I love the little creases around his eyes.

"Is Danny still sleeping?" I ask, pouring some orange juice, trying to distract myself from how hot he looks in his tight T-shirt and gray sweatpants.

"Yeah, I poked my head in when I woke up, and he was still out cold." He cracks some eggs into a bowl and skillfully whisks them up for my scramble, snipping some chives into the mix. He always could make an excellent breakfast.

As if he heard us talking, Danny wanders sleepily into the kitchen, still in the clothes he had on yesterday minus his sneakers, holding a bundle of sheets in front of him.

"Hey there buddy. Are you hungry?" Chris asks, looking up quickly from the frying pan. "What you got there?"

I can see Danny's cheeks pink up, and his chin starts to wobble, and I know exactly what's happened.

"Chris, why don't you carry on making breakfast and Danny and I will get cleaned up?" I hop down off the stool and move quickly, holding out my hand which I'm relieved Danny takes, and I walk him back down to his room.

"Is everything okay, poppet?" I ask, kneeling down in front of him, noticing that he still hasn't let go of the bundle of sheets.

Danny shakes his head, and tears start rolling down his cheeks. "I had an accident," he sniffles, finally dropping the sheets. "I'm so sorry. I couldn't remember where the bathroom was."

"Oh Danny, it's alright." I hold my arms open, and he steps into them for a hug that doesn't last more than a few seconds before he pulls away, swiping his arm over his eyes. "Come on, let's get you out of these clothes. I'll show you how to work the shower, and you can get cleaned up. I'll take care of your sheets. How does that sound?"

Danny just nods, and I take him to the bathroom, showing him how to use the shower and where to find the towels and soap. Once he's settled, I wait outside until he hands me his clothes and then I gather up the soiled sheets from his room and put them in the laundry.

"Is he okay?" Chris asks when I return to the kitchen, a concerned look on his face.

"He had a little accident, so he's in the shower, and the sheets are in the laundry," I explain, washing my hands at the kitchen sink.

"Shit!" he curses, slamming the spatula down on the counter. "I should've left the bathroom door open so he'd know where to go."

"Hey," I say, resting my hand on his thick forearm. "It's not your fault. It's just one of those things you have to think about in future. It was his first night in a strange place. He'll get used to it."

Chris lets out a huff and picks up the spatula, scooping scrambled eggs onto three plates alongside the bacon and toast. "This is gonna take a lot of getting used to."

"You're doing great," I reassure him, accepting the plate, my stomach growling with hunger. "And this looks amazing. Thank you."

Just as I grind pepper onto my eggs, Danny comes back into the kitchen dressed in basketball shorts and a T-shirt, his curly black hair still damp from the shower.

"Come and get your breakfast, buddy," Chris says, smiling and pulling a stool out. "You like eggs and bacon?"

Danny nods and clambers up onto the high stool, looking hungrily at the plate of food before digging in. I notice the smile of satisfaction spread over Chris's face, but I can tell he's still feeling a little bit awkward.

"So, who is your favorite basketball player?" I ask Danny, trying to get the conversation started.

"I like LeBron," he replies quietly. "He's my favorite."

We have a slightly stilted conversation about basketball while we eat, and afterward, I help Danny do the dishes while Chris has a shower.

"I should go," I say quietly to Chris while Danny

plays with some Legos on the coffee table. "I have a meeting this afternoon and some calls to make, but I can come back in time for dinner at Bugs and Cam's tonight."

"Shit," he curses, shaking his head. "I forgot that it was tonight. Do you think it's too soon to introduce Danny to people?"

"No, I think it'll be good to start socializing with him. Plus it's only Bugs and Cam, not the whole team." I laugh. "Hey Danny, I have to go to work, but I'll be back later, okay?"

Danny looks up from his Legos, and I can see the slight apprehension in them. "You promise you'll be back?"

I go over and sit next to him. "Of course I will, poppet." I gently rub his back. "I just have to go to work, and then I'll be back so we can go to dinner with some of our good friends. They have a little baby daughter called SJ, and Bugs is a hockey player just like Chris."

Danny nods a little sadly, but I can see the determined set of his chin, and I know he's going to be okay.

"Thanks, Trixie," Chris says as he shows me to the door. "You're really great with him."

I laugh a little self-consciously. Kids have never been in my life plan, and I never thought I'd be any good at it since I had such a shit example in my own mum.

"Don't forget Madeline will be here at 3 so try to keep him alive until then," I say, raising an eyebrow and smirking at the look of horror on Chris's face. "I'm joking! You'll do fine. Just remember to feed him."

Chris laughs as well and gently pushes me out of

the door. "Okay, Mary Poppins. Thanks for the advice. Get outta here."

As I ride the elevator down to the parking garage, I can't help the slightly worried feeling in the pit of my stomach. Should I have left them? Will Chris be able to handle being alone with Danny when he has zero experience with kids?

But as the elevator doors slide open, I scold myself for having so little faith in Chris. He's an intelligent, grown-ass man who can certainly take care of a little kid for a few hours on his own.

However, as the day passes, I can't help checking my phone constantly in case I miss a call from him asking for help.

"Trixie, are you listening to me?"

I look up from my phone after checking it for the millionth time and see Kyle Hammer, the NFL linebacker I represent, looking at me from across the my desk with a quizzical look on his face.

"Yes, sorry, Kyle," I splutter, locking my phone and putting it on the desk face down. "So you want to renegotiate your deal with Nike? Right?"

I manage to get through the rest of the meeting without checking my phone, but as soon as Kyle leaves, I open it and panic. There's a message from Chris.

"Oh shit," I curse as I fumble to unlock the phone and open the message.

The relief that washes over me when I see a photo of them holding up a fantastic Lego model is palpable. Chris is smiling like a fool, and I can see the hint of a smile on Danny's face.

I quickly send a message telling them I love the

model and then call my assistant, Kristen, to go over my schedule for the next week. With training camp starting soon, I'm busy, but I have to make time to spend with Chris and Danny, especially while the nanny settles in.

"You know I really appreciate you helping out like this," I tell Kristen when we're done scheduling.

"It's no problem," she replies, closing her laptop. "I really want to be an agent some day so all this experience speaking to clients is fantastic, but..." She looks down at her fingers, twirling the rings around nervously.

"But...?"

"Are you sure spending all this time with Chris Ford is such a good idea?"

I take a deep breath in. "We have it under control. We've made a deal to be friends. That's all."

"Just be careful," Kristen replies, smiling kindly. "I've been your assistant for three years, and in those three years, you've made it very clear that if Chris Ford is at a function, you want to avoid it if possible. I don't want to see you get hurt."

"I appreciate that, love," I reply, touched by Kristen's concern for me. "But I've got this under control. Chris Ford is firmly in the friend zone."

After our chat, I spend another hour making calls and returning emails, but during that time, her words keep ringing in my ears. I know on the surface I'm all about keeping Chris at arm's length, but in my heart, it's getting harder every time we're together. But I made him a promise, and more importantly, I made a commitment to Danny. I'll be there for as long as it takes for them to settle in, and then I hope we can continue to be friends. I just need to keep my stupid heart locked down.

I end up spending a lot longer at the office than I initially planned, and when I look up and see it's already five o'clock, I send Chris a panicked text to say I'll meet them at Bugs and Cam's and then I rush home to get ready. I shower and spend way too long deciding what to wear. I don't want to be too dressy or look like I'm trying to impress Chris. So in the end, I choose my smartest pair of skin tight jeans and a cute blouse teamed with my favorite red pumps.

Making sure I choose a good bottle of merlot from my wine collection, I drive across town to Bugs and Cam's place which sits in a gated community. It still takes my breath away when I pull up to their huge mansion, but I know how hard they work for it, so I'm nothing but thrilled for them. And from previous visits I know this isn't a soulless museum like so many of the other palatial houses my clients live in. It's a home full of love and comfort, and as hard as they try, there are always a few baby toys laying around.

When Cam opens the door, I'm happy to see she's smiling and doesn't look too stressed and covered in baby puke. However, she is holding back their very boisterous Alaskan Malamute, Juneau, who seems eager to greet me with one of his big sloppy kisses.

"Hey Trixie, c'mon in. Bugs and Chris are out back firing the grill up, and Danny is playing with SJ." She closes the door and lets go of the dog, who immediately sniffs my crotch. "No, Juneau! Go to your bed."

He looks a little sad and slumps off to wherever his bed is, and Cam laughs. "Sorry about that. He's a great dog but has terrible manners."

I laugh and brush dog hair off my jeans. "Is Danny okay?"

"He's great. Isn't he just the cutest?"

"He is," I reply. "I have to admit I was a bit worried he'd be really shy."

"Oh, he was when they first arrived," Cam explains as she leads me through the impressive foyer and into the open plan living space. "He barely said a word, but as soon as SJ toddled over to him and handed him her favorite squishy, they were besties. It's so adorable I feel like crying." And as if to illustrate the point, her eyes glisten, and she swipes them with her fingers. "Jesus, I put mascara on for the first time in a week. I will not ruin it with tears."

I pat Cam on the back. "You look lovely, and in the future maybe think about waterproof mascara." We both laugh. Cam fixes me a glass of prosecco, and I go over to say hi to Danny.

I shoo Cam's cat off the couch and sit next to him and SJ, both of them playing with a pile of colorful blocks. I watch Danny build a tower and then he lets SJ knock it down, her gleeful giggle making both of us smile.

"How was your day, poppet?" I ask. "Did you have fun playing Legos with Chris?"

"Yeah, this is funner though," he replies quietly, building the tower again while SJ claps her hands

106

together in anticipation.

"Was it good to see Madeline?"

"She asked me lots of questions, and I had to tell her about…" He looks up at me and his cheeks pink up. "…you know."

"That's okay," I reply, gently rubbing his shoulder. "It's good that you can tell her things like that. And no one is angry at you, okay?"

Danny nods and places the last block on the tower just in time as SJ sweeps her chubby arm through it. She sends the blocks flying, almost hitting the cat who gives her a shitty look and slinks off somewhere safer. It's so great to see a genuine smile on his face. I know what it's like to grow up an only child, so I decide to leave them to their game and go out to see the guys at the grill.

"Hey, it's the Daddies Club." I laugh as I see Bugs and Chris at the grill flipping steaks and slabs of eggplant.

Bugs turns to face me and grimaces. "Why does that sound so dirty when you say it?"

"Hey, it's your filthy mind that made a perfectly innocent comment into something naughty, so don't put the blame on me." I smile at Chris as he turns around, and my smile just broadens when I notice he's wearing the same "Kiss the Chef" apron as Bugs. "You boys are adorable."

Chris scoffs and rolls his eyes, leaving his steaks to sizzle as he approaches me and pulls me close for a hug. He smells like smoke and cooking, and underneath that, I can still detect his own special smell that causes parts of me to sizzle uncontrollably.

"I think you'll find cooking meat with fire is very butch and manly."

"Sure," I laugh.

"How was work?" he growls in my ear, and I swear that innocuous question asked in his rough voice makes my nipples diamond-hard.

I cough and pull away slightly to get some space because I just can't stop this man's effect on me.

"Yeah, it was fine. Got everything done, so now I'm mostly free for a few days." I take a swig of my drink and sink into one of the large outdoor sofas organized in a U-shape on the terrace.

While the guys cook, Cam and I watch the kids through the open bi-fold doors and talk about the upcoming season—the Fan Event on Saturday, training camp starting on Monday, and then the exhibition games which include a week-long road trip.

"How are you feeling about Chris going on the road?" Cam asks. "I know Bugs is always so anxious if I have to come too, and we need to leave SJ with the nanny. I mean Chloe is amazing, but there's always that fear and the mom-guilt gnawing at the back of my mind."

"I know he's really anxious about everything at the moment," I reply quietly. "We're meeting the nanny tomorrow so she can spend some time with Danny to see how they get along. I think once that's sorted, he'll feel a little more relaxed. Then he just needs to get Danny enrolled in school, and hopefully they can get into some kind of routine."

"Well, I think it's amazing what you guys are doing," she replies, giving me a soft smile. "And it's so nice that you've managed to … reconnect." Suddenly, that smile turns a little bit wicked, and I know exactly what she's getting at.

"I'm here to help with Danny, nothing else," I whisper-hiss as the guys come toward the table with a tray of delicious steaks and eggplant.

"I'll go and get the kids," I say helpfully, getting up and heading back into the house. The sight that greets me makes something inside my stomach flip and ache—the children are sitting on the couch, and Danny is reading one of SJ's baby books to her while she sits transfixed next to him. It's such a beautiful scene, I don't want to break it up, but before I can make a move, Chris comes in behind me.

"Come and get it, kids!" he calls, and I see Danny jump in surprise. He closes the book and quickly tosses it aside, his little cheeks going pink with embarrassment.

Danny nods and helps SJ down from the couch, and he walks next to her as she toddles out onto the terrace into Cam's open arms. Chris goes out ahead of us, and when he's out of earshot, I lean down and whisper to Danny, "That was a really lovely thing you did. It looked like SJ was really enjoying it."

He looks up at me, and I see the faint hint of a sad smile. "My momma used to read to me."

And with that heart-breaking statement, he rushes over to the table to take his seat next to Chris as he serves the food.

When I take my seat on the other side of him, Chris must notice the fact that I'm on the verge of tears. "Everything okay?" he asks quietly.

"Yep," I reply, stabbing a slab of char-grilled eggplant

before I start sobbing all over it.

He gives me a quizzical look and doesn't press any further, but I know there'll be a conversation about it at some point.

During dinner, the conversation turns to the Fan Event on Saturday. It's something the Whalers do every year before the season starts. Season ticket holders are invited, and there's a lottery for the other tickets. It's a chance for the fans to meet the players and the coaches, and there's always a skate in the afternoon especially for the kids. It's one of those lovely things that I know the players really enjoy, especially the single ones because there are plenty of puck bunnies handing out their numbers.

"Have you ever skated?" Bugs asks Danny while Cam serves up New York style cheesecake and fruit for dessert.

Danny shakes his head because he's just stuffed a huge strawberry into his mouth.

"Ah man, you're a terrible guardian!" Bugs laughs, pointing at Chris. "The kid's been here more than twenty-hours, and you haven't gotten him on the ice yet!"

"I didn't wanna overwhelm him with too much stuff," Chris replies, looking a little embarrassed.

"Ah, I'm only yanking your chain, dude," Bugs says, smiling. "Why don't I meet you guys at the rink, and we can get Danny fitted for some skates? My treat."

Danny's eyes go as big as saucers, and he looks between Chris and Bugs expectantly. "Can I?" he asks quietly.

"Sure thing, buddy." He ruffles Danny's curls. "We have to meet your new nanny in the morning, but then

I'm sure we can head over to the rink after that."

Danny smiles broadly, strawberry juice making his lips bright red, and I'm yet again astonished at how naturally Chris is taking to being a father.

It just makes my feelings for him so much more confusing. Am I having some kind of weird hormonal reaction to this because I'm of a certain age, and my biological clock is ticking? Surely that must be it—I can't possibly be considering settling down and playing happy families, can I? I'm at a crucial point in my career plan, looking to expand to have an office in Los Angeles in the next year. There's no way I can do that if Chris and I decide to make this into a real relationship, a real family. I can see it now. He'll surely expect me to slow down my career to look after Danny while he sees out the last years of his.

It'll be Memphis all over again, and I barely survived that.

No. I need to keep these ridiculous feelings on lockdown and stick to the plan—settle Danny in and slowly extract myself from their domestic situation and hopefully stay friends. I don't want us to start a relationship out of some kind of desperation on Chris's part to have a mother-figure for Danny or because of some hormonal imbalance that I seem to be suffering from.

11

Chris

"**H**ow do they feel? Too tight or too loose?" Greg, our equipment manager, asks as he finishes lacing Danny's new blades.

"I can't move my ankles," Danny replies quietly, trying to move his feet.

"That's good. It's how they should feel." Greg folds the top of Danny's thick socks over the top of his skates. "As long as you can wiggle your toes, they're a good fit."

I notice Danny sticks his tongue out the side of his mouth like he does when he's concentrating, and then he says, "Yeah, I can wiggle them just fine."

"Perfect!" I clap my hands together and reach out so I can help Danny stand up. He wobbles a little at first, and we walk back and forth a few times on the rubber floor of the equipment room so he can get his balance.

"Looking good there, champ," Bugs says with a great big smile on his face. I know he's desperate to get SJ on the ice. He's already scheduled her first skating lessons for as soon as she's more steady on her feet.

Danny's face beams with pride, but I can see that little glimmer of hesitation in his eyes.

"We don't have to skate today if you don't want to," I whisper in his ear. "Wanna go and see if there's a milkshake with your name on it in the players' lounge?"

He nods enthusiastically, so I let Greg unlace his skates and show Danny how to take care of the blades and how to fit the safety covers.

"He's got great balance," Bugs says quietly. "Could have a future Whaler in the making."

I laugh. "I think the kid wants to be a basketball player more than anything."

Bugs scoffs and slaps my back. "I'm sure we'll soon change his mind. When I was six, I wanted to be a grizzly bear so who knows what the future holds?"

"You're a very strange man, you know that?" I reply, shaking my head.

"Keeps it interesting." Bugs shrugs. "C'mon, Danny. Let's go find that milkshake."

"Thank you for my skates, Uncle Bugs," Danny says shyly as he carries them past us, and Bugs grips his chest and pretends to collapse. I hold him up and then punch his arm good-naturedly.

"You're welcome." Bugs ruffles Danny's hair. "Now hustle. I need a strawberry milkshake."

We head up to the players' lounge, and I love the way Danny looks at everything with his eyes on stalks. We pass a few players and coaches on the way, and they all greet him warmly, asking him about his new skates, and by the time we make it to the lounge, he looks like his brain is on overload.

Once he's settled at one of the tables with his shake and a muffin, watching one of our games on the big TV, Bugs and I move over to the large floor to ceiling windows.

"How'd it go with the nanny?"

I nod my head while I sip my espresso. "Yeah, as good as it could go for a first meeting. He was pretty shy, having to meet another new person, but Annie brought some cool art stuff with her so they painted a picture, and then he showed her his room."

"Sounds good, man," Bugs replies. "You want them in a routine before we have to start going on the road. Believe me, the first time you have to leave will just kill you."

"Does it get easier?" I ask, dreading that moment.

"I'm not gonna lie: it doesn't. And if I'm honest, the older SJ gets, the harder it becomes." Bugs looks down into his coffee cup. "I swear she can sense when I'm getting ready to go. It just cuts me to the core."

"Shit," I grumble, not sure I'm ready to handle that part of fatherhood.

"But it's a month before we go on the road. You'll be in a routine by then." He smiles reassuringly, but I know he's already thinking about what it'll be like to start leaving SJ again.

"Uncle Chris, I'm done." Danny's soft voice interrupts our conversation as he appears between us holding up his empty cup.

"Great job, buddy." I take it from him and dump it in the recycling bin. "Shall we go home and then head out to the courts for a quick game before dinner?"

At the mention of his beloved basketball, Danny lights up, and he nods vigorously.

Bugs gives Danny and I high fives and then heads up to Coach Casey's office for a meeting, and we make our way home so we can change into our sweats and walk over to the park a few blocks from my apartment. We shoot hoops and play two on two with a couple of neighborhood kids, and it's the first time I've really seen Danny come alive like a little kid should be. His voice is strong and loud when he calls his plays to me, and my heart just bursts with pride at how amazing he is. My mom died when I was an adult, and I still fell to pieces without her. I can't even imagine how he's coping with it at the age of six.

When the sun starts to set and the other kids go home, we take a slow walk back to the apartment in a comfortable silence. I don't want to push him to open up to me, but I hope someday soon he will. As much as my feelings for my dad are toxic, I don't resent Danny's mom. She didn't ask to be born into that situation. However, I do regret not knowing about her sooner. I wish she'd felt she could've reached out to me before the worst happened. At least then I could keep reminding Danny what she was like. But she's a stranger to me, and I feel helpless at trying to keep her memory alive for him.

While things seem to be going well right now, I'm under no illusion; we're still in the honeymoon period, and there are definitely rocky roads ahead.

When we get home and wash up, I make spaghetti for dinner, and Danny manages to get more sauce on his face and shirt than in his mouth. So it's another shower before pjs and a few cartoons before bed.

As I tuck him in, he opens the drawer in his nightstand and takes out the picture of his mom that he put in there on the first day. He looks closely at it for several minutes and then he puts it back in the drawer, looking up at me.

"Anything you wanna talk about?" I ask quietly, sitting down next to him on the bed.

Danny presses his lips together and shakes his head. "I just forgot what her hair looked like."

My heart kicks in my chest, and I swear I feel like crying for the tenth time today. What the fuck is up with that?

"You know you can keep the picture out all the time," I reply quietly. "That's why I put it there."

Danny shakes his head again. "No. I just don't want to forget her. But it makes me sad to look at her all the time."

I put my hand on his shoulder. "I understand. You do whatever you need to. It's all okay."

"I'm tired," he says and snuggles down under the sheets, and I realize the conversation is over.

"Good night, buddy. I'll leave the hall light on like usual." And as if I've been doing it all his life, I lean over and kiss his forehead. It feels so natural to do it, but it does startle me a little.

"Good night, Uncle Chris." Danny rolls over and I creep out of the room, leaving the door ajar so the light from the hall doesn't leave his room completely dark. I lean back against the wall until my heartrate evens out, and I scrub my hand down my face.

What the hell is this kid doing to me? For years, my heart has been a black hole in my chest. I had no use for it once I lost Trixie and my mom. But now it seems to have come back to life with a vengeance. I'm feeling *everything*, and to be honest, it's fucking terrifying. I thought that if my heart was off the table, I'd never get hurt again. But I can't do that now, not with Danny.

And I guess as a consequence of that, I'm letting Trixie back in too. If I thought she was a knockout ten years ago, she's a game changer now. Her poise and confidence takes my breath away. The way she's handled our reconciliation and then Danny coming into my life has been incredible. She's not flinched or shied away from any of my requests.

I grab a beer from the fridge and flop down onto the couch, flicking on a baseball game, and I see the guy making a run for the home plate is one of Trixie's clients.

She's made such a success of her business that I think our breakup was the best thing for her. If she'd followed me to Canada, would she have had the same success? I guess we'll never know the answer to that.

Thinking about Trixie makes my mind wander to the make-out sessions we shared in Memphis and then back in my apartment. Jesus, her skin was like satin, and when I held her throat and she made that growly sound, I swear I instantly got hard. I want her so much, but as we've discussed, it's not the right time for us. No matter how much we want it. I can't put a confusing relationship into Danny's world. It's selfish to put my needs ahead of his. I learned that sacrifice is part of parenthood—my momma made her share of sacrifices for me, and now it's my turn.

As much as I want Trixie, I need to be happy with her friendship. She's made it clear that that's all she can give me, so I'll have to be satisfied with that.

At least for now.

Perhaps when Danny goes to college, we can think about being together.

I snort a laugh into my beer and adjust my semi-hard dick, a state I always get into when she's on my mind. I turn my attention to the game on the TV and try to stop thinking about her sexy blue eyes and heart-shaped ass.

Good luck with that.

The next few days are a whirlwind—I officially hire Annie, and she comes by every day to spend a few hours with Danny while I go to the gym or catch up on paperwork for the charity I run in Memphis. I'm happy when I come out of my office for a drink, and I see them building Legos or painting.

I finally enroll him in school, and we take a trip there so he can meet his new teacher and some of his classmates. As usual, he's really shy to start with, but after a while a little girl with braids and scraped knees comes over and asks him to play on the jungle gym. After a nod of approval from me, they run off together, and I watch as he stands back at first, watching the little girl swing upside down from the bars. After a while, he gains more confidence, and they play together until it's time for us to leave.

Madeline made her final visits and seemed happy with the progress we've made. We had a Zoom meeting with the judge in Memphis, and after Madeline's report, he was happy that Danny was in a safe, happy home, and he signed over guardianship to me.

"Mr. Ford, this order is still subject to visits by a social worker for the next six months. We will assign you someone in Seattle, and they will be making spot checks, which means they could show up at any time."

"Yes, sir," I reply, sweating slightly. "I understand the terms you've set out."

"Very good." The judge nods. "Having a child is a very special responsibility, and I hope you're ready for what's ahead."

"I am." And for the first time, I kind of believe it.

It breaks my heart and terrifies me in equal measure when Madeline says goodbye to Danny. They share a long hug, and I can see tears rolling down his little cheeks. He's relied on her so much, and if I'm honest, so have I. But now we're going to be alone together, and we have to get on with it and make our mistakes.

Once Madeline is gone, Danny retreats into himself, and even our trips to the basketball courts have become mostly silent events. The confidence he seemed to have gained has just melted away, and I'm at a loss as to what to do.

I've mentioned this on our team WhatsApp chat, and the guys have been as helpful as they can be with advice, but I'm not sure taking him to our local hangout, O'Connell's, and buying him a beer (Knox's suggestion) will help.

As we're eating a quiet dinner on Friday night, I tell Danny about the Fan Event we'll be going to tomorrow.

"It's really fun," I say, working my ass off to get any kind of reaction out of him. He's just been so sad since Madeline left. "There's a Ferris wheel and other carnival games, a huge moon bounce, and then we can try out your new skates."

He just nods silently and puts the last piece of fish stick into his mouth, putting his fork down.

"Can I go to my room?" he asks, not looking up at me.

"Sure," I reply, feeling completely lost as to how to deal with this change in his mood. Should I just let him be alone or try to talk it out? "I was going to watch the new Spiderman movie after I've cleaned up if you want to come back out."

"No, thank you." Danny slides down off the high stool and disappears into his room, and I slump against the counter, resting my forearms on the cool marble. I huff out a deep breath and go about cleaning up after dinner, loading the dishwasher and wiping the counter tops.

Just as I'm cutting up some mango for dessert, my phone rings, and I see Trixie's smiling face fill my screen. Despite my low mood, I can't help but smile as I answer.

"Hey Sugar," I growl, unable to keep the arousal out of my voice.

"Hi," she replies, and I can't help but notice the slight breathless quality to it. "How did it go saying goodbye to Madeline today?"

I take a deep breath and scrub my hand down my face. "It's not good. Danny's completely shutting me out. It's like we're back to day one all over again."

"It's understandable that he's going to have attachment issues," she says in a soothing voice. "Madeline has been his one constant since his mum died, so of course he's going to feel bad when she leaves. You just have to be patient and show him that you're

120

not leaving."

"I know. I just wish he'd talk to me." I'm so frustrated, I'm sure she hears it in my voice.

"Chris, he's a six-year-old boy. He probably couldn't articulate his feelings even if he wanted to," she says a little sternly, and I know I'm being a pussy about this whole situation.

"You're right." I sigh. "I'm the adult, so I just need to give him space and let him come to me when he's ready."

"That's true, but don't distance yourself too much or he might see that as you not wanting to be around him. Where is he now?"

"He's gone to his room."

"Okay, why don't you see if he wants to do something together? If he doesn't, at least get him to come and play in the living room so he knows you're still there," Trixie suggests.

"Yeah, that's a good idea." I take a deep breath and exhale. "Thanks. I wish I knew what to do in these situations. You're so good at it. I'm lucky to have you."

The husky sound of her laugh fills my ears, and I remember how much I love it. "I don't have a fucking clue what I'm doing. I'm just using common sense. You can do this. Just make sure you stop and take a breath before doing or saying anything."

"Again with the good advice. Thank you." I wait a beat before I ask my next question. "I was wondering if you wanted to come to the Fan Event with us tomorrow? I have to do my shift at the signing station, so I don't want Danny hanging around while I do that. If it's not good for you, I can always ask Annie to work…" I know I'm rambling nervously, but Trixie seems to have that effect on me recently.

"Chris, stop!" Trixie laughs. "I'd love to come with you."

It's ridiculous how my heart soars when she agrees to come. I mean it's not a date or anything, but I suddenly feel as nervous as a teenager with his first girlfriend.

"That's amazing. We can pick you up."

"That would be lovely." I can hear the smile in her voice, and it's my new favorite sound.

We talk for a few more minutes, confirming the plans for the next day, and when we end the call, I feel slightly less worried about how to handle Danny and so excited to see Trixie, I can't wipe the stupid grin off my face.

Trixie

I've tried on three different outfits, and I just can't decide what to wear. Chris and Danny will be here any minute, and I'm still flapping around in my underwear, trying to decide between a pretty summer dress and gladiator sandals, or jeans, sneakers, and a Whalers jersey.

I chastise myself for caring what I'm going to wear—this isn't a date, so it shouldn't matter. But part of me loves the lusty look Chris gets on his face when he appreciates what I'm wearing.

But this is an outdoor event with part of it taking place in the rink, so I go for the jeans and jersey option because the weather in Seattle can be very changeable, and I don't want to be caught in a downpour in a flimsy summer dress.

I'm just pulling my sneakers on when the doorbell rings, and I leap up to answer it, finding Danny standing before me holding out a cute little posy of flowers.

"Oh my!" I gasp. "Who is this handsome young man at my door?"

Danny doesn't answer but holds the flowers out

more so I can take them from him.

"Thank you, Danny." I smell the pretty blossoms. "They're beautiful." I look up and lock eyes with Chris, enjoying the cocky grin on his face and yet again feeling the crackle of sexual tension between us.

When I look back at Danny, I notice he's doing a little jig on my doorstep. "You okay, poppet?" I ask.

"Can I use the bathroom?" he replies, biting his lip.

"Of course. Go through the kitchen. It's out the back." I stand aside to let him rush past. "The flowers were very sweet, thank you."

"Don't thank me. It was Danny's idea. We passed someone selling flowers on the drive over, and he asked if he could get some for you," Chris explains. "Looks like the kid's a little romantic at heart."

"What a little cutie." I smile and smell the flowers again.

"Like uncle, like nephew," Chris says, leaning in to kiss my cheek. "Loving the Whalers jersey, by the way…" He puts his hands on my shoulders and turns me around. "Well, that just won't do," he tuts.

"What?" I ask, trying to look over my shoulder in case there's a mark or imperfection on the back.

"I can't believe you're gonna wear Bugs' number on your back. It's such a kick in the nuts," he growls, crowding me up against the door frame.

"It's the only jersey I have," I breathe, feeling my nipples harden at the close proximity of his big, hard body. Why the fuck does he always smell so good?

"I was gonna get Danny a jersey when we get to the event, so I guess I'll have to get one for you too. I can't have you walking around with me wearing that douchewaffle's number."

I giggle huskily at how alpha he's being, and I must admit it's turning me on no end.

"Okay," I whisper, sliding away from him to give myself some space. I also need to get the flowers in a vase before we leave.

Danny reappears shortly, and I grab my purse. We drive over to the Whalers rink, bypassing the lines for the public lot and parking in Chris's space in the underground levels. We walk quickly to the elevator, and Danny is almost vibrating with excitement. He walks slightly ahead of us once we get out of the elevator, and I take the opportunity to ask Chris how he's been.

"I did what you suggested and asked him to come and play his iPad in the living room which he did. And after about ten minutes, he sat on the couch with me, and we watched Spiderman," he explains. "We didn't talk about it, but he seemed comfortable just to hang out."

"That's good," I reply. "You just need to be there for him when he's ready to talk."

"Thanks for the advice." Chris puts his hand on the small of my back as we walk toward the merchandise store, and I swear I can feel the heat of his touch through the material of my jersey.

When we reach the store entrance, Danny is waiting, his eyes taking in all the merchandise available.

"Right then, buddy, we need to get you and Trixie new jerseys, so go and pick out the one you want."

Danny nods and runs off, immediately going to the stand displaying the Ford #45 jerseys, looking through them for his size.

"See, at least the kid has some loyalty to me," Chris whispers in my ear, his breath making goosebumps ripple down my neck and peak my nipples.

"He shares your name, so it's an obvious choice for him," I reply, trying to hide my arousal behind my sassy attitude.

"Is that a hint you wanna get married?" He chuckles, and I think it quickly dawns on him what he's said. "I mean, obviously we're not gonna get married. It was just a joke."

I laugh loudly at how awkward he's suddenly become. "Don't get your knickers in a twist, Romeo." I pat him on the back. "I'm not expecting a proposal in order for me to wear your number."

The look of slight relief but also a hint of disappointment on his face makes me very confused, so I stride over to the rails with the women's jerseys and grab one with Chris's number on the back, shoving it at him.

"I need to find my rookie before he goes onto the signing station. I'll meet you at the Ferris wheel in about an hour?" I splutter, suddenly feeling like I need to get some space.

"Yeah, sure." He looks even more confused than I feel. "Trixie, I didn't mean to upset you."

I laugh a little too loudly. "You didn't! I just need to make sure my rookie knows the rules about not taking girl's numbers and hitting on the fans. See you later."

I turn on my heel and literally run through the building toward the huge outdoor parking lot where the event is being held. They haven't let the fans in

126

yet, but I can see them lined up outside the chain link fencing waiting to meet their heroes.

I'm in such a rush to get away from the awkward situation with Chris that I don't look where I'm going and smash straight into Mila, Coach Casey's assistant.

She lets out a loud *oof* as we collide, and her armful of autograph photos of the players flutters to the floor in a total mess.

"Bloody hell, Mila. I'm so sorry. Let me help you." I squat down and start to gather all the pieces of glossy paper that are now totally muddled up.

"Thanks," Mila huffs and I can tell she's pissed at me. "In a bit of a hurry, are you?"

I sigh and sit down on the floor, holding a promotional photo of Chris in my hand. "You could say I'm in a hurry to get away from someone," I confess, looking at the photo.

Mila catches the look and also sits down, forgetting the pictures for a minute. "How're things going with you two?" she asks kindly.

"Very confusing, I have to admit." I rest my arms on my bent knees and let my head flop between them.

"Matt's told me a little about your situation," Mila confesses. "It sounds like you have a lot of stress on your new relationship with Danny and all. It's bound to be a bit tense."

"It's not just Danny," I say, deciding I need to confess how I feel to someone, just to relieve the pressure. "My feelings for Chris are becoming ... complicated. We agreed to be friends, but I can tell he feels more, and I sure as shit do."

Mila smiles. "When Matt and I found out we were

working for the same team and tried to do the friend thing, it was okay for a while. But the strain of trying to deny your feelings will eventually get the better of you both."

"So how did you deal with it?" I ask, hoping her experience can help me find a solution.

"We gave in and followed our feelings." She shrugs. "It seemed stupid to deny what we wanted. I mean we had the complication of Coach not wanting any of his players to date within the staff, but he got over that once he saw the depth of our feelings. He even persuaded me to give Matt a second chance when he screwed up."

"But Chris and I have so much history, so much pain, I don't know if that will all come back to bite us on the arse."

Mila giggles and then covers her mouth. "I'm sorry. I'm not laughing at your situation. I just love the way you say 'arse.'"

I roll my eyes and laugh as well. It's been good to share how I've been feeling, and I realize I probably over-reacted to the marriage joke in the store.

As I help Mila pick up the last pictures, we walk out to the event together, and I spend some time helping her sort them into the correct piles until I spot my rookie and excuse myself.

"Trixie, look how tall I am!"

I see Danny weaving his way through the crowd, balanced on top of the broad shoulders of the Whalers'

6'6" goalie, Thor. I can see Danny is now wearing his Whalers jersey and is sporting a huge foam hand and a Whalers ball cap.

"Hey buddy," I reply when they're close enough to hear me. "You've become a giant since I saw you last." I slap my hands to my cheeks in fake astonishment, and I see Chris roll his eyes good-naturedly as he appears from the throng of people milling around the Ferris wheel.

"No!" Danny laughs as Thor reaches up and lifts him effortlessly from his shoulders, placing him carefully on the ground. "Uncle Thor gave me a ride because all the people kept bumping me."

Thor laughs loudly and lifts Danny's ball cap off his head so he can see his face. "I did suggest he start body-checking people, but Uncle Chris gave me shi… I mean, a hard time about that kind of advice."

"Well, I think giving him a ride was the better option," I agree, smiling at Chris, but sensing a bit of a frosty reception from him.

"It was so much fun," Danny giggles, and it's so nice to see him having a good time.

"You good to take over while me and Thor do our shift at the signing station?" Chris asks while Thor tries to wrestle Danny's foam finger off him.

"Yes, of course." I take a deep breath. "Is everything okay? I'm sorry I was weird earlier."

He barely looks at me, and I know he's upset with me. "It's fine. Forget about it." He steps away, and I feel a cold chill slither down my spine. "C'mon, man. We're gonna be late, and Cam will have our asses."

Thor looks up from where he's holding the foam

finger just out of Danny's reach and nods. "Here you go, kiddo. Have fun."

Once the guys disappear toward the signing tent, I squat down next to Danny so we're face to face. "Have you had a good time? What do you want to do next?"

"Can I have a hot dog?" he asks shyly.

"That sounds like an amazing idea." I stand and reach my hand out, which Danny takes without hesitation, and that surge of hormones floods my system again.

God damn it, I need to lock this shit down.

But as I spend the next hour chasing around after Danny, wiping mustard off his chin to avoid it dripping on his new jersey, watching him on the moon bounce praying he doesn't barf up the hot dog, holding his hand as we ride the Ferris wheel because I'm scared, and seeing the glee on his face as he shoots hoops and wins a stuffed bear that's as big as he is.

"Wow!" Chris laughs when we meet him behind the signing tent. "Looks like you two had a great time."

"We did! We did!" Danny gushes. "Trixie is the coolest. Can she come skating with us? Can she?" He looks between Chris and me, and it seems neither of us can deny him.

"It's okay with me, but you know Trixie can't skate." The cocky smirk on Chris's face is like a red rag to a bull.

"Oh really?" I say, propping my fists on my hips. "Is that a challenge?"

"It sure is," he replies, mirroring my stance and narrowing his eyes. He knows full well I'll never back down from a challenge, especially from him.

"Challenge accepted." I stick my hand out for him

to shake, and Danny jumps up and down, clapping his hands. It seems that my humiliation will bring him immense happiness, so I guess I'm okay with that.

As we walk toward the parking lot to collect the boys' skates from the car, I seriously regret not wearing my summer dress, then I'd at least have that excuse to get out of this. Even though I love sports, I was always more of a spectator than a player. Apart from a stint on the school netball team, I was firmly on the sidelines. So the prospect of strapping knives to my feet and wobbling around on hard, cold ice is terrifying to me.

"Suck it up, Cavendish," Chris whispers in my ear as we enter the rink, and I get my first sniff of that distinctive smell of the ice. "I always tried to get you out on the ice, and now my dream is coming true."

I side-eye him as we approach the skate hire, and Chris asks for a pair of skates in my exact size.

"How do you remember what size shoe I wear?" I ask, a little taken aback.

Chris steps in close in order to hand the skates to me and whispers in a growly voice, "You'll be surprised at what I remember about you, Sugar."

Oh holy shit balls! I think I just had a teeny tiny orgasm, and despite the chill in the air, my cheeks are burning by the time he pulls away, our fingers touching as he hands me the skates.

"Are you able to help Danny lace up while I head to the locker room to change?" he asks, seeming very pleased that he's made me even more flustered.

"Sure," I croak, taking a seat next to Danny while he slides his sneakers off and pulls on his special skate socks.

"I'll see you out there, champ. Take care of Trixie for me."

"I will," Danny replies, waggling his legs excitedly.

"Thanks, Uncle Chris," I say sarcastically, smiling through the pain of what's about to happen.

It takes longer than I'm proud of to get Danny and me into our skates, and by the time we wobble our way to the edge of the ice, the place is packed with excited squealing kids and equally excited parents.

"When is Uncle Chris coming out?" Danny asks, gripping my hand so tight, I feel like he's cutting off the circulation.

"Any minute now." I check my smartwatch to see the time and notice the alert to warn me my heartrate is high.

No shit, Sherlock!

Suddenly all the lights go out, and Danny grips my hand even tighter. House of Pain "Jump Around" starts blasting out of the speakers, and the blue and yellow lights begin to flash.

"What's happening?" Danny yells, looking a little bit freaked out.

"This is how they introduce the team," I yell back. I squat down as best I can in my skates and point. "Look over there at the tunnel, and you'll see the players come flying out like rockets!"

The MC starts to announce the players, starting with Bugs, and Danny almost explodes with excitement when he appears out of the smoke, and power skates up the ice, holding his stick in the air. The MC then announces Matt, Nate, Knox and Thor, who appears like a giant in his full goalie gear.

"And finally, for this shift, I'd like you to give a huge Whalers welcome to Chris Ford!" the MC shouts into the microphone, and Danny literally clambers up the barrier to get a better look.

"UNCLE CHRIS! UNCLE CHRIS!" he shouts at the top of his voice, and I think it's just adorable how excited he is.

I watch Chris do a circuit of the ice, waving at the fans, and then he heads toward us at full speed, skidding to a halt with a spray of ice. Danny staggers back as if he thinks Chris won't be able to stop, but when he realizes he's safe, he looks utterly thrilled.

"Can you teach me to do that?" he yells at Chris through the plexi-glass, and with a nod, Chris indicates the gate where Danny can enter the ice. I follow him on wobbly legs and watch as Chris holds out his hands and helps Danny take his first cautious steps.

"You comin', Sugar?" he asks, standing still so Danny can get his balance.

I laugh nervously. "No, you boys go first. I'll just watch for now." I make a shooing motion with my hands, and Chris starts to skate slowly backward while still holding Danny's little hands.

I always think it's amazing how quickly kids can pick things up. After as little as twenty minutes, Danny is skating forward on his own, and even when he falls down, he gets straight back up and keeps going. In fact, the ice is full of little kids doing exactly that, and I feel like a great big chicken for being scared.

I watch as Chris introduces Danny to his teammates, and I'm nervous at how small he looks compared to the guys, all of them standing way over six feet tall in their skates. But Danny stands his ground and seems to grow in confidence by the minute as Bugs shows him how to hold a stick and Matt teaches him to bounce a puck on the end of it.

When Thor joins the group, I really am afraid that Danny will panic at the size of the massive Swede. However, he's a total champ, and when Thor starts teaching him how to body-check, I can see the huge smile on Danny's face. The goalie is a really good sport, and even falls over a few times when Danny barges his little body into his pads as fast as he can skate.

"C'mon, man," Nate jeers when Thor takes a particularly hard "fall." "Don't cry. He's just a little kid."

"You'd better watch your spot on the team, Halsted," Thor yells back. "Looks like mini Ford here could take it from you. He certainly hits harder than you."

I can't help laughing at the banter between these guys. They have such a strong connection, and I'm glad Chris found such a good team. When my eyes find him again, I notice he's handing Danny off to one of the coaches, and he skates casually toward me, that damn sexy grin splitting his face. All of a sudden, it's ten years ago, and I'm back at the Memphis Jazz game where I first laid eyes on him, skating into the Sin Bin after a fight.

Jesus, I think I fell for him at that moment, and the vivid nature of the memory—the smell of the ice, the chill in the air, the look on his face—brings me back to the feeling of that night.

And if I'm completely honest, I realize right then that my feelings for Chris have never gone away. I'm as in love with him now as I was then.

It's that simple.
But with absolute clarity, I know it's anything but simple.

13

Chris

"**I** think he had a great day," Trixie says as we drive home through the darkening Seattle evening.

I flick my eyes to the rearview mirror and see Danny fast asleep in his booster seat, hugging the foam finger Thor bought him earlier. Next to him is the gigantic teddy he won, and I quickly wonder where the hell it's going to go.

"He really did," I reply quietly. "He's such a natural skater. The kid is a prodigy or something."

Trixie giggles. "I think every parent thinks their kid is the best at everything they do."

"I'm serious!" I say loudly, flinching a little when Danny stirs but doesn't wake up. "Even Coach said he has great balance for his first try. The kid's fearless—reminds me a lot of me at that age." I can't keep the melancholy out of my voice as I think back to all the times my mom gave up things for herself to make sure I could skate. I'm so glad I can support Danny in anything he wants to pursue, even if it's not hockey.

"Well all I can say is that he's a hell of a lot better than me," Trixie says, the venom clear in her voice. "My arse is still throbbing after that last fall."

I chuckle when I remember how hard she stacked it, the cute pouty look on her face as she sat there with her arms crossed, waiting for me to help her up. I know from experience that Trixie hates failing at anything, so this afternoon must have been torture for her. But she was a good sport, and she could see how much Danny was enjoying it.

And I must admit, I didn't hate it when she clung to my arm or grabbed my jersey to steady herself, the smell of her perfume making me feel drunk. At one point I slipped my arm around her back and the feeling of the top of her ass under my palm made me hard inside my cup, which is not a fun experience.

I spent weeks trying to get Trixie on the ice during our relationship, and today made me realize why she was so reluctant. She has the coordination of a drunk baby deer. But it felt great to support her and teach her something new, and it made me think about what our life could be like together—teaching and supporting each other. And I guess that's what I couldn't get my thick head to understand ten years ago—it shouldn't have been about whose career was more important; it should have been about us compromising to make it work. I never even considered doing the long distance thing while Trixie finished her internship. She'd talked previously about working in whichever city we ended up living in, but I was too stubborn, thinking that if she didn't come to Canada with me that minute then she didn't love me enough.

I was a fucking idiot.

"You're in deep thought." Trixie's slightly husky

voice pulls me back to the moment, and I realize I've automatically driven to my apartment.

"Ah shit, Sugar. I can take you home if you want," I say, annoyed that I was too busy daydreaming to drop her at her place.

"It's okay. I can get an Uber." She shrugs, and if I'm not mistaken, she seems a little disappointed.

"Or we can get the little guy into bed and have a glass of wine. I think your ass could do with it." I can't help but smirk when I notice the mortified look on her face, remembering her clumsy falls.

She swallows and looks me right in the eye, her navy blue irises sparkling. "I think a glass of wine is the least you owe my bruised derriere."

"You got it, baby." I reach over and squeeze her knee. "You grab the massive teddy, and I'll grab the kid."

We nod at each other and jump out of the car, quietly opening the rear doors so Trixie can pull out the ridiculous teddy, and I carefully unclip Danny from his seat belt. The kid is out for the count—full of hot dogs and cotton candy and exhausted from all the skating and running around. He'll definitely sleep well tonight.

We manage to get into the elevator without waking him up, and when we get to my floor, Trixie unlocks the front door, and we enter the dark apartment. I don't put any lights on, allowing the light from the city skyline to illuminate my way down to Danny's room where I carefully remove his sneakers, socks, and jeans and cover him with his comforter.

"Good night, buddy," I whisper, leaning down to kiss his forehead.

138

"I had a really good day. Thank you, Uncle Chris." His quiet words melt the last shard of ice inside my heart, and I know that this experience will be the most important of my life.

I slowly make my way back out into the kitchen, still deep in thought.

"I poured you a drink. It looks like you could use it," Trixie says quietly, holding the glass of red wine out to me, a big smile on her face.

Suddenly, I'm nervous. I want Trixie so bad it hurts, but I just don't know how she'll react if I make a move. I could end up with a face full of merlot and a slap, and that would ruin whatever this is that we have going on between us.

"Thanks," I say, taking a huge swallow of wine. "You wanna sit?" I nod my head toward the couch.

"Sure." Trixie looks at me as we make our way over to the couch. "Are you okay? You seem a little distracted."

I flop down and drain the last of my wine. "I'm okay, just tired. That kid has so much energy." I let my head fall back onto the couch and close my eyes.

"I think you're doing an amazing job," she says, and I notice her voice seems very close to my ear.

Slowly, I open my eyes and turn my head, and Trixie is right there, her legs curled up underneath her, her arm resting on the back of the couch, her inquisitive eyes stripping me bare.

With my heart in my throat, I decide it's now or never. I can't hold back one more moment. I have to kiss her.

As if sensing my intentions, Trixie's eyes flick to my

lips, and I see her lick her own, making them glisten and so damn tempting. That's all the invitation I need. I lean slowly toward her, keeping my eyes on hers, reeling us both in.

Just as our lips are about to touch, I hesitate and pull back. "Wait," I whisper breathlessly.

"What?" Trixie asks, her eyes pleading with me.

"Do you remember what I said to you last time we kissed?" I reply, gently running my fingers up her arm, over the slightly rough material of her jersey, and onto the satiny soft skin of her neck. When I wrap my fingers around the elegant column, she gasps and her eyes become hooded with desire.

"Chris, I can't think straight when you do that to me," she growls and that husky quality to her voice makes my already hard dick ache to be inside her.

I lean in so I can whisper in her ear. "I said I wouldn't kiss you again until you asked me to." I need to hear her say the words, to give me the green light to start this thing up again. I need her to be on the same page as me, otherwise I'll back off.

When I sit back a bit, I can see the slight conflict in her eyes—her heart and head are in an epic battle, and I know that the next move she makes will tell me which one is victorious.

"Chris Ford, will you get your arse in gear and kiss me?" she murmurs, her voice quiet but pleading and full of need.

"Thank god," I chuckle and press my lips against hers, lightly squeezing the hand around her neck, knowing that will make her wet and ready for what I have in mind.

The first slide of her tongue against mine makes me feel like I've come home, and I move my hand to the back of her head, gripping the blonde hair at the base of her neck, holding her against me as we rediscover each other.

Trixie rises up and straddles my lap, not breaking the connection between our hungry lips, and it's as if no time has passed. This was always our go to position for a great fuck. She loved being on top, in control, and it always turned me on so much to let her take on that role. She settles down, and I can tell by the whimper that she feels the steel rod pressing against her core.

As our kissing reaches fever pitch, I slide my hands down her back and grip that fantastic ass, urging her on to grind against my painfully hard dick, needing more of that delicious friction we're creating.

"Are you sure Danny's asleep?" Trixie gasps, not stopping the insistent motion of her hips.

"He's dead to the world, but we should probably be quiet," I whisper, trailing my lips down her neck.

"Well, if my memory serves, I'm not sure I can guarantee that," she replies, leaning back slightly, gripping the hem of her jersey and pulling it up over her head. Her gorgeous globes bounce in my face, encased in navy blue lace that almost perfectly matches the stormy color of her eyes. She tosses the discarded jersey behind her and rests her hands on my shoulders, her usually perfect hair slightly messed up and wild.

"Fuck, Sugar," I moan, reaching up to cup her full tits in my hands, her hard nipples pressing against my rough palms. She lets her head fall back as I massage them, pushing them together so I can kiss down the line of her cleavage. I roughly pinch her nipples until she whimpers, but if I remember correctly, she's feeling immense pleasure right now so I don't stop. I keep working her, kissing and tonguing her nipples through the lace until she claps her hand over her mouth, her hips finding a rhythm of their own as she cries out into her palm.

It's only when Trixie's still that I let up on her, allowing her to settle her head on my shoulder until her breathing evens out, and I feel her lips against my Adam's apple.

"Well that's never happened before," she whispers, reaching between our bodies to work my belt open.

"What's that?" I ask, lifting my ass so she can shuffle my jeans down.

"I've never come that way before. You know, with just my boobs."

The pink tinge of her creamy cheeks betrays her vulnerability at sharing this with me—it certainly never happened when we were together before, so I feel the stupid swelling pride in my chest that we can still discover new things about each other.

"Well, now I know that, I'm gonna try and find plenty of other ways to make you come." I chuckle as she slides off my lap, onto the floor between my feet.

"As tempting as that sounds, I think you've earned a little treat of your own," she growls, dragging her short nails up my bare thighs to the edge of my boxer briefs which are obscenely tented by my erection.

Trixie's eyes are fixed on my dick, and as she pulls my boxers down, I'm pleased to see them widen slightly as she reveals me.

"You keep looking at my dick like that, and I'm gonna have to fuck you with it." I sigh, noticing the bead of pre-cum pooling at the tip. I'm so desperate to be inside her—in her mouth or her pussy, I don't care. I just have to be connected with her.

With a wicked smile, Trixie dips her head, and I know which option she's going with. As her pouty lips purse together and gently kiss the head of my cock, I can't help but jolt like I've taken a hundred volts to the balls. The feeling of her lips on me is incredible, and as her light kisses trail down my shaft, all the muscles in my abdomen contract and pulse.

"Oh fuck, baby. Please…" I beg just as she takes my glans into her warm wet mouth, and I think I've died and gone to heaven. I let my head fall back against the couch as she works more of my length into her mouth, sliding off and taking a little more each time. I'm not a small guy, and Trixie takes as much as she can before gagging slightly, returning her attention to the tip while she fondles my balls with one hand and traces the ridges of my abs with the other.

The familiar tingling sensation begins deep in the pit of my stomach as Trixie settles into a rhythm that's going to have me coming in no time. I gently fist her hair to encourage her but never pushing her down. I learned early on that that was a hard no for her.

Trixie begins to moan, and I know it's because she can feel my cock swelling in her mouth, preparing for release, and it feels so amazing I never want it to end. But I want that sweet release. I want to see her swallow every drop like a good girl.

"Oh baby, I'm coming, I'm coming," I gasp, jerking

my hips up as my cum sprays the back of her throat. Trixie keeps gently sucking my cock until I'm finished, and it thrills me that she remembers that I like to soften in her mouth, so she doesn't move off immediately. It's like she's savoring every second of our union.

"Jesus Christ. That was incredible," I whisper, helping her up off her knees so she can snuggle into my side, my boxers and jeans still bunched around my ankles.

She giggles breathlessly and gently strokes my abs, which are still twitching and contracting with aftershocks.

"Call me crazy, but it was never that good before," she replies, looking up at me.

"I mean, it was pretty fucking hot before, but you're right. I don't know what's changed, but whatever it is, I like it."

"I can tell." Trixie sits up and rubs her hands up and down her bare arms, looking around for her discarded jersey.

"Are you cold?" I ask, pulling up my boxers and jeans, standing so I can go and retrieve her shirt.

Trixie nods and smiles when I hand her back her jersey, and she slips it back on, suddenly looking a little awkward.

"Do you want more wine?" I ask, trying to ease the tension that seems to have filled the space between us.

"No, I should probably go home." She stands and adjusts her clothes, smoothing down her hair. "I don't want to confuse Danny by being here when he wakes up."

Despite the sudden sharp pain of rejection in my

chest, I smile and walk her to the door.

I open it but stand in the doorway, blocking Trixie's exit. "Please stay." I hate myself for begging, but I'm not ready for her to leave.

The conflict flashes across her face again, and she sighs. "Not tonight." She reaches up and gently strokes my scruffy cheek, making me lean into her touch. "It's not that I don't want to. You have no idea how much I want to. But I just don't want to rush into things and confuse Danny. He needs stability, and if this blows up in our faces, I don't want him caught in the crossfire."

I know she's being the rational one, but it still hurts that she's walking away. I gently kiss her palm and then pull her in for a hug, taking in the softness of her breasts against my hard chest and the smell of her hair.

"Good night, love." Trixie pulls away and ducks around me. "I'll call you tomorrow."

"Sure thing." I watch her walk down the hall toward the elevator, and as she turns the corner, she flicks her hair and looks back at me, smiling broadly.

I slowly close the door and lean against it, closing my eyes, trying to recall every second of our time together. Just thinking about the touch of her lips and fingers makes me hard again, and I curse myself. Now I've refreshed my memory on how Trixie's lips taste, what she looks like when she comes undone, I need it like an addict. I don't know how I'm going to keep my hands off her when we're together, but I understand what she means about keeping things discreet for Danny's sake. The poor little guy doesn't need any more confusion. And if things don't work out between us, that's another person he'll lose from his life.

I know that it's my job to protect him, so I need to keep my head and not end up like a love sick fool.

Danny and Trixie deserve more.

With thoughts of how this thing might work, I take a bottle of water from the fridge and settle down on the couch, pretending to watch a movie. But what I'm really doing is reliving the last hour, shamelessly holding a throw pillow to my face because it was the one Trixie leaned against, savoring the ghost of her scent.

"Get a fucking grip, man." I laugh, tossing the pillow back on the couch. I think it's time I go to bed and stop acting like a goddamn maniac.

14

Trixie

The start of the Whalers training camp is such a busy time for me that I don't know whether I'm coming or going. I have four clients on the Whalers team—Bugs, the reserve goalie, and two rookies, one of which, I'm afraid to say, looks like he'll be starting the season on the farm team.

My eyes scan the field and see the first line working on their sprints—each one tied to a bungee cord to offer resistance while they run a hundred meters up the track. I laugh when the coach holding Thor's bungee gets dragged along behind him once it reaches its maximum extension. But then my eyes settle on Chris, and my heart flutters in my chest. He looks so hot in his tight Whalers T-shirt and athletic shorts, a backward cap covering his sandy blond hair. Even though he's one of the oldest guys on the team, he's still one of the fittest and he's luckily escaped any serious injuries.

I know I should be watching my players, but I'm mesmerized by the flexing of Chris's muscles and perfect grace and athleticism of his body. I can't help but remember our time together after the fan event, and my pussy tingles at the memory. He knew exactly how I wanted to be touched, and it's like we'd never been apart. It was comforting but also new and exciting.

We haven't been alone together since that night, and I can feel myself craving his touch; it makes me ache inside. I don't usually attend as many days of training camp as I have this season, but I just can't stay away. Chris is so focused that I don't want to be a distraction, so when he sends me a message or a picture of him all sweaty and beaten after a day at camp, my heart soars like a teenage girl with her first boyfriend. We've spoken on the phone every night this week, and sometimes he puts Danny on to tell me about school or what art project he and Annie have been working on. I love how he's keeping Danny involved. My fear that he's just using me to support him with this life change has disappeared now they're settling into a routine.

For just a moment, I let myself imagine what it would be like to be a real family—the three of us against the world. It's a long shot and probably an unrealistic fantasy to have, especially if Chris expects me to shelf my career like he did before. But perhaps he's changed. I know I have in the last ten years. My career is still very important to me, but if this reunion has taught me anything, it's that all the success in the world means fuck all if you've got no one to share it with.

A cheer of loud voices brings me back to the moment, and as I watch my rookie throw up in the trash can for the third time today, I wonder how he ever made it this far. The team have had a brutal week of physical tests and trials, medicals and afternoons on the ice. At the moment, some of them are doing a bleep test and my rookie is the first to tap out, puking his guts up while one of the coaches hands him a bottle of water.

"Looks like your kid can't take the heat." The slimy voice in my ear makes me cringe and pull away automatically.

I flick my eyes in the direction of the voice and see Blake standing next to me in his expensive suit, his black hair slicked back with way too much product, just adding to the overall sleazeball image.

"Good afternoon, Blake," I say as politely as I can manage. "You don't usually lower yourself to come along to training camp. Don't you have an intern that can do this type of work for you?" My voice is dripping in sarcasm, but this douchebag just brings it out in me.

"Well, if you must know, Your Majesty, I want to keep a special eye on Chris." The venom in his voice is unmistakable. "He's got a lot of new distractions in his life at the moment, and I need to make sure he's keeping his eye on the Cup."

"That's so supportive of you," I scoff, flashing him a fake smile, knowing he's having a very obvious dig at me. "I'm sure Chris is thankful for all your help." I make a move to walk away because having this guy in my personal space is making me feel sick.

"Keep your eyes on your own players, Beatrix," Blake calls after me as I march away, pissed off that I let that wanker get anywhere near me and that I let him get under my skin. I check on my rookie and make sure he's okay, but the poor kid looks completely deflated. I leave him in the capable hands of his coach and then I notice Chris jogging toward me, looking hot and sweaty, but so fucking handsome I have to concentrate on breathing.

"Hey, Sugar. You enjoying the show?" He flashes that cocky grin at me and then grabs the hem of his T-shirt, lifting it up to wipe the sweat from his face, giving me a good look at his ripped abs and slim hips. Fuck me, he's an absolute masterpiece of male perfection, and I can't help but lick my lips and think about dragging my tongue over it all.

I must have slipped into a momentary sex coma because suddenly Chris is snapping his fingers in front of my eyes to get my attention.

"Huh?" I ask, blinking several times to clear the filthy thoughts out of my brain.

"I asked if you wanna come to the zoo with me and Danny on Saturday?" he asks again, smirking because he caught me fully gawping at his body.

"Yeah, sure," I reply in a croaky voice. My mouth is suddenly very dry. "What prompted a visit to the zoo?"

"We watched Madagascar the other night, and he laughed like a loon at the lemurs, so I've arranged a surprise meet and greet for him. You know, so he can feed the lemurs and get up close with them."

I can't help my heart from soaring at how attentive and generous Chris is with Danny. Some might think he's over-indulging the boy and spoiling him, but I just think that he's taking a real interest in what Danny likes.

"That sounds amazing. I'd love to come with you." I can't help the stupid grin that splits my face.

Suddenly Chris leans in close. I can smell the clean masculine scent of his sweat, and my nipples peak underneath my blouse. "I'm gonna ask Annie to come and babysit on Saturday night, so how about you and me go on a little date of our own?"

I swallow loudly and take a deep breath, the thought of a real date with Chris making me all kinds of giddy.

"I'd like that a lot," I say breathlessly.

"Annie also said she could do the whole night if we needed. You know, like a trial run for when I go on my first road trip." He takes a step back and the lust in his eyes is hard to deny.

I bite my lower lip as I think about spending the whole night with him, and I press my thighs together to try and subdue the ache at my center.

"I think that's a good move," I reply. "Annie should have a night with Danny before the first road trip. You don't want him freaking out when you're halfway across the country."

Chris chuckles and lifts his ball cap to run his fingers through his sweaty hair. "Yeah, that's exactly why I've asked her to stay the night." He leans back in and whispers in my ear, so only I can hear. "It has nothing to do with the fact that I want to fuck you so bad, it's making me a little crazy."

His dirty confession makes me take a deep breath, and I have to step back before I leap into his arms and do things to him that would get me into all sorts of trouble.

"What time were you thinking on Saturday?" I ask, innocently looking around to make sure no one is watching our exchange too closely, especially Blake.

I can tell by the look on Chris's face that he knows he's had the desired effect on me, but I know he also understands that I'm here in my professional capacity so he backs off as well.

"We'll come and pick you up at nine. I thought we could get some breakfast first."

"That sounds perfect." I smile because it really does. I never in a million years thought a day at the zoo with my ex and a little kid would be a perfect Saturday— mine are usually spent at a spinning class, getting coffee, and then catching up on work.

This sounds much better.

"See you then, Sugar." Chris winks, grabs a bottle of Gatorade from the bucket of ice I'm standing next to, and runs back to the team, ready for their next torture session.

I decide to head back to the office because if I stay here watching Chris work out, I won't be responsible for my actions. I flash my glance over to Blake who's lurking by Coach Casey, talking animatedly, but his dead shark eyes are fixed on me. I can't help the shiver that runs down my spine as I walk away. I have no doubt he'll try to make trouble as soon as he finds out Chris and I are dating again.

"Don't you think you've put enough syrup on that waffle, buddy?" Chris asks as Danny reaches toward the jug that is just out of his reach. We're sitting in a roadside diner that we spotted on the way to the zoo. It's a little hole in the wall, but I swear the mushroom omelet I've just devoured is the best thing I've eaten in a while.

I sip my tea and smile as the boys have a little back and forth about the amount of syrup Danny has already poured over the enormous waffle in front of him. It has to easily be as big as his head, and I can clearly see the little square holes are already filled to capacity with golden sweetness.

"A little help here," Chris whispers in my direction as I notice he appears to be losing the battle. I shake my head and put my tea down, smiling kindly at Danny.

"How about you eat what you have already and if you feel like you still need more syrup, we can renegotiate then?" I say, raising my eyebrow to see what Danny comes back at me with.

He scrunches his eyebrows together and thinks really hard for a minute. "If I knew what renegotiate means, I might say yes."

Jesus, this kid kills me. I look over at Chris, and he looks like he's about to bust a gut laughing.

"Okay, why don't you tell me what you think it means, and if you get it right, you can have as much syrup as you want?" I fold my arms across my chest, pretty sure I've just ended the discussion, but I notice Chris looking slightly panicked next to me.

Danny also folds his arms, mirroring me, and his little tongue pokes out the corner of his mouth in the way it does when he's concentrating. He scrunches his eyes up, and it's so cute how hard he's thinking about it. He must really want the syrup.

"Is it like when you have a deal, but you make a new, better deal?" His little voice breaks the silence, and my eyes widen, my mouth dropping open in shock. I look from Danny to Chris, and he has the same shocked expression on his face.

"How the H.E. double hockey sticks do you know

that?" Chris laughs in surprise.

"Don't say hell, Uncle Chris. It's a swear." Danny shakes his head in disapproval, and it makes me laugh so hard I feel like I might pee my pants.

"I'm sorry, buddy. I won't say it again," he apologizes. "But seriously, how did you know that?"

Danny just shrugs and smiles. "Momma used to say that if you don't know what a word means, listen to it in the sentence and find the clues. That's all I did." He looks between Chris and me with those big green eyes, and I just melt inside. "May I have the syrup, please?"

Chris laughs again, but this time in defeat. "Sure thing. A deal's a deal." He pushes the jug of syrup toward Danny and then he shoots me a look. I can tell he's pissed but only a little bit.

When we finish breakfast, we get a very excited Danny into his booster seat and drive the rest of the way to the Woodland Park Zoo, arriving just in time to see the Humboldt penguins feeding. Danny laughs gleefully as he throws the slimy little fish into the penguins' hungry beaks and presses his whole body against the glass wall as they swim past him at amazing speed.

After that, we watch them training the tigers and I can't help feeling a little bit scared for the poor keepers who are in the enclosure with them. Chris seems to sense my tension, so he reaches around and holds me close to his side, his hand curling round my hip. I instantly start to relax and enjoy the show until it's over and Danny is grabbing both our hands and pulling us toward the rhino reserve.

"What time do we have to be at the lemurs?" I

ask quietly as we watch Danny stare at the rhinos in their wallow.

"In about twenty minutes, so we'd better get moving." Chris smiles at me and shocks me a little when he leans in and gently presses his lips against mine in a chaste kiss. "Thanks for coming today."

I bite my lower lip and look up into his beautiful open face, and I know I'm falling hard for this man—this intoxicating mix of the old version of him and the new man he's growing into.

Before I can reply, a small family approaches, the little girl and boy wearing Whalers caps, and they ask Chris for his autograph and a picture. I move out of the way and stand with Danny, making sure to stand in front of him in case they want to take a snap without Chris's permission.

Chris is always so gracious with the fans, but I know if they were to take a picture of Danny, he would go full Papa Bear on them.

Once the family moves away, we let Danny know that he has a special treat that we need to get ready for, and he literally bounces all the way across the zoo, asking us what the surprise is. When he sees we're approaching the lemur exhibition, he can hardly contain himself.

The keeper comes out to meet us, and she explains to Danny that he has to be very calm and quiet when he meets the lemurs, and he promises to do exactly as she says. We then follow her inside the enclosure where at first all I can see are trees and bushes.

"I think the lemurs are a little bit shy today," the keeper whispers to Danny, and his eyes begin to get shiny with tears as if he thinks he won't get to see them. "How about you shake this food bucket and see what happens?"

She hands Danny a bucket of chopped up fruit and little wiggly worms that smell rancid, but he grabs it with both hands and shakes up and down enthusiastically. As if by magic, we're suddenly surrounded by black and white ring-tailed lemurs, all scrabbling at Danny's feet wanting some treats from the bucket.

The keeper instructs Danny to walk around the enclosure, dropping the contents of the bucket as he goes, and he follows her directions perfectly. He reminds me of the Pied Piper from the fairy tale, except he's being followed by lemurs instead of rats.

Once the bucket is empty, Danny and the keeper sit together on a log and watch the lemurs eat their snack. Chris is being so cute and taking hundreds of pictures on his phone, so when the keepers asks him to come over and sit with them, I take over the role of photographer. As the lemurs finish their food, they become interested in the visitors, and soon Danny and Chris have lemurs clambering all over them, jumping off their shoulders. One even starts to groom Chris's hair which makes me giggle uncontrollably.

"C'mon, Sugar. It's your turn," Chris says as he gets up and makes room for me to sit next to Danny.

I take a deep breath and put my brave girl knickers on—it's one thing watching from the sidelines, but now it's my turn to get crawled all over.

As if he can sense my hesitation, Danny says, "It's okay, Auntie Trixie. They are sort of gentle. Don't be scared."

Now how the hell can I refuse that invitation? I hand Chris his phone back and walk slowly over to the log, being careful not to stand on any of the lemurs as they run around my feet. I sit next to Danny, and he reaches out to take my hand just as a lemur leaps from a nearby tree onto my shoulders. I let out a little yipping sound, and he holds my hand tighter.

"It's okay," Danny whispers, and I look over at this little boy who has more bravery in his little finger than I do in my whole body.

Once I relax, I actually start to enjoy it, but all too soon, our time is up, and we have to leave. The keeper kindly lets Chris take her place on the log, and she takes a few pictures of the three of us on his phone.

"How was that, Danny? Did you have fun?" Chris asks as we exit the enclosure.

I look down and see that Danny looks a little bit sad. "Hey, what's wrong, poppet?"

Danny looks between us, and his little chin starts to tremble. "Momma used to love it when the lemurs in Madagascar sang that song. I'm just sad they didn't sing."

Chris squats down so he's on Danny's level and holds his arms gently. "It's okay to miss your momma."

Suddenly Danny flings his arms around Chris's neck and hugs him so tight, I feel my nose sting with tears. Chris looks up at me and gently rubs Danny's back while he cries quietly into his shoulder, little heaving sobs that break my heart. In the end, I have to turn away and wipe the tears from my eyes. It won't make Danny feel any better to see me bawling like a baby.

I listen as they have a quiet conversation, Chris

gently wiping away Danny's tears with a Kleenex from his pocket. I don't know what they say to each other, but Danny hugs him again and they stand side by side, Danny's little hand fitting naturally into Chris's large, rough one.

I believe I've just witnessed a real transition in their relationship, and it warms me that they're growing closer every day.

15

"**Y**ou have my cell number, and the hospital and Trixie's number?" I say, pulling my leather jacket on, taking another look at my Rolex. I can't be late picking Trixie up for our first official date. That's not the impression I want to make.

"Yes Chris, I have all the numbers," Annie says, stirring the pot of marinara sauce on the stove. "And if they don't work, there's always 9-1-1." The little smirk that tilts her lips shows me she's busting my balls, but I can't help but be a little anxious. It's the first time I'm leaving Danny overnight, and even though I'll only be across town and not out of state, it's still another big milestone for us all.

"Okay, okay." I hold my hands up in defeat. "I know I'm being a neurotic jerk. But please call me if there are any problems." I adjust my collar and grab my keys, phone, and wallet from the kitchen counter. I decided to keep it casual tonight, so I've paired my dark jeans and biker boots with a button down shirt and leather jacket.

"We'll be fine, I promise," Annie reassures me.

"We're gonna have meatballs for dinner and then make the Batmobile Lego set you got him. He'll be in bed by 9 at the latest."

I exhale loudly and scrub my hand down my face. I never thought I'd be this anxious about leaving Danny for one night. I fully sympathize with how stressed Bugs and Cam look on road trips.

"Okay, thanks Annie." I smile at her, feeling so lucky to have found her. I've heard some horror stories about other players and their nannies so I'm really happy she seems perfectly normal and not at all interested in jumping into bed with me.

"I'm heading out now, buddy," I call to Danny, who's coloring at the coffee table.

"Bye, Uncle Chris," he says, waving at me but not looking up from his art.

I laugh quietly and shake my head. "I guess he's happy enough that I'm going out. I'll call at 9 to say goodnight," I tell Annie.

"Sure thing. Have a good time, and we'll see you in the morning. There's no hurry. I don't have to be anywhere until lunchtime."

"I'll be back early," I reply firmly, heading for the door. "See you tomorrow," I call again, reluctantly opening the door.

"Byyyyeeeeee," Danny calls. "Annie, come and see my dinosaur!"

And just like that, I'm free to leave. So why does my chest hurt as I walk slowly toward the elevator? If I think back to my life before Danny, I was free to do whatever I wanted. I had no one to answer to or think about, and I thought my life was perfect.

But now I know something different. I know what it feels like to care deeply for someone else, to worry more about their welfare and happiness than my own. It's fucking scary. However, I have to admit that I'm kind of loving it.

On the drive to Trixie's, I try to stop obsessing and think about the evening ahead. I'm taking Trixie downtown to my favorite soul food place and then to listen to some jazz. We used to love to do that when we lived in Memphis, and I hope it'll bring back some good memories for us both.

The nerves have really taken hold by the time I pull up outside her cute little house, and I have to take a minute to calm my shit down before I knock loudly on her front door. It's ridiculous to be so nervous about this date—Trixie and I have been on countless dates in the past, but for some reason, this one has more at stake. This really could be the start of a new relationship for us, but it's so much more complicated than before. We have Danny to consider in everything we do. Our relationship has a direct impact on his life, and I know that neither of us would do anything to hurt him.

Thankfully, before I spiral any further, Trixie opens the door, and I'm spiraling all over again. She looks breathtaking—her blonde hair is smooth and shiny, skimming her jawline, and her makeup is subtle yet classy. Her body is hugged by a scarlet dress that fits her like a second skin, showing off the perfect amount of leg, shoulder, and cleavage, and she's added a few inches to her height with a pair of sexy heels.

"Wow," I gasp, not even trying to hide the fact that I'm checking her out from head to toe. "Baby, you look amazing." I reach out and slide my hand around her hip, pulling her flush against my body, kissing her red lips.

Trixie lets out a little whimper as I slip my tongue against the seam of her mouth, and she opens for me, bringing her hands up to grip the lapels of my leather jacket as my palms get their fill of her glorious ass.

When the kiss ends, we're both breathless, and I don't know about Trixie, but I'm horny as hell. From the pink tinge on her cheeks and the wild storminess in her navy blue eyes, I'd say she's feeling it too.

"That was one heck of a hello." Trixie giggles, grabbing her purse and jacket from the console table, pulling her front door closed behind her. "I think we should get somewhere public pretty quickly, otherwise I might just drag you inside and have my wicked way with you."

"I'm down with that," I growl as I walk her to the passenger side of my Tesla, my hand on the small of her back, the magnetic connection impossible to deny.

"Hold your horses," Trixie says, turning around and pressing her hand to the center of my chest, suddenly very serious. "We're doing this right—dinner, dancing, and then we'll see where it goes from there. We're not going to fuck this up by shagging in the back seat of your car."

"Yes, ma'am," I laugh, taking her hand from my chest and gently kissing the butterfly tattoo on the inside of her wrist. I just love how she phrases things in her very British way, and even though I don't always get what she means, on this occasion, she's being perfectly clear. She's as worried about fucking this up as much as I am.

On the drive across town to the restaurant, we talk

about everything from our day at the zoo, how training camp has been, and our upcoming exhibition games. Trixie fills me in on her expansion plans in L.A. and I can see how excited she is at the prospect. She's already managed to secure an investor and will be taking a trip down there to look at office space next month.

"That's so great, Sugar."

"Thanks." She looks over at me and smiles. "I have a few clients in L.A. and San Diego so it makes sense to have an office in California."

We're silent for a while, and I know that I'm thinking about what our lives would have been like if we hadn't parted ways back in Memphis. It's impossible to predict what might have happened, but a part of me thinks Trixie wouldn't have had the success she's had if she'd followed me around the country. After a season in Canada, I played in Florida, Kansas, and New Jersey before finding my place with the Whalers, and all that moving around would have been brutal on her career. So even though it hurt like a bitch to lose her, I know in some ways it was the best thing for both of us. All I can hope is that we're older and wiser, and we can make this second chance work.

When we pull up outside the soul food restaurant, I look over at Trixie and love the huge grin on her face.

"Oh my god, I've wanted to come here for ages," she cries, clapping her hands together.

I laugh. "You've lived in Seattle for six years. Why haven't you come here before?"

Suddenly she looks a little sad, and her eyes drop to her lap where she plays with the thin strap of her purse. "It always felt too painful," she replies quietly, still not looking up at me. "It was our thing so it felt … wrong to come here with anyone else."

Oh shit! I've completely fucked this up.

"Hey." I lean over the center console and take Trixie's trembling chin in my hand, lifting her face toward mine so she can see the sincere apology in my eyes. "I'm so sorry. I thought it would be a trip down Memory Lane, but we can go any other place you want."

Trixie closes her eyes and shakes her head. "No, it's okay. It was a really sweet thought, and I've been dreaming about catfish and cornbread for years."

I slowly lean over and kiss her soft pouty lips, loving the taste of her, the smell of her in the enclosed space of the car. The kiss is gentle and sweet, but for me, it feels like a homecoming. When I pull away, Trixie's eyes are shiny with tears, and she turns her face away to take care of it while I hop out and move around to open her door for her. I hold my hand out and she takes it, standing taller in her heels so her eyes are almost on a level with mine.

"You know that if they don't have catfish on the menu, I'll never bloody forgive you," she says quietly, a cheeky little smile on her lips, and I breathe a sigh of relief that she's still happy to come inside with me.

Now I just have to pray they have plenty of catfish in tonight.

"I can't eat another bite," Trixie huffs, pushing her mostly empty plate away from her. "Darlene, I swear to god I lived in Memphis for six years, and I never had food that good." She looks up at the chef who has come over to ask how the food was. I've been coming here ever since I moved to Seattle, and Darlene and I know each other well.

"Well that's the best compliment I've had all night," she beams, winking at me. "Your girl has good taste. You keep hold of this one."

Trixie flashes me a stern look and then she says to Darlene, "Oh, he brings a lot of girls here, I take it?"

I almost laugh out loud at the panicked expression that crosses Darlene's face, and she begins to tug on the dreadlocks that are hanging from underneath the bandana she wears in the kitchen. "Hell no!" she cries. "Chris has been coming here at least once a week for years, and he's always flying solo, never even brings his teammates along which I keep encouraging him to do."

"Hey, I thought I was your favorite Whaler?" I reply, enjoying the banter.

"You are, but it wouldn't do my business any harm to have the rest of the team here once in a while. You know how much hockey players eat." She laughs loudly and claps me on the shoulder. "I'll send over some pecan pie bites and coffee, my treat."

"Thank you, Darlene." I stand and give her a warm hug, loving the familiar mix of spices and cooking smells that cling to her, reminding me of my mom. "Don't forget you have a standing pair of tickets at Will Call for you and your boy, whenever you wanna come to a game."

"Thank you, baby. It means a lot to Kenny. I'm sure we'll see you at some of the exhibition games."

"It was a wonderful meal," Trixie says, and before

she can say anymore, Darlene literally pulls her out of her seat and hugs her close, whispering something in her ear that makes her giggle and blush.

Once Darlene has returned to the kitchen, I lean over and ask, "What did she whisper to you?"

Trixie raises an eyebrow and sits back in her seat. "Well, I think that's between me and Darlene and none of your bloody business." She reaches for her glass and drains the last of the beer, but I can tell by the shape of her mouth that she's smiling at me.

I'm so relieved that after the slightly shaky start to our date, we've settled into easy conversation and plenty of overt flirting—little touches here and there, her foot brushing my leg under the table, our fingers linking between courses. I can't help looking at her mouth as she talks, and every time she drags her little pink tongue across her lower lip, I swear I feel it on my dick which is obscenely hard under my napkin.

We continue to catch up on the last ten years while we eat the pecan pie bites and sip cafe au lait, and before I know it, Darlene is looking to close up. So we pay the bill, promise to come back soon, and I leave my usual generous tip because I know how hard everyone works to make the place a success. Before we leave, I quickly call Annie again to check in on Danny, and she assures me he went to bed an hour ago, and she just checked him, and he's fast asleep. I've tried really hard not to obsessively text or call tonight, but every time Trixie excused herself to use the restroom, I will admit I looked down at my phone to make sure I hadn't missed a call from Annie, the hospital, poison control, the fire department, or the FBI. But now I know he's safely asleep, I can return my attention to the beautiful woman on my arm.

"So where to now?" Trixie asks as I open the car door for her, holding my leather jacket over her head because Seattle hasn't failed to bring the rain to our date night.

"There's a jazz, funk, and soul night at the Sea Monster, so I thought we could go and check out who's playing." I close the door and rush around to my side, shaking the rain off my jacket before throwing it in the back seat and jumping in. "I hope that's…" But before I can get the rest of the sentence out, Trixie's lips silence me, insistent and needy, her tongue stroking my mouth open to receive it. My hand automatically closes around her throat, and she growls into my mouth, tilting her head so our kiss deepens to new erotic depths. I swear to god, if the center console of my car wasn't in the way, I would be pulling her against my body, just so every part of me can touch every part of her.

But it is in the way, and her words from earlier about not "shagging" in the car come rushing back, and I pull away, unsure of my levels of self-control if we keep kissing like this.

We both stare at each other, breathing hard and wild eyed, and I really, really want to take her home to her bed, but I also want to finish the date. So I do the sensible thing, press the ignition button, and put the car into drive.

"Let's go get our groove on, Sugar." I laugh as we drive off down the slick Seattle streets. Trixie lets out a little whoop of excitement, and her smile lights up the inside of my car, even in the darkness. She really is the most perfect woman for me, and I can't believe what a lucky bastard I am to get another chance at having her in my life.

16

Trixie

The pulsing beat of the music seems to be rising up through the floor, the heels of my pumps, my legs, and making my chest vibrate. It's an electric feeling, and the band on stage are rocking the place so hard I can't help but move my body to the hypnotic rhythms. Chris is standing behind me, his arms around my waist, his hand resting on my stomach in a spot that is almost too hot for me to bear. We weave together, perfectly in sync, and I can't seem to keep my mind out of the gutter, imagining his hand sliding unseen by everyone else to the place I'm desperate for it to be. It seems to be an appetizer for what I hope will come later in the evening when we get back to my place. And if the flirting, touching, and that searing hot kiss in his car are anything to go by, I think I'll be getting exactly what I want.

As the evening has progressed, I know without a doubt I want Chris Ford—fully, completely, and in every way possible. He's just proved to me what a gentleman he is—opening my door, being so kind and friendly to everyone at the restaurant, holding his very expensive leather jacket over my head so my hair didn't get all frizzy in the rain. And none of these things were done to overtly impress me; he's just like that every day.

I love the date he planned for us. Even though I was a little taken aback by his choices, it was very sweet to consider all the things we used to love to do together. He could have just taken me to O'Connell's for drinks and a movie, but he took me to places that he loves and that mean something to him. He wanted to share those parts of himself with me and that means so much.

"These guys are fantastic!" Chris yells in my ear over the music, and I just look over my shoulder at him and nod and smile, leaning up on my tiptoes to kiss him softly. When I slowly pull away, I know that we've both had enough of this portion of the date, and it's time to leave.

Without a word, Chris takes my hand, and we push through the crowded club toward the exit, grabbing our jackets from the coat check and rushing out into the darkness. The rain has stopped, but the streets are shiny and we splash through puddles, running and laughing hand in hand toward his car.

There's definitely an urgency about the next twenty minutes as Chris drives quickly through the thankfully quiet city streets to my house. I'm working so hard to control my breathing, trying to keep myself from panting with excitement at the prospect of finally spending the night with him. As I look over at Chris concentrating on the road ahead, I catch him sneaking a quick glance at me, and he looks as wild as I feel.

By the time we reach my house, the rain has started again, and it's really coming down. I don't wait for

Chris to be a gentleman and open my door. I just slip my heels off and leap out with my keys ready to let us in. We're both dripping wet and laughing madly once we get inside, Chris shaking his jacket off and hanging it on the back of one of my dining chairs. I drop my heels on the floor by the front door and walk slowly toward him, loving the way his biceps strain against the material of his shirt as he runs his fingers through his hair.

I stand as close to him as possible, and I immediately notice the change in his green eyes—the laughter has disappeared, and he's now predatory and hungry, ready to claim me. The urgency from earlier is just bubbling beneath the surface as I reach up and brush his damp hair from his forehead where it's fallen again. His Adam's apple bobs as he swallows, and I can tell he's holding on by a thread.

Our eyes lock, and we slowly lean in toward each other. I wet my lips with my tongue as my heart hammers against my rib cage. The anticipation of what's going to happen is driving me mad, but I also love the slow burn of it. I can feel his breath on my damp skin just before our lips touch, feather light and tentative to begin with, but it quickly deepens as my arms snake around his neck, pulling him close, crushing my breasts against his chest.

Chris groans into my mouth when his hands slip around my waist, palming my ass and pulling me even closer, close enough that I can feel his hard arousal against my stomach. Our slow, lazy kisses are quickly becoming deep and desperate, hands roaming everywhere as the urgency to be connected takes over.

My trembling fingers begin to undo the buttons of his shirt, but I'm so full of adrenaline, I can't seem to make them work. I huff in frustration, and he just chuckles against my lips.

"I got it, baby," he growls, momentarily breaking our kiss, pulling his shirt out of his jeans and ripping it open, sending buttons flying around my living room like little bullets.

"Oh wow," I sigh as his chest is exposed, perfectly sculpted from years as a professional athlete, almost as if the gods had carved him themselves. I reach my palms out and press them against his pecs, spreading the sides of his destroyed shirt away, smoothing over the light blond hair that covers them. I admire his perfection, letting my eyes travel down his torso, taking in his abs and the darker hair that leads from his belly button and disappears under his leather belt.

Chris places his hands on my upper arms, running them over my shoulders and up my neck, sending a cascade of goosebumps down my spine as he cups my face, caressing my cheeks with his thumbs.

"You're so beautiful," he whispers, leaning in to kiss me again, his warm tongue sliding against mine, giving me a preview on how he'll hopefully use it on other, more needy parts of my body.

His words help to lift me higher, and I'm sure I won't be able to take this slow build up much longer. I know from experience that Chris can fuck hard, just how I need it, and I'm eager to see that side of him. So I reach up and push his shirt off his shoulders and down his arms, letting it fall to the floor, and then I begin to work his belt buckle, desperate to get this thing moving.

But he pulls away and covers my hands with his. "I know what you need, Sugar," he growls, fixing me with a hot stare. "Believe me, I thought about it plenty of times over the years. But I'm taking charge of this."

My eyes widen and I nod. All I can manage is a squeak of acceptance as Chris reaches around and pulls down the zipper at the back of my dress, helping me wiggle out of it. Then I'm left in nothing but my red bra and lacy panties, suddenly feeling a little shy. My hips are wide and my breasts are large. My belly is soft and my thighs rub together. I've always loved that I have curves, and over the years, I've realized as long as I'm confident, it will shine through. But I'm also ten years older than I was when Chris and I were last fully naked together, and I have a few more stretch marks and dimples of cellulite than I did then.

"Hey, where did you go?" Chris asks, lifting my chin so I can look at him. With that one look, all of my insecurities melt away. He's looking at me like I'm a delicious snack he can't wait to tuck into, and my confidence soars.

"Just in my own head, for a minute," I confess. "It's okay. Let's go upstairs."

I reach out and take his hand, leading him to the ladder up to my bedroom. As I begin to ascend, I feel Chris's hands grip my hips, halting my progress.

"Wait just there," he orders. "I really wanna eat your pussy, right here."

I look back over my shoulder in surprise, but I can tell he's deadly serious, and it seems my lady parts know it too because I feel them flood with desire.

"Okay," I breathe, gripping the rungs of the ladder to brace myself.

Chris slowly hooks his fingers into the sides of my panties and pulls them down my legs until I can step out of them. He then runs his fingers up the backs of my calves, the backs of my knees and slowly toward my inner thighs. Carefully, he lifts one of my legs so that foot sits on a higher rung than the other, and I'm suddenly very aware that I'm now completely exposed to him, completely vulnerable. Despite this revelation, I still can't help the fluttering of my pussy as it anticipates his ministrations.

"Fuck me, your cunt is so sweet and wet," Chris growls, and he must be close because I can feel his breath on my slick skin.

"Please…" I beg, unashamedly pushing my ass out, desperate to get closer to him.

"I got you, baby." And then his face pushes between my legs from behind, and I enter a whole new stratosphere of sensation. He holds me firmly at the hips and eats me out like it's his mission, his long skillful tongue plunging in and out so quickly I'm sure he'll get a cramp. But the guy is a machine and soon one of his large hands slides from my hip and down my belly, his thick index finger spreading my folds until it finds my needy little button.

"Oh GOD!" I cry as he presses my clit and then begins a slow circular movement, the combination of his tongue and finger bringing me higher and higher. I circle my hips to match his movements, and I can feel the familiar tightness in my lower belly that means my orgasm is on the way.

Just as I'm getting ready to come all over his face, he pulls a new move out of the bag and suddenly his tongue is no longer in my pussy. I feel it slide backward and then he's circling my tight little hole, a sensation I never expected to like or need. But damn, his tongue on my butt and his fingers on my clit makes me come so hard, I feel a rush of moisture soak my inner thighs and stars burst behind my eyelids. He doesn't stop, and my orgasm just keeps going until I have to let go of one of the rungs and push his head away.

"Oh god, oh god, oh god," I groan, resting my forehead against the ladder, unsure how I'm still holding on because I'm completely boneless after that.

Chris just chuckles and begins to climb the ladder behind me, somehow lifting me up and helping me onto my bed.

"You liked that, huh?" he asks, standing next to the bed while I lay there, completely destroyed. I moan and nod and then watch as he slowly unbuckles his belt and pulls the buttons of his jeans open. As he pushes them over his slim hips, I lick my lips when I see the large tent in his black boxer briefs. When he kicks off his boots and jeans, I watch, fascinated as he grips his cock and gives it a squeeze, his eyes closing with need.

"I want you so fucking much," Chris growls as he falls onto the bed beside me, pulling me close so we're laying face to face. We begin to kiss slowly. I can taste myself on his tongue, and it really turns me on. I reach behind me and flick the clasp on my bra, wriggling out of it and tossing it away. Without breaking our kiss, Chris rolls me onto my back and palms my breasts, pressing them together, trapping my erect nipples between his thumbs and forefingers. I moan and arch my back, trying to get more of my tits into his large hands. My nipples are so sensitive that it's almost painful, but I know from experience that if I just push through, it will be worth it.

Trailing kisses down my neck and across the mounds of my breasts, he finally latches his mouth onto the hard pink flesh, rolling it between his teeth. I become frenzied with the sensation and begin to tug at his hair and claw at his back, grinding my center against the bulge in his boxers. We roll around together, both frantically pushing his boxers down and I finally get my hands on his perfect hockey butt—Jesus, it feels like it's sculpted from granite. I squeeze it and feel him chuckle against my breasts.

"Why are you laughing?" I gasp.

"You always loved my butt."

I release a throaty giggle and hold Chris's face in my hands. "I do, but right now I need your dick in me, so stop messing around and fuck me."

"Yes, ma'am."

But suddenly the fire dies in his eyes a little. "I don't have a condom." The disappointment in his voice is evident, and it makes my heart ache because I know he feels like he's messed up. "I can't believe I came out on this date without packing protection. What an idiot!"

"Hey, relax," I whisper. "I have some in the medicine cabinet."

Quick as a flash, Chris leaps out of bed and disappears into my small bathroom. I hear things falling into the sink with a loud clatter as he searches for the condoms.

"Don't make a mess in there!" I laugh, shifting up the bed so I'm resting against the pillows, laid out ready for him.

When Chris reappears in the bathroom door, his large cock bobbing against his stomach, I feel my center flood with a fresh rush of moisture. He's holding the box of condoms that have been in my cabinet for an embarrassingly long amount of time, and I pray they've not expired.

"Get your sexy arse back over here," I growl, patting the empty space on the bed next to me, and it seems he needs no further instructions. He rips open the box and tears open a condom packet with his teeth, looking down as he concentrates on rolling the latex down the impressive length of his thick shaft.

I have to keep pressing my thighs together because I'm sure I'm leaking all over my comforter, the desperation to have him on top of me, inside me, claiming me is becoming too much to bear. Slowly, Chris stalks toward me and crawls up the bed, looking like a panther approaching his prey. I part my legs and allow him to kiss his way up my legs, pressing his lips to my mound, my belly, my ribs and my nipples before he cradles his hips against mine, and I can feel the tip of his cock notch at my entrance.

There are no more sassy words or jokes from me. All I can do is plead with my eyes, open my legs wider, and tilt my hips to try and encourage more of him inside me. But that cocky grin on his face shows me he's going to take this at his pace, which to begin is going to be so maddeningly slow I'll want to scream.

Despite my hands on his ass pushing him forward,

he won't be rushed. Chris feeds his cock into me an inch at a time, pulling back and pushing forward a little more each time. I begin to feel the slight burn as I stretch to accommodate his size, and I crave it, wrapping my legs around his hips.

When he's finally fully seated inside me, we just lay there, holding each other's gaze, relishing in the feeling of it.

"Are you ready?" he asks, pressing a surprisingly soft kiss against my lips.

I nod my head and moan as he brushes his fingers across my breasts and then up to my neck, where he holds my throat lightly. Thank god he remembers that I love this, and as he begins to move inside me, his hand on my throat squeezes and it quickly builds the pressure between my legs.

As he finds his stride, we move in sync with each other, the sound of our sweaty flesh crashing together accompanying the moans and gasps. I grab his ass to pull him closer and harder, and all the reasons he was such a good lover come rushing back—he knows how to turn me on, he's considerate and giving, and my pleasure is forefront in his mind.

"Oh fuck, Trixie," he gasps, sweat beading at this temples and on his upper lip, his eyebrows scrunching together. "I can't go much longer. Your pussy feels so fucking good."

I grunt and double down, thrusting my hips up to meet his and chase the precious friction between us. But it's not quite enough.

"Rub my clit," I beg and Chris quickly shifts position so he's kneeling between my legs, giving him unfettered access to my button. Continuing with his relentless rhythm, he matches it with his fingers, and my orgasm goes from just out of reach to right on the surface.

Never breaking eye contact, I reach up and grab my breasts, rolling my nipples between my fingers, adding that little bit extra to tip me over the edge.

"Chris, Chris, yes, yes!" I cry as the wave crashes over me, and I'm submerged in pleasure, swirling in the vortex, scared I may never resurface. But as I'm coming, I feel Chris swell and explode inside me, grabbing my legs behind the knees, holding me open so he can watch my pussy flutter around his cock. His sinewy muscles strain with his release, and when it passes, he collapses, just managing to hold his weight off me with shaky arms.

"Fuck me, Sugar," he gasps, reaching down to hold the condom as he withdraws. "That was something else."

I laugh and run my fingers across the sweaty ridges and valleys of his chest. "It sure was. It's like we were in the minors before and now we've made it to the show."

"Damn straight." Chris presses a kiss to my lips and then disappears into the bathroom to dispose of the condom. He returns with a glass of water that we share and a damp washcloth that he uses to gently clean me up.

When we're both a little more hydrated, we snuggle under the comforter, and I rest my head on Chris's chest, his heartbeat thumping against my cheek. We don't have a lot of pillow talk, but the silence is comfortable and familiar. We talked so much on our date I don't think we have anything left to say, for now.

I slowly allow my post-orgasmic haze to pull me under, and as I'm falling into the abyss, Chris's fingers glide up and down my spine and he whispers two words that I only just hear before I fall asleep.

17

Chris

"**I**'m sorry."

As the words wisp past my lips, my eyes fly open, and I wonder where the hell they came from.

I try to recall our breakup ten years ago, and I don't ever think I said those words to her. I never apologized for running out on us. But why do I feel the need to say them now, after that mind-blowing, life-altering sex? I'm so confused. So many feelings are swirling in my brain I can't order them or make sense of them. I'm holding this goddess in my arms, her breath ghosting across my chest, her hand splayed across my abs, and I feel at peace. And all I know is that I've had one of the best nights of my life. It surpasses any date I've had with her or any other woman. It makes me think that Trixie could be it for me—Will I ever get this feeling again with anyone else but her? Am I just in a post-sex euphoric state, or could these feelings be genuine?

Is it love?

I lift my head slightly to see if Trixie is awake, but her gentle snore indicates that she's already slipped into sleep.

My heartbeat begins to regulate, and I take a few deep breaths. I don't think she heard me, and while most of me is relieved, a small part of me is disappointed. The rational part of me knows it's madness to think this could be love, but the dumbass romantic fool in me wants to run out into the rain, naked, and tell everyone I meet that I love Beatrix Cavendish.

But that's not the way I need to play this. Trixie could be spooked so easily, and there's so much at stake. There's no way I'm going to rush into this like an idiot. I need to play the long game and make sure we're both one hundred percent on board, not just for the protection of our hearts, but for Danny as well.

I must drift off to sleep because when I wake up, I'm spooning against Trixie's back, our legs entwined and my hand cupping her breast. My dick is hard again, and it's nestled deliciously between her generous butt cheeks. From the slow steady rhythm of her breathing, she's still out cold so I nuzzle into her neck and drift back off into a warm dreamless sleep.

When my eyes flicker open again, Trixie is looking down at me in the pre-dawn light. I can't hear the rain splattering against the window pane anymore.

"Good morning, Sunshine," she says, smiling, her usually perfect hair disheveled, giving her a thoroughly fucked appearance. The caveman in me beats his chest because I did that. I try to hide my smirk at the thought and lean up and kiss her. "Hope my morning breath isn't too minging." She giggles when we part, covering her mouth with her hand.

"Remind me of 'minging' again?" I ask, not remembering this particular piece of British slang.

Trixie blushes. "You know, like gross or disgusting." She covers her mouth again, and I move it away, pulling her in for a long, deep kiss that makes my already semi-hard dick throb painfully. At first she resists, her concerns about her morning breath clearly worrying her, but I don't give a fuck. Every part of her tastes like strawberries and cream to me, and I can't get enough.

Trixie finally gives in and settles into the kiss, her palm presses against my heart, and I let my hand slide down her smooth back and grip one of her soft ass cheeks, urging her on top of me.

When the kiss ends, I smile up at her. "No, I don't think your morning breath is minging."

She smiles as well and presses her face into my neck, wrapping her arms around me, and it feels so fucking good, I never want to move. But I quickly flick my eyes over to the clock on Trixie's night stand and see that it's five in the morning.

Not quite time to go yet.

So I roll over and grip Trixie's wrists, holding them above her head, spreading her legs with my knees, pressing myself against her core.

"Oh," she gasps, her navy blue eyes flashing with lust. "Do I get a little morning delight, Mr. Ford?"

"Why yes you do, Ms. Cavendish," I reply, working my way down her body, kissing a trail toward her pert nipples, her belly button, her hips, and finally the soft tuft of sparse hair between her legs.

My heart soars when she moans as my thumbs part her lips, and I lap at her clit with the tip of my tongue. Her legs flop open lazily, and I continue to work her slowly, in no rush to make her come. I want to keep her on the edge until she's begging me, and soon I get my wish. Her fingers thread into my hair, and she starts to grind against my tongue.

"Oh please, Chris, please…" she moans, drawing her knees up to her chest to open herself further, and a fresh surge of honey coats my tongue. I don't know how much longer I can keep her on the precipice, so I slide two fingers into her throbbing channel and curve them up, finding that spot inside that makes her grunt and bear down, almost suffocating me with her pussy.

I'm on the point of passing out when she finally cries out and comes all over my face, letting go of my hair so I can pull away and catch my breath.

"Fuck's sake, you're so good at that," Trixie pants, pulling up into the fetal position and then slowly unfurling as her muscles relax.

I wipe my hand over my face and shift up the bed so I can hold her close as she comes down from her high. "I aim to please." I chuckle.

"Well, you certainly do." Trixie rolls over so she's facing me, and I can tell by the little furrow between her brows that she's thinking about something really hard.

"What's on your mind, Sugar?"

She huffs out a breath, and I can feel her body tense in my arms.

Shit, this can't be good.

"I was just wondering how this thing is going to work once the season starts properly," she says quietly. "I mean, everyone knows I'm helping you with Danny, but I think it would look a bit shady if we were openly … dating. What do you think?" She bites her plump bottom lip and lowers her eyes from mine, like she's embarrassed for asking this.

But I understand her concerns. "I know what you mean. I don't want to confuse Danny. He seems settled having you around, but if we add that extra element of a romantic relationship into the mix, he might feel insecure."

"What about the team and everyone else, especially Blake? He'll have a field day if he finds out, and he could even accuse me of trying to steal you away…" Her voice has taken on a high-pitched quality, and I know she's beginning to panic.

"Hey, hey." I pull her close and kiss her forehead. "I want you to know one thing—I don't give a fuck what anyone thinks about us. The only people that matter are you, me, and Danny. If he's good with whatever this turns into, then everyone else can go to hell. Especially Blake."

The memory of Blake's harsh words about Trixie fills my mind, and my blood still boils. Perhaps it's time to move on from him. I liked his drive and cutthroat attitude when I was young and hungry for a Cup win, but all that seems so insignificant now I have new priorities. Don't get me wrong. I still want to hold that enormous cup over my head before I retire, but maybe Blake's way isn't the way to go.

My words seem to calm Trixie, and we drift off back to sleep in each other's arms until my phone alarms jolts me awake, and I know it's time to get home and relieve Annie from her babysitting duties.

Before I leave Trixie's bed, I make sure to kiss her and give her one more orgasm with my fingers, leaving her panting and sweaty.

"What's your week looking like?" she asks, laying on her side, head propped on her hand, looking like a fucking goddess.

"I'm free today so Danny and I are going sneaker shopping, and we'll probably go and shoot some hoops." I pull up my jeans and button them, loving the fact Trixie's eyes are following my every move. "This week I have a physical with the doc, conditioning training, physio, and we'll go over the travel plans and game plays."

"Wow, sounds busy." She flops back on the pillow. "My week is crazy too so I guess we won't get a chance to see each other."

I can see the look of disappointment in her eyes so I sit on the edge of the bed and cup her face in my hands.

"Do you have time to come and eat dinner with me and Danny one night this week? I can't promise a sleepover, but I know he'd love to see you."

And so would I.

"I'd really like that. I'll check my schedule and see which night is best. I have a few client dinners this week." She smiles brightly and my heart stutters in my chest.

"Sounds good." I lean forward and kiss her again, feeling like shit for leaving. "I'll call you later."

"Okay," she replies on a breath, leaning back on the pillows, her cheeks and chest flushed. "Thank you for the lovely date."

"You're welcome. We'll go back to Darlene's again soon. Maybe we can take Danny and give him a taste of home."

"That sounds perfect."

I quickly kiss Trixie again and grab my boots. "We need to think about this ladder situation." I laugh, carefully reversing down it. "Seriously, I could end my career on this thing."

Trixie giggles and waves at me as she disappears from view, and I let myself out, heading home to see my kid, feeling on top of the world.

18

"Trixie, it's four o'clock. You asked me for a time check so you don't run late for dinner." Kristen's voice at my office door makes me look up from the spreadsheet I've been studying for hours. I push my glasses up onto my head and stretch my arms above my head, hearing my back crack.

"How is it that time already?" I groan, rubbing my eyes. "I feel like I've been looking at the costs for L.A. all day." I close my eyes and sigh, the numbers still swimming behind my eyelids in a confusing jumble.

"I can take a look at them tonight if that'll help," Kristen offers kindly.

"No, that's okay. You go and enjoy your evening." I smile at Kristen and mentally thank god she's so amazing. I really couldn't do half of what I do without her.

"Oh, by the way, I picked up the tiramisu from Bakery Nouveau. It's in the fridge," Kristen explains, pulling on her jacket. "Don't forget."

"Did you get three?" I ask, logging off my laptop.

She laughs and nods. "I literally bought every

tiramisu they had—I know how much hockey players can eat."

"Thanks, love. I really appreciate you doing that. I've just been swamped today." I pull on my jacket and slide my laptop into my bag. "I'm not even going to get home to change. I'll have to go straight there now."

"Hey, it was no hardship going to that amazing bakery." Kristen laughs. "You know I love their almond croissants."

"Well I know you're over qualified to run my errands, so I really do appreciate it."

"It's not a problem, really. Have a good evening." The cheeky smile on her face as she leaves makes me wonder if she overheard me on the phone to Chris this week. Since our date, we've talked every day, and on Wednesday, we had a very hot, sexy call during my lunch break. He recounted, in agonizingly vivid detail, everything he did to me the night we slept together. It made me so wet and needy that I couldn't help slipping my fingers down the front of my pants and into my knickers, rubbing myself to a muffled orgasm.

"Fuck me," Chris moaned after he came too. "Why is the sound of you coming so goddamn sexy?"

"I don't know, but it really wasn't appropriate for me to do it in my office," I giggled.

We chatted for a few more minutes, and once I hung up and left my office to use the bathroom, I noticed that Kristen was back at her desk with a knowing look on her face. As I walked past I tried not to die of embarrassment that my assistant might have heard me coming.

Now it's Friday, and I finally get to spend some

time with Chris and Danny. Matt has invited the first line over for game night, so even though we won't be alone, it will still be good to see them. I must remember that our blossoming relationship is still just between us, so we'll have to keep the PDA to a minimum.

Thankfully, the traffic isn't too bad, and I get to Matt's house on the Sound just before 5. Mila answers the door wearing a post-it note stuck to her forehead that reads Katy Perry, and she gives me a big hug, taking the bag of desserts from my hand.

"Come in. We're just warming up with a game of *Guess Who*." She ushers me into their main living space, and I find everyone sitting on the large U-shaped couch and on the floor around the coffee table. They all have post-it notes stuck to their foreheads, and it looks like it's Nate's turn to try and guess who he is.

"Auntie Trixie!" Danny comes sprinting up to me, slamming into my legs, wrapping his arms tightly around them. "Guess who I was? I was Superman! Isn't that awesome?"

"Hey poppet," I huff as he knocks the wind out of me. "That *is* awesome." I smile down at him and love how excited he is.

"Come on. We saved one for you." He grabs my hand and drags me across the room as I say rushed hellos to everyone. Danny leads me to the couch where there's a spot right next to Chris, who's looking so hot in jeans and a light blue checked button down shirt with the sleeves rolled up to the elbow. I sit next to him. His clean linen scent wafts into my nostrils, and I become hypnotized by the fine blond hairs on his thick, muscular forearms.

"Hey Sugar, glad you could make it," Chris growls, his hand reaching out to squeeze my knee so quickly I don't think anyone notices, but the spot where his palm touched my bare skin is now on fire.

"I wouldn't miss game night, you know that," I reply a little breathlessly, not daring to look to my right in case looking into those sexy green eyes causes me to push him to the floor and take him in front of all our friends.

Bloody hell, I need to keep this under control. I'm not ready for our relationship to be out in the open yet. I still don't know what it is, so I'm not ready to try to explain it to other people.

"Here you go, Auntie Trixie," Danny says, holding out a post-it note, ready to stick it to my forehead. "Can I stick it on?"

"Go for it," I laugh, thankful for the distraction from the warmth of Chris's thigh up against mine.

Danny leans forward, sticks the note to my forehead, and sits on the floor next to my feet, giggling adorably.

"Am I Michael Jordan?" Nate guesses and everyone cheers as he finally gets it right.

"Jesus kid, we literally served that answer to you on a silver platter." Bugs laughs, taking a swig from his bottle of beer. "I guess so many hits to the head will take its toll eventually."

"Hey fu … fudge you, man," Nate replies good-naturedly, removing the post-it from his forehead and screwing it into a little ball, tossing it at Bugs.

"Nice save on the F-bomb," Thor chuckles under his breath.

Nate's cheeks pink up a little. His eyes dart to Chris,

and he mouths an apology before excusing himself to get another beer.

Conversations and games continue, and the whole time Chris keeps some kind of contact between us—his thigh against mine, his hand on the small of my back, slipping down the back of my skirt to caress my bare skin. All of this out of sight of our oblivious friends.

Or so I thought.

Once *Guess Who* ends, the girls decide to go to the kitchen to make cocktails while the guys have a game of pool. And that's when my hope of keeping things between Chris and me private goes to hell in a handbasket.

"So Trixie, tell us what's up with you and Ford?" Beth asks, lifting her tiny frame onto one of the high bar stools at the kitchen island. She raises a blonde eyebrow and crosses her arms across her chest.

I've taken a swig of margarita so start to cough on it at her brash question.

"For god's sake, Beth," Mila scolds her best friend. "We weren't just gonna come right out with it like that." She quickly pats me on the back as I try to regain my composure and come up with a story to explain the obvious sexual tension between Chris and me.

"What?" Beth asks, fluttering her eyelashes innocently. "What's the point of beating around the bush? We might as well just get on with the interrogation."

"Hey, c'mon you guys. Give Trixie a break," Lana interjects. "As the newest member of this weird little group, I know how intimidating ya'll can be."

I flick Lana a thankful look, remembering all the

drama around her arrival to Seattle—fleeing France and an abusive ex, falling for Thor but having to keep it secret because her brother, Matt, had made it clear that he would murder any of the guys if they hit on her.

"What Beth is trying to ask, with the subtlety of a sledgehammer, is are you and Chris a thing again?" Cam says, sipping her virgin cocktail.

I huff out a breath and take another quick sip of my drink for Dutch courage. These women are my closest friends in Seattle, and I could really do with some advice about what Chris and I have going on.

"Okay, yes, we have kind of started seeing each other," I say as quietly as I can because the guys are just in the next room, and I don't want Chris to think that I'm in here gossiping.

Sensing my need to keep this conversation on the DL, the girls all smile and clap quietly, holding their glasses into the middle of the counter so we can clink them together.

"But it's very new. We've only been on one real date without Danny, and I don't think either of us know exactly what we want it to become."

"That's so exciting," Mila sighs. "Second chance romance is my favorite kind of book to read." She looks wistfully into space, and I can only imagine she's recounting her own romance with Matt—their one night stand turning into a friendship and then an epic love story.

"And how does Danny fit into everything?" Cam asks, her mothering instinct shining through. I know she cares a lot about that little boy.

"I know that Danny is at the forefront of everything

Chris does, and we won't make any decisions about our relationship without considering the effect on him first." Just saying this to the girls makes me realize how naturally Chris has adapted to fatherhood and how easily he puts Danny first.

"And how's the sex?" Of course this is the first question Beth asks, a cheeky little smirk on her face.

I can't help the nervous giggle that escapes me, and my cheeks start to heat up as I remember our night together after our date.

"Let me just say, Chris was an amazing lover ten years ago, but I can safely say his skills in the bedroom have moved from rookie to Stanley Cup winner since then."

This comment elicits whoops of glee from the girls, and I make a shushing noise in case the guys decide to come and investigate the excitement in here.

"So why are you keeping it quiet?" Lana asks. "I mean I'm the queen of secret relationships, but that's because my brother would've ended up on a murder charge if he'd found out about Alex and me before we were ready. But you and Chris have a history. No one would blame you for getting back together."

I think hard for a moment—I guess I know why we aren't going public, but Chris and I haven't really had this conversation yet.

"We're just trying to protect Danny," I finally say. "What if we break up again? I'd feel so guilty about leaving after all the trauma he's been through with his mum."

"But what if you don't break up?" Mila, the ever optimistic romantic of the group, asks. "What if you and

Chris can give him the stable, loving family he really needs? And you can give each other the relationship you were denied all those years ago." She takes a big gulp of her cocktail as we all look at her aghast.

"Jesus, Doctor Phil in the house." Beth laughs.

I laugh as well to try and break the tension, but Mila's words swirl around in my head—what the hell are we so afraid of? Why am I so sure this relationship will end horribly? Why can't I open that last part of my heart to the possibility that Chris, Danny, and I can have a future together?

Before the conversation can continue, Danny comes into the kitchen holding the baby monitor. "Auntie Cam, I can hear SJ crying on the monitor. You said if I did I should come get you."

"You did a great job, buddy," Cam says to him, taking the monitor and holding it to her ear. "Do you wanna come and see what she needs?"

"Sure," Danny replies enthusiastically, grabbing Cam's hand as they head upstairs.

"Oh my god, he's just the sweetest little guy," Beth gushes, clutching her heart. "Perhaps it's time I let Nate knock me up."

We all laugh loudly, and Mila shakes her head. "The day I see you with a baby is the day hell freezes over."

"Hey, no need to be a bitch about it," Beth replies, pouting. "I think I'd make a good mom, but I have to admit I'd be terrified about giving birth to Nate's massive baby." She grimaces and crosses her legs.

"You'd make a wonderful mom," Mila says, hugging her bestie. "But yes, I would worry that your vagina would never recover."

While we're still laughing about the possibility of tiny Beth trying to give birth to a fifteen pound baby, Matt walks in and heads to the fridge.

"Sounds like you ladies are having fun in here," he says, his head buried in the fridge. "What's the topic of conversation?"

"Just talking about Thor knocking up your baby sister," Beth replies, smirking when Matt's head whips around, and he growls low in his chest.

"What?"

"Beth, that's not funny!" Lana scolds.

"Take it easy, baby," Mila soothes, going to Matt and nestling into his embrace. "We weren't talking about that." She shoots Beth a shitty look. "In fact, you might want to go tell Nate that Beth is really excited for him to knock her up."

The look of terror on Beth's face is priceless as Matt laughs and rushes into the other room, closely followed by Beth, trying to grab at the back of his shirt in a vain attempt to slow him down.

Lana comes over to me and puts her hand on my arm. "If you want some advice from someone who was in a secret relationship, you and Chris have an undeniable chemistry, and I think you're gonna struggle to keep it quiet. I mean, if we all noticed…" She shrugs. "All I mean is, why not give it a chance? Danny loves you, and I think he'd be thrilled to have you in his life. But you can't deny yourself love because you're scared. Believe me, I almost gave up the best man ever because I was scared of what I'd experienced before him."

Her words of wisdom hanging in the air, Lana disappears outside, leaving me in the kitchen with my thoughts.

Before I can spiral too much, I feel a strong pair of arms slide around my waist from behind and soft lips on my neck. I can't help my body quivering at the feeling of his chest against my back and the bulge of his dick against my ass.

"How's my girl doing?" he growls into my ear, and I moan, leaning back against him.

"I'm okay," I sigh, turning around so I can look up into his beautifully imperfect face. "I've really missed you." I'm a little shocked at my honesty, but the look on his face confirms that he feels the same.

Chris leans down and gently presses his lips to mine, softly caressing them with his tongue, encouraging me to open for him, which I do willingly.

"I missed you too," he replies once our kiss ends. "Danny's been asking every day when you're coming around again."

My heart stutters in my chest as all my doubts about moving forward with this relationship come flooding back. It seems Danny is already invested in me being in his life, so even if I end this now and walk away, he'll still be hurt and confused.

So I decide to take a leap, even though I'm absolutely terrified. "Perhaps I can take him to the first exhibition game on Saturday, and I can sleep over afterward?" I suggest, holding my breath in case Chris doesn't think it's a good idea.

But his face splits into a huge grin. "I think that would be amazing. He hasn't stopped talking about the game. He's so excited."

The relief washes over me. "That's a date then."

"It sure is, Sugar." He leans in close so I can feel his lips against my ears. "And you know how hard it'll make me having you in the crowd wearing my number. That's so fucking hot. Everyone will know you're mine."

I moan at his words and press myself against his body, wanting him so much it aches.

"So you want people to know about us?" I ask expectantly, again terrified at his reply.

But Chris just cups my face in his hands and lands a breathtaking kiss on my lips, stealing the last sliver of doubt from my heart.

"I want the world to know I'm your man, but obviously we need to speak to Danny about it first. I'm sure he'll be thrilled. He's completely besotted with you."

His words make me absurdly happy, and I struggle to hold my shit together as he leads me into the living room, only dropping my hand when we're in the company of the others. I mourn the loss, but I understand his reasons—it's only fair we have a proper talk with Danny and not just drop this on him in front of all our friends. He deserves more than that.

I can't seem to wipe the stupid grin off my face for the rest of the evening, and when it's time to leave, I give all the girls big hugs and whispered thanks. I hug Danny and Chris at the car, promising to pick Danny up on Saturday to take him to the game.

"Do you mind if I talk to Danny about the possibility of us being together?" Chris asks once Danny is safely in his booster seat. "I just wanna get a sense of how he feels about it and then perhaps we can talk to him together after the game."

I take a deep breath. "I think that's a good idea."

Chris quickly kisses my lips and gets into the car, Danny waving like a lunatic as they pull out of the driveway and onto the street.

When I get home, I potter around unstacking the dishwasher and putting some laundry away, but the whole time I'm smiling and humming soppy love songs to myself. I try to work for a while, looking over the spreadsheet again, but I just can't focus; the numbers have beaten me today. So I decide to have a glass of wine and treat myself to a long hot bath, slipping into the comforting water and allowing myself to indulge in the fantasy of a life with Chris and Danny and all the joys that could bring.

19

Chris

Waking up on Game Day is like being a kid on Christmas morning every single time. I always thought to myself that if I ever stop getting the nervous excitement in my stomach, I should quit.

But it's still there, and as I run a few miles on my treadmill before Danny wakes up, I run through the pre-game briefing we had yesterday. Coach Casey always records it and sends us the video so we can review it again and concentrate on the parts that pertain to us in particular. I watch the penalty kills on my iPad because this is what Coach really wants me to focus on this season, and I memorize the plays we've been practicing.

Once I finish my run, I rub down with a towel and knock on Danny's door to tell him I'm fixing breakfast. This gets a grunt from inside the dark room, and I can't help smiling, leaving the door open so the smell of frying eggs will eventually raise him from his bed.

It's kind of weird doing my game day routine with Danny here. I've arranged for Annie to be here even though it's Saturday, but I will have to go to the rink for a practice skate and game briefing, and I need a nap so she's agreed to take him out to the little book store he likes for a few hours.

It's definitely an adjustment, but I'm thankful I have the means to make sure Danny has cool things to do while I'm not around. I'm still really anxious about the first road trip in a week, but we'll cross that bridge when we come to it.

Right now I have to focus on tonight.

"Good morning, sleepy head." I laugh as I slide a fried egg onto a piece of toast, the yolk wobbly and runny just how he likes it.

"Morning, Uncle Chris," Danny yawns, rubbing his eyes, his hair a jumble of black curls. I can already tell it hasn't seen a comb this morning, but I'll let him eat before I bust his chops about that.

As I continue to cook, I decide to broach the subject of Trixie and me dating.

"So, you like Trixie, right?"

Great start, jack-ass.

"Yeah, she's nice, and I like that she knows a lot about sports for a girl," he replies through a mouthful of toast and egg.

"Hey, girls can know a lot about sports just like guys. Sometimes they know even more," I say. I don't want him to grow up with the attitude that sports are just a guy thing.

"I know that." He looks up at me with a slightly sad look. "My momma loved basketball so much, she could tell me the lineup of every Memphis team since forever."

My nose tingles with emotion hearing him talk about his mom, but I'm glad he still drops her into conversations.

"That's impressive. Your momma must've really loved that team."

"She did, but we never had enough money to go and see them in real life." Again, he drops his eyes from mine and concentrates on his eggs.

"Well perhaps some day we can go and see a game. I'd really like that," I say.

Danny shrugs. "Sure. So why do you wanna know if I like Auntie Trixie? Is it because she's your … girlfriend?" He smirks a little and seems embarrassed by the word.

His honesty and insight floor me for a second, but then I regain my composure.

"How would you feel if Trixie was my girlfriend? Would it be okay if she hung out with us more or slept over sometimes?" I ask, not sure how to ask a little kid if he's cool with my girlfriend sharing my bed.

"Sure. It would be fun to have her here more." He shrugs again and finishes his orange juice. "I mean, you have another bedroom, so she wouldn't have to sleep on the couch."

I press my lips together so he can't tell I'm about to burst out laughing. What a cute little guy—his innocence is so refreshing.

"That's very true," I say with a smile. "I'm happy you're okay with it. Trixie really loves hanging out with you."

Danny just nods, and I guess the conversation's over. I'm so relieved he's on board with Trixie being around a lot more, I can't wait to tell her and I can't wait to sleep with her in my arms tonight.

"You have to eat all that?" Danny asks, his eyes wide when I serve myself a four-egg spinach omelet and a cup of blueberries with a whole wheat bagel covered in peanut butter.

"I sure do," I laugh. "I use a lot of energy on game day so I need to make sure I have enough fuel on board. It's like being a race car—if I don't have enough gas in the tank, I won't go as fast as I can go."

Danny nods to show he understands just as I hear the key turn in the lock and Annie lets herself in.

"Good morning, guys," she says cheerfully as Danny jumps down from his stool to greet her with a hug.

"Hi, Annie. Thanks for coming over so early," I say, popping a blueberry into my mouth.

"It's no problem," she replies. "I have an awesome day of fun planned for me and Danny, and we'll be sure to give you some quiet time for your nap this afternoon."

"I really appreciate that."

"Young man, look at this mop on your head." Annie laughs, turning her attention to Danny, ruffling his hair. "I'd say it's time you hit the shower, so hop to it."

He salutes her, and she laughs as she hustles him down the corridor, leaving me to finish my breakfast and clean up.

I have a game day superstition that I don't shower until I've had my nap, so in order not to stink out the locker room, I use a liberal amount of deodorant, change into my clean Whalers sweats, and pack my bag for my session with the physio and our workout.

"Make sure you have a good day, buddy. And listen to Annie. She's the boss of you today, you hear me?" I say to Danny once he's done with his shower.

"Yes, Uncle Chris," he replies. "What time is Auntie Trixie gonna be here?"

"She'll come over at 6. She wants to take you for a burger, and then she'll bring you to the rink. That okay with you?"

Danny nods enthusiastically, and it warms my heart that he loves Trixie so much. I guess both the Ford men are crazy for her.

"I'll see you at the game. Make sure you shout extra loud," I say.

"Annie's going to help me make a great big sign to hold up so you can find me," Danny explains, and I ruffle his hair, feeling so much love for this kid I can't even put it into words.

"I can't wait to see it." I lean down and kiss the top of his head, throw my duffle over my shoulder, and make my way to the rink.

After a morning of drills, stickhandling, and off-rink shooting practice, reviewing game footage from last season and plays for this game and a brutal physio session to work out the kinks in my hamstrings, I meet the guys in the player's lounge for lunch.

We're all eating salmon, brown rice, and salad when Thor comes in looking wrecked after his session with the goaltending team. Like me, he's one of the older guys on the team, and if he's feeling half the pain I am, then I know he's hurting like a bitch.

"So the word on the street is you and Trixie are

dating again, and I don't mean the fake dating we talked about before," Matt says before taking a long drink of water, holding my gaze.

I finish chewing so I can order my thoughts before I reply. "And what street did you hear that on?"

"The street where all the women in our lives stand around and gossip." Bugs laughs, rolling his eyes. "The girls were talking to Trixie at game night, and she might have mentioned that you too were all hot and heavy again."

I huff out a breath. I love this group more than anything, but these guys are the worst gossips. But perhaps it's time to come clean.

"Okay, fine. Trixie and I went on a date, and it was fucking incredible. Are you goons happy now?" I slam my fork down on the table and cross my arms, pissed that they've forced me into a corner. I don't need the distraction today of all days—I've been trying my best to keep Trixie's satiny skin and slick pussy out of my head, but now she's all I can think about.

I guess my face must tell the guys exactly how I'm feeling because they all look a little sheepish, and I don't get my balls busted about keeping a secret from them.

"Well, that's great to hear, man," Nate says, looking around the table where the guys all nod in agreement. "We're happy for you."

"I second that," Thor agrees through a mouthful of spaghetti.

"Okay, great," I say, pushing my plate away. "Now I have the blessing of the group, can we get back to the task at hand, beating the shit out of the Saxons tonight?"

"Fuck yeah!" The guys high five, and I immediately

feel the energy in the room ramp up a notch. There really is no feeling like it.

We hang out in the lounge for a while and play pool, and once our huge lunches have gone down, we head off to continue our own pre-game routines. Mine involves going home for a nap and a shower, but as I reach my car, my phone pings with a message.

I pull my cell out of my pocket and see Trixie's name, my heart immediately kicking in my chest. Even a damn message from her makes my dick thicken with desire, so I quickly adjust it as I get into the driver's seat and open the message.

[TRIXIE: I don't want to distract you, but I just want to wish you luck for tonight. You'll be amazing, and I can't wait to wear your number. T x]

I read the message three times, smiling like a lovesick idiot as I type out my reply.

[CHRIS: Thanks, Sugar. I can't wait to see you either. We'll definitely be having a private post-game party for two later.]
[TRIXIE: Does that mean I have permission from the little man to sleep over?]
[CHRIS: You sure do. But he has one condition.]
[TRIXIE: ???]
[CHRIS: You're in the spare room.]

I smile as I hit send, anticipating her reaction.

[TRIXIE: He's a tough one. But if those are his rules, I guess we'll have to obey.]
[CHRIS: The fuck we will. As soon as he's asleep, you'll be in my bed and I'll be buried in that sweet pussy all night long.]

I watch the three bubbles start and stop for at least a minute as Trixie types out her reply.

[TRIXIE: Bloody hell, that's made me so wet for you.]
[CHRIS: Save it for later, Sugar.]

And then I quickly send her another message.

[CHRIS: Leave your car at my place and get an Uber to the game, then we can all travel home together.]

Once I hit send on the message, I read it back and see that I used the word home. It's a simple, innocuous word that we use everyday, but in this instance, it seems weighted with meaning. I do see Trixie as home, and if I'm completely honest with myself, I feel at home when I'm with her. I guess that's why I never tried to make my apartment into a home until she came back into my life.

As I drive, I allow myself time to imagine a life and home with Trixie and Danny, eating together and going on trips. It seems like a simple thing to wish for—a family—and I guess I never really allowed myself to believe I'd have that.

But with Trixie and Danny, it seems like it could

be possible. As long as I don't screw it up like last time.

As I pull into the garage, I put a hold on my fantasy. I know that if I keep thinking about it, I'll be too distracted to sleep, and I certainly can't have this muddling my head once the game starts.

Focus is what I need right now.

When I get up to the apartment, all is quiet and tidy. There's something propped up against the wall with an old sheet over it and a sign in Danny's handwriting reading, "DO NOT TOUCH—THIS MEANS YOU, UNCLE CHRIS," and it makes me smile. It also makes me miss him like crazy.

But I have to keep to my routine, and right now, I need a protein shake and a nap.

20

I grip Danny's hand like my life depends on it. I've been to the Whalers rink on game day a thousand times, but I don't ever remember it being this crowded or full of potential kidnappers. I'm on high alert as we make our way through the crowds of people moving around the concourse doing perfectly normal things—buying beer and snacks, queuing up for merchandise, meeting friends.

However, my normal excitement is replaced with a weird protective instinct. I'm in full Momma Bear mode, and every time someone innocently bumps Danny as they pass by, I'm ready to eviscerate them with my bare hands.

"This is so cool," Danny says, looking adorable in his Whalers jersey, staring at everything with curiosity and delight.

He'd been pretty excited when I picked him up from Chris's apartment earlier. He and Annie showed me the huge sign they'd made, and the look of pride on his face almost made me lose my composure.

After I managed to get it into the Uber without the

driver freaking out about the amount of glitter that was falling on his upholstery, we went to a diner across the street from the rink and had burgers and shakes along with almost every other Whalers fan in the city.

We talked about the game and what it would be like, and Danny asked me lots of questions about Chris's position and scoring record. He's such a sponge for knowledge and took in everything I told him.

Just before we finished our meal, he looked at me with those familiar green eyes and asked, "Are you and Uncle Chris boyfriend and girlfriend?"

Why do people have a knack of asking me killer questions when I have a mouthful of food? I quickly chew my burger and swallow so I don't accidentally choke to death.

"How do you feel about that?" I reply, deciding to see how he feels before I answer. Chris already told me he was cool about it, but I need to hear it for myself.

"It's okay, I guess." He shrugs and takes a big slurp of his extra thick shake. "Uncle Chris is happier when he sees you. He smiles and looks off into space a lot. I like it when he smiles."

I swallow hard at his honesty and wonder how someone so young can say all the things we, as grown ups, find so hard to see.

"Well then, yes, we're boyfriend and girlfriend." I can't seem to stop smiling when I finally admit it out loud.

Danny smiles too and points his straw at me, dripping milkshake onto the table. "He smiles just like that." And we both laugh, finishing our meal before walking the short distance to the rink.

Now we're approaching the Will Call to collect our tickets. Chris made sure his Friends and Family seats were available for us. The line is short, and once our tickets are securely in my jeans pocket, we go to the concession to get soda and popcorn before going down to our seats.

As soon as we enter the rink, the cold air hits me, and the smell of the ice brings back all kinds of memories. I love the roar of the crowd and sound of sticks clattering against the ice as the teams have their pre-game warm up.

It's the first game of the pre-season, and the place is already packed, mostly with Whalers fans, but I can see a few blocks of seats with people in black and silver Saxons jerseys.

"C'mon, poppet. Keep a tight hold on my hand," I say as we head down the stairs toward the rink side, and I try not to hit people with the giant sign I'm holding in my other hand. It's so strange sitting with all the other friends and family of the players. I usually sit in my corporate seats on the other side behind the penalty box. But here I am, shuffling past wives and children of other players toward the seats that are occupied by my friends.

"Hey, Trixie! Over here!" Beth calls, standing up so she can be seen.

"Hi, everyone. Sorry we missed most of the warm up," I apologize when I'm in earshot. "It took us ages to get a seat at the diner." I look sadly at the ice as the players start making their way back to the locker rooms.

"No problem," Lana says, moving her purse so Danny can sit next to her. "The guys were looking strong. I still freak out whenever Alex makes a save and goes into a box split. It seems impossible for a man that big to be so flexible."

I laugh and place Danny's sign up against the seats in front of us. "He's definitely still one of the best goalies in NHL history."

"He holds the NHL record for most saves in the 2018-19 season," Danny states, and Lana nods, looking extremely impressed.

"Are Cam and Mila coming to sit with us or are they busy?" I ask.

"No, Cam has corporate guests in the box to entertain, and Mila needs to be rinkside with Coach Casey," Beth replies. "They said they'll try and duck out between periods if they can."

We continue to chat and catch up as the loud music plays while we wait for the teams to come back out. Danny continues to ask questions and reel off stats, and even a few of the people sitting around us start asking him questions about different players.

"So I guess you're ready to come out as Chris's girlfriend tonight?" Beth asks quietly, pointing to my jersey. Both she and Lana are wearing the jerseys of their guys, so I guess I have to admit it.

"Yes, we are now officially a couple. With Danny's blessing, of course." I look down at him and ruffle his hair.

He playfully knocks my hand away. "Don't mess with the hair, Auntie Trixie." He laughs, and I pull him against me, kissing his forehead and feeling so much love for this kid.

Before the game starts, we have a tactical bathroom break so he doesn't miss any of the game, and as we're making our way back to our seats, the lights dim and the music blares, the MC taking to mic to introduce the players.

Just as we get back to our seats, Chris is introduced, and I help Danny climb up onto his seat and hold up his sign, holding his legs because he's jumping around like a loon, and I don't want to be responsible when he falls and breaks something.

I keep my eyes on Chris as he does his lap, holding his stick up in the air, and I pray that he sees Danny and acknowledges him. As he comes to our side of the rink, he skids to a halt right in front of us and points his stick at Danny, causing the little boy to yell his head off and jump so hard I'm afraid he's going to break the folding seat.

And then Chris drops his stick to the ice, shakes off his gloves and makes a heart with his two hands, holding my gaze the whole time. I swear to god the whole world becomes silent, and everyone disappears so it's just the two of us. I can feel my heart beating hard against my chest, and I blow him a kiss like I used to when I watched him play in Memphis. He always told me he held that kiss for the whole game and that it was his good luck charm.

"That boy is head over heels in love with you," Lana yells in my ear as the MC introduces the next player, and Chris picks up his gear and skates to the bench, leaping over the boards to take his seat next to Matt.

I can't help smiling and hope that she's right. I know how I feel, and if I'm honest, I don't think I ever stopped loving him despite all the pain he caused me. But that seed of doubt is still there—the fear that all of this is just a reaction to suddenly becoming a father figure and that he just wants a ready-made family for Danny and I'm a convenient option.

As the game begins, I try to push those fears aside and enjoy it and Danny's reactions to the action. There's nothing like witnessing someone's first ever hockey game.

"Uncle Chris! Uncle Chris!" Danny yells, running down the corridor as Chris comes out of the locker room. I try to keep up, but he's bloody quick for such a little kid.

"Hey, buddy, how did you like the game?" he asks as Danny flings himself into his arms, forcing him to drop his duffle bag.

"You scored such a good goal, and when you had that fight, I just knew you'd win. You're the best," Danny enthuses, barely taking a breath.

Chris laughs and touches the developing bruise under his eye. "The goon got one good shot in, but I kicked his butt, didn't I?"

"Yeah, you did. It was so awesome!" They start having a little fake fight, and it's the cutest thing I've ever seen.

As I reach them, I notice Chris's expression changes from playful to predatory, and he pulls me into his arms, planting a deep, searching kiss on my lips. I struggle at first because the corridor is busy with players, coaches, and fans, not to mention Danny is right next to us. But I just can't help sinking into the kiss, wrapping my arms around his strong shoulders and tilting my head so the kiss can deepen.

"Are you guys gonna do that all the time? Because if you are, I'm not sure I want you to be boyfriend and girlfriend." Danny's voice breaks up our passionate embrace, and we both look down at his serious little face.

Shit, have we gone too far too soon in front of him?

But then he cracks up laughing at his own wit, and Chris roars with laughter, picking him up and turning him upside down.

"You think you're a comedian, huh?"

"Put me down! Put me down!" Danny squeals, but I can tell by the laughter in his voice that he loves it.

Chris tips Danny the right way up and grabs his duffle, flinging it over his shoulder so he can hold both our hands.

"Let's go home."

21

"**I**'m getting too old for this shit," I groan as I slump into the deep cushions of the couch and accept the glass of red wine from Trixie. I've just put Danny to bed, and thankfully, he was so tired from his busy day that he was almost asleep before he got undressed.

I stretch my long legs out and moan, feeling every muscle scream in protest. My face is throbbing where the black eye is developing, and my shoulders are burning with the exertion of the game.

But as soon as I take a sip of wine and feel Trixie's fingers gently stroking my hair away from my forehead, I feel at ease. I lean back and close my eyes, allowing her to softly kiss my face, my neck and finally my lips.

"You were amazing tonight," she growls in my ear, and despite how tired I am, one part of me is very much awake.

"Will you dance with me?" I ask softly, wanting to feel this gorgeous woman in my arms.

"I'd love to," she replies, taking my hand and standing up, slipping her arms around my neck, my

216

hands finding the curves of her hips and ass.

"Alexa, play Otis Redding," I say, and the soulful sounds of his voice fill the room, making us automatically begin to move to the slow rhythm of the song.

Trixie rests her head on my shoulder as we sway together, feeling so connected to each other, it's like we have one heartbeat. As the song progresses, I slide my arms around her back and look down into her beautiful blue eyes, hypnotized by the gold flecks.

I slip my hands down her back, pulling her close, so her lips finally connect with mine, and I sigh with relief. I want her so much it hurts and it terrifies me all at once. I know how much it hurt last time things didn't work out, and I can safely say I didn't feel as strongly then as I do at this moment—slow dancing with her in my dark living room, feeling her heart beating against mine as we kiss tenderly.

When the song comes to an end and the next one begins to play, I break our contact and scoop her up into my arms, making her squeak in surprise.

"The couch or the bed?" I growl, carrying her easily.

"I need you so badly, but we can't risk Danny waking up, so take me to bed, you sexy bastard."

I laugh. "You got it, Sugar." I walk down the corridor to my bedroom, still carrying Trixie bridal style and push my bedroom door open with my foot, trying to be quiet so we don't wake Danny up.

I drop her onto the bed and quickly cover her with my body, desperate to be joined with her. Our lips find each other, and our kisses are deep and frantic, tongues stroking, teeth biting gently.

Trixie pulls my shirt out of my pants and starts

unbuttoning it from the top, but her fumbling frustrates me so I grab the back and pull it over my head while she wiggles out of her tight jeans and kicks off her sneakers.

I stand up at the base of the bed and grab her foot, ignoring her giggling protests because I know she's ticklish there. But despite this, I raise her foot and kiss her insole, her ankle and run my tongue up her calf, kissing behind her knee.

"Chris…" she gasps as I run my hands up the soft skin of her thighs, sliding them inward so I can open them up for me. I bite my lip when I see the sheer white fabric of her panties covering her mound, and the memory of her tangy taste fills my mouth, making it water.

"First, I'm gonna eat your pussy until you're right on the edge," I growl, looking her right in the eye. "And then I'm gonna fuck you, hard and slow just how you like it."

"Oh bloody hell," Trixie moans, trying to squeeze her thighs together, but I continue to hold them open, denying her the friction she's craving.

"Will you be a good girl and come for me?"

She bites her lip hard and nods quickly, her eyelids hooded with excitement at the prospect of our game.

Trixie reaches for the bottom of her Whalers jersey, but I cover her hands with mine. "No. Leave it on. I'm gonna fuck you while you wear my number. Then I know you're mine."

Again, she nods and lets her arms flop out to the side, surrendering herself to me.

Now the game has begun, I hook my fingers

into the edge of her panties and slowly draw them down her thighs. The smell of her desire makes me desperate to get my mouth on her, her pussy looks so pink and tempting.

But as desperate as I am, I want to prolong the anticipation, slowly kissing and nibbling her inner thighs, her hip bone, her stomach. I feel her tense up slightly because I know she's sensitive about that part of her body, but as I continue to trace around her belly button with my tongue, I gently begin to stroke her pussy.

Her sighs and moans start to become more frantic when I move down and shoulder her legs wider, parting her pretty pink lips so I can get to the juicy interior. I can't hold out any longer. I have to taste her. I have to cover my tongue in her sweet nectar.

When I bend my head and kiss her mound, Trixie threads her fingers through my hair and spreads her legs wider so I can lick the entire length of her, feeling her swollen little bud when I reach the top, circling it with my tongue, eliciting a deep growl from her when I know I've found the correct pressure.

Fuck me, I love eating her pussy. She's so wet and hot, I just get lost in the movement of my tongue and the rhythm of her hips, the grip she has on my hair as her arousal climbs and builds.

It's only when she's getting close, I realize how loud her moans and cries have become, and I suddenly worry that we'll wake Danny up.

"Sugar, let's not wake the kid up, huh?" I growl, lifting my head.

"Fucking hell, Chris," she cries. "Don't stop! I'm

almost there."

I chuckle and reach up, covering her mouth with my hand, getting back to work with my tongue. Her breath is hot as she pants against my palm, her moans making the skin vibrate, her pleasure reaching its peak. Trixie squeezes her thighs around my head when she crashes over the edge, a fresh gush of her juices coating my lips, her pussy convulsing against my tongue.

As she comes down, I gently kiss her thighs and mound, knowing from experience that her clit will be throbbing and too sensitive to touch for a few minutes. Her fingers slowly release their death grip on my hair, and she strokes it, my hand slipping from her mouth, allowing her to sigh with deep satisfaction.

I, on the other hand, am hard and aching, desperate to slip my cock into that juicy pussy. While Trixie catches her breath, I get up and remove my pants and socks, leaving my boxer briefs in place despite the fact they're tented at the front, barely covering my solid erection.

Trixie rolls onto her side and props her head on her hand, looking greedily at me.

"You're so fucking beautiful," she whispers, licking her lips. "Take those undies off and get your sexy arse over here." She pats the bed and looks at me with those deep blue eyes, always challenging me, but she doesn't have to ask me twice. I push my boxers down my legs and kick them off, not caring where they land, falling down onto the bed next to Trixie.

She quickly pushes herself up so her hands are pressing into the bed on either side of me, straddling one of my thick thighs.

"You've worked very hard tonight," Trixie growls, gently kissing the side of my face and down my neck, causing my skin to break out in goosebumps. "You scored that amazing goal, so I think you deserve to relax and let me take control."

She licks up the side of my neck and sucks my ear lobe, making me moan deeply. The prospect of Trixie riding my dick makes it bounce against my abs, and I feel her mouth smile against my neck.

"Someone likes the thought of that," she giggles, reaching down to grip my cock at the base, squeezing it how she knows I like.

"Fuck me, you'd better get on top of me now before I bust a nut all over your hand."

"Patience, my love. Patience."

Before I can speak again, Trixie moves quickly down my body and takes the head of my dick into her mouth, flicking the glans with her tongue. It feels like my head's going to rocket right off my shoulders as she works more of it into her mouth, gagging slightly before drawing her lips back up to the head.

A few more repetitions of this, and I'm almost out of my mind. "Baby, please. I can't take it anymore. You have to stop."

Trixie looks up, her hair all messed up, and she's never looked more beautiful. I'm sure she can tell from the desperate, pained look on my face that she needs to move this thing along before I embarrass myself.

"Do you have a condom?" she asks and I indicate the nightstand where she retrieves a small foil packet, ripping it open with her teeth and rolling the latex down my length.

Then, to my immense relief, she finally climbs on top, straddling my thighs and gripping my cock at the right angle so she can rise up and notch it at her wet entrance. We both let out animalistic groans as she finally begins to work my length inside, sinking a little, then lifting up and sinking some more. I definitely don't have the kind of dick you can just slam down on, so it takes a few agonizing minutes until Trixie is fully seated, her eyes slightly glazed, her bottom lip clamped between her white teeth.

Slowly, cautiously, Trixie starts to move her hips back and forth, my hands holding her thighs, sliding up and down the satiny skin. I can tell that her confidence is increasing as she picks up the pace. Keeping her jersey on is not only sexy as fuck, but I know she's not distracted by worrying about her body. Trixie can let go and concentrate on making us both come, squeezing my cock tight, her hips taking on a frantic rhythm as we both climb toward our release.

"That's it, Sugar," I growl breathlessly. "Ride my cock. Make me fill you up with all my come."

"Oh god, that's so bloody hot," Trixie moans, closing her eyes tightly, not lessening up the pace of her thrusts, pressing her palms against my abs.

I can feel my balls drawing up tight, a sure sign I'm about to come, so I grab Trixie's plump ass and squeeze the globes before slipping a finger between them. I remember how much she liked me eating her ass so I press my digit against her tight little hole, and her eyes widen, her mouth hanging open.

"That's it! Let go," I command, and like a good girl, she surrenders and her orgasm washes over her, my cock in her pussy and my finger in her ass, both places contracting and squeezing. She stuffs the sleeve of her jersey in her mouth to stifle her cries and claps her other hand over my mouth as mine get louder and louder.

The tightness of her pussy sets off my own release, and I fill the condom in throbbing spurts that make stars explode behind my eyelids as I groan into the palm of her hand.

As Trixie's muscles turn to jelly, she flops down onto my chest and nuzzles my neck, both of us panting and sweaty. We lay there in a tranquil silence for a few minutes before I get up to take care of the condom, and Trixie pulls off her jersey and snuggles under the comforter.

"Why do you look so fucking sexy laying in my bed?" I ask when I return from the bathroom.

"I dunno," she mumbles sleepily, cuddling deeper under the covers.

I chuckle and shake my head. Out of the pair of us, I should be the one dead on my feet, but I'll let her sleep. I'm way too pumped now, so I kiss her forehead, her light snores already filling the air, pull on my sweatpants, and quietly close the door. Before I go to the kitchen, I poke my head into Danny's room and find him sleeping soundly—thank god for that.

As I wander around the kitchen, fixing myself and Trixie some glasses of water, I think about the game tonight. It was amazing, but I have to admit after the second period, I was hurting. In normal terms, I'm still young, but in the hockey world, I'm an old man, and tonight proved to me that I may not have much longer left at the top flight.

It's a fucking depressing thought. I mean, what the hell will I do if I don't have hockey? I suppose I could go into coaching. I've always enjoyed mentoring the younger players, but in my mind, I don't feel ready to retire. It's my body that's telling me time is almost up.

Perhaps I should talk to Coach Casey and see how he feels about my performance and longevity. He might even have some suggestions about what comes next. He made the successful transition from player to coach so it can certainly be done.

With these thoughts swimming in my head, I go back to the bedroom and put a glass of water on the nightstand next to Trixie. When I see her sleeping face, so peaceful and angelic, I have no other thought but her. So I quietly slip out of my sweatpants and climb into bed behind her, snuggling up to her warm, soft body and immediately falling into a deep, dreamless sleep.

22

Trixie

"I can't be late," I grumble to myself, applying mascara to my lashes in jerky swipes. "Oh bollocks!" I stab myself in the eye and end up having to clean the smudge of black off and start again.

It's the night of the Whalers Charity Gala, the one they have every year after the end of the exhibition games to raise money for the team's Foundation. Chris and I are attending as a couple, and apart from a few dates to O'Connell's with the rest of the team tagging along, this is our first official outing. We're ready to say to the world that we're together, and I'm so excited to not have to hide it anymore.

I know there will be plenty of my peers at the event who will be skeptical about our relationship, but I'm willing to take the heat. Chris is totally worth a few raised eyebrows and curious looks.

The one person I'm not looking forward to seeing is Blake. I overheard Chris on the phone to him the morning after the last exhibition game where Chris was sent to the penalty box twice for high sticking and slashing. From what I could ascertain from his side of the conversation, Blake was pissed off at him.

"Being with Trixie is not affecting my game," he growled into the phone as I hid behind the bedroom door, listening in. "No, you fucking listen to me. I don't care what your opinions are about me and Trixie. That has nothing to do with your position as my agent. You don't get to dictate who I sleep with. If you can't get onboard with that, perhaps it's time I find a new agent."

I must admit, I got a little zing of pleasure to hear Chris declare all of that to Blake, but I know if I see him tonight, he'll say his piece to me.

Oh well, a showdown with that misogynistic tosser is long overdue, so bring it on.

I finally get my eye makeup right, sweep some gloss over my lips, spray my perfume into the air, and step through it a few times.

The navy blue, strapless, fishtail gown I chose for tonight is extremely tight, but I know Chris will love the fact it accentuates my curves, so the lusty look on his face will all be worth it. Wisely, I dressed in the living room because there is no way I'm negotiating that ladder in this outfit, so I slip on my strappy navy blue heels and make sure all the essentials are in my clutch bag.

I have just enough time for one more look in the full-length mirror before the loud knock on my door announces the arrival of Chris and the car service.

Even though this is our second time around, my heart still flutters in my chest at the thought of seeing him tonight. The last few weeks have been a whirlwind of road trips and games so we haven't had much chance to go out on any proper dates—although that hot night in a hotel room in Tampa certainly made up for it.

When I open the door, Chris is standing in front of me, dressed in a tuxedo that fits him perfectly, holding an umbrella in one hand, because of course it's raining, and a single red rose in the other.

For a moment, we just stare at each other—I can't get over how handsome he looks all dressed up, just the faint yellow of a fading bruise on his cheek. I know it's crazy, but that just makes him more attractive to me.

"Goddamn it, Trixie. You look so beautiful." He sighs, holding the rose out for me to take, but as I reach for it, he grabs my wrist, pulling me against him under the umbrella. Our lips press together, and his tongue slips in, making all my special places tingle with desire.

When we part, I don't even care that he's messed up my lip gloss. I'm completely turned on. If it weren't mandatory for the Whalers to attend the gala, I'd be dragging him inside and fucking his brains out.

"I know that look, Sugar," he chuckles, pulling the door closed behind me. "There'll be plenty of time for that later." He holds the umbrella up so we can make a dash for the car without getting too wet in the Seattle drizzle.

We talk and flirt all the way to the fancy downtown hotel. Chris's hand never leaves my thigh, and I love how tactile he is, always wanting a connection between us. It makes me slightly dizzy.

"You ready?" he asks as we pull up to the red carpet. The rain hasn't deterred the photographers, and they crowd the door to the limo as the driver comes around to open it for us.

"I'm ready," I whisper, feeling a little unsure. Soon

our picture will be all over the fan blogs and Instagram, and then the comments will begin. I'm not sure how I feel about that.

"You look stunning." Chris leans over and kisses my cheek, squeezing my thigh, and that's all the reassurance I need. Fuck what other people think. I've always had that attitude. I don't know why being with Chris sometimes brings out my insecurities.

Before I can completely freak out, the door opens and Chris gets out, my hand firmly in his, flashes going off all around us. Thankfully, I don't fall on my face, and we walk up the red carpet, Chris's hand on the small of my back, keeping me close and protected as we pose for a few photos and then head into the safety of the hotel lobby.

"Fucking vultures," Knox slurs, standing in the marble lobby watching the action, a tumbler of brown liquor in his hand. "Don't they ever get tired of following us around?"

Chris laughs and slaps him on the back. "When you stop giving them a show, they'll stop following you around, kid."

Knox scoffs and wanders away, perhaps looking for his date for the night.

"That guy is gonna get another fine from Coach if he's not careful."

I squeeze Chris's hand. "It's so sweet that you worry about him, but he's a big boy and needs to make his own mistakes."

"Would you say that if you were his agent?" He laughs as we make our way into the function room.

"Fuck no!" I scoff. "If I was his agent, he'd be at

home tucked up in bed with a hot cocoa by 10."

"I bet he would, Sugar." He kisses my head then pushes open the door to the function room, which is decorated in Whalers team colors, a small band playing soft jazz music while people mingle with cocktails and canapes.

We walk through the room, stopping to talk to people—players, coaches, benefactors and a few celebrities who have attended. Chris seems perfectly at ease, but I'm on high alert, waiting for Blake to make an appearance. The word on the agent grapevine is he's gunning for me, and it would be just his style to make a scene tonight.

"You feeling okay?" Chris whispers as we take flutes of champagne from a passing waiter.

I don't want to worry him so I plaster a grin on my face and take a long drink. "I'm fine. This dress is just really tight, and I think it's cutting off the circulation to my legs."

He leans in so only I can hear what he says next. "Well I think you look fucking spectacular, and I'll happily rip that dress off you with my bare hands later."

Bloody hell, that's hot!

All I can do is release a breathy giggle as we arrive at our table where our friends are already seated.

"Hey, it's the happy couple!" Bugs gets up from his chair to shake Chris's hand and give me a hug. "You look really happy, Trixie," he whispers in my ear, and I can't help but smile broadly.

We go around the table and greet everyone, finally taking our seats just as the appetizers start to come out. This is such a great group of people to hang out with—all the guys bust each other's balls and the women just roll their eyes at how juvenile they can be when they're together.

By the time we're eating our entrees, my sides are literally hurting from laughing so hard, and as I haven't seen Blake yet, I begin to relax a little. Perhaps he won't show up.

"I'm just popping to the loo," I whisper to Chris before the desserts are served. He smirks and kisses my cheek.

"I love your cute little British words."

I laugh and shake my head. "I refuse to call it a bathroom," I tut. "I mean the word insinuates that there's a bath in there, and I doubt this hotel is that fancy. So I'll call it the loo if you don't mind."

"I don't mind at all, Sugar." Chris presses his lips to mine, and we smile as the table erupts into whoops and wolf whistles. "You guys suck!"

I quickly get up and leave the table before they can start with another round of "Take the piss out of the new couple."

I stop and say hi to a few agents who are sitting at other tables and finally make it to the double doors that lead into the corridor where the toilets are. I take my phone out of my clutch to check my messages, and I'm momentarily distracted until I feel a large hand grip the top of my arm, squeezing it tightly.

For a second, I think Chris has followed me for a little bit of naughty fun, but as I spin around ready to give him a sassy mouthful, I suddenly feel a cold chill spread over my skin.

Blake.

He's still gripping my bicep, but his eyes look unfocused, and he's swaying slightly, an ugly grimace on his face.

"Hello there, Beatrix," Blake slurs in a terrible English accent. "Having a good evening?"

"Yes, thank you," I reply in a controlled voice. I will not let this snake see how uncomfortable he makes me. "Obviously not as good as you, it would seem."

He barks out a laugh, but I can hear the venom in it and the cold glare in his eyes.

"Don't be such a stuck up bitch," he snarls, pulling me closer, but I manage to back away slightly.

"What do you want, Blake?" I ask, trying not to let my voice quiver. I glance over his shoulder, willing someone else to come into the corridor.

He doesn't answer me, but I feel his hand grip my upper arm tighter, holding me in place. Then suddenly he's right up in my face.

"Now you listen to me," he growls, a fleck of spit flying out of his mouth, landing on my cheek. "I've worked with Chris for many years. I've invested time and money into having a Stanley Cup winning hockey player on my resume. He's running out of time, and I won't have this little fuckfest derail that."

I shake my head. "That's not what this is," I protest, but my cheeks begin to burn.

"Don't treat me like a fucking idiot," Blake spits, his eyes blazing. "I have eyes everywhere, and I heard about the pair of you at the first exhibition game, dragging that orphan along like you're a real family."

At his poisonous mention of Danny, my hackles rise and I attempt to rip my arm out of his grip, but he's ridiculously strong. He just pulls me in closer, so close I can smell the whiskey on his breath, and it churns my stomach.

"Get the fuck off me," I hiss, desperately trying to maintain eye contact to show him he's not intimidating me

"I know all about your plans in L.A. I have a lot of influential friends down there who could seriously fuck things up for you if you fuck this up for me. So if you and your uptight British cunt or that little mongrel get in my way, I … will … destroy … you. Do I make myself clear?"

We stare each other down, and I don't answer him. I'm trying not to shake with the fury I feel burning inside me.

"Trixie? Is everything okay?"

I finally break eye contact with him and see Mila approaching down the corridor.

I rip my arm away from Blake's steel grip and square up my shoulders. "You have no right to interfere in my business or our relationship, and if I ever hear you talk about Danny like that again, you'll have every player on the team hunting you down. But not before I remove your scrotum with a very blunt knife. Do *I* make *myself* clear?"

Blake visibly blanches at the mention of his balls, and he looks like he might throw up. I don't wait around to see the show. I just stride away, grab Mila's arm, and hurry off down the corridor to another toilet.

Once inside, Mila looks at me with a quizzical expression, and I need to lean against the vanity to steady myself.

"What the hell was that all about?" she asks as I turn around and run my wrists under the cold faucet, trying to calm down.

"It was nothing," I lie, flicking my eyes at her in the mirror.

"It didn't look like nothing," Mila says. "Look at the mark he left on your arm."

I look down and she's right. There's an angry red mark around my bicep where he held me so tightly.

Shit, Chris will definitely notice that.

I spin around and hold Mila's shoulders. "I need you to keep this to yourself. If Chris knows Blake did this, he'll go nuts, and I don't want to cause a scene. If he asks about the mark, can you just say I tripped on my heels and you grabbed me to stop me falling?" I look at her with pleading eyes.

"I don't know, Trixie," she replies, looking unsure, biting her lower lip. "I have absolutely no poker face. I fear I'll crumble under questioning. Chris should know that Blake was bullying you like that."

I laugh, not very convincingly I fear. "It wasn't that. It was just agent banter. It was nothing to do with Chris. Please, Mila. Please don't ruin the evening over nothing."

She sighs and nods. "Okay. I'll try my best."

"Thank you." I pull her into an awkward hug, and we go back to the group where they've just served the dessert.

"You ladies have a good time in the bathroom?" Matt chuckles, greeting Mila with a kiss. "I don't understand what you have to talk about in there. Guys just go in, do our business, and get out."

"Truth!" Thor replies loudly, receiving a shove from his tiny girlfriend that barely moves him an inch.

"Is everything okay?" Chris asks, a crease forming between his eyebrows. "You were gone for a while."

"Everything's fine. This dress is a bugger to go to the loo in," I reply, smiling, thankful he's sitting on the opposite side to my injured arm.

He seems satisfied, but as we eat dessert, he keeps glancing over at me, and I have to work my ass off to keep upbeat, but every now and again, I scan the room to make sure Blake isn't staging his next attack.

However, as the evening progresses, it seems he's crawled back into his hole, and the red mark on my arm fades. So when Chris asks me to dance, I accept and allow him to hold me in his arms and spin me round until I'm dizzy and happily tipsy.

But Blake's vicious words stay in my head all night, only briefly quieting when we're home and Chris makes love to me. Afterward, as he sleeps peacefully beside me, I go back to obsessing about Blake's threats, and I don't get a wink of sleep.

23

Chris

Something isn't right, and I can't quite figure out what it is.

In the days since the gala, Trixie has been a little distant. We'd planned to go out for brunch the following morning with Danny and then to a little bookstore to buy him this new adventure series he wants to start. But when I woke up, Trixie was already pulling on a pair of my sweatpants and T-shirt, apologizing for having to run to an unexpected work emergency.

I offered to drive her home, but she said she had an Uber waiting downstairs, and then she ran out of my apartment like her ass was on fire.

She left my messages unread all day, and it made me so unsettled even Danny commented on it.

"Are you okay, Uncle Chris?" he asked when we were browsing in the bookstore.

I shook away the unsettling thoughts that had been plaguing me all day and looked down at him. His eyebrows were bunched together in concern, and I felt like a complete shit for ruining this for him.

"Everything's fine, buddy." I took one of the books

from him. "So tell me about this book then."

Trixie finally replied later that evening, apologizing for being busy, but she still seemed distant and not her normal warm self. I asked if she wanted me to call; however, she said she was tired and was going to bed.

Then she went offline, and I was left feeling even more unsettled.

Now it's three days later and we've had minimal contact—just good morning messages and a few checking in during the day. Tonight, she called to speak to Danny because he'd had a playdate with a friend from school, and she wanted to ask him how it went. We talked briefly, and she confirmed she'd bring Danny to the Vikings game tomorrow night; however, that uneasy feeling just won't shift.

"Is everything okay, Sugar?" I have to ask because it's driving me crazy. Have I done something? Did something happen at the gala? Is it work pressure?

"Yes, everything's fine," she replies in a tense voice. "I'm just so busy with work now the pre-season is over. And with L.A. picking up pace, I'm swamped."

"If you don't have time to bring Danny to the game, I'm sure Annie can…"

"No!" she cries. "Of course I'm bringing him to the game. I know how important the game against the Vikings is for the Whalers. It's like when Spurs play Arsenal."

I laugh. "I assume you're talking about soccer."

"It's called football," she says seriously, but I can hear the smile in her voice. "I miss you."

I'm surprised for a moment. She's been so distant, but now she's saying she misses me. I don't get what the fuck is going on.

"I miss you too, Sugar," I reply quietly. "Are you going to stay over after the game?"

There's a pause, and my heart stutters in my chest. "I should be able to, but I have to go to L.A. to look at some office space so I'll have to leave early."

"No problem. Just so long as I get you in my bed," I growl quietly so Danny doesn't overhear. "I've missed the smell of your skin and how wet your pussy gets when I kiss your neck."

I hear her suck in her breath, and I'm satisfied I've turned her on, but that little gasp also hits me straight in the dick which starts to swell at the thought of being inside her.

"I should go," she replies in a raspy voice. "Tell Danny I'll see him tomorrow."

"Good night," I say, but she's already hung up.

I throw my phone down onto the couch and run my fingers into my hair, gripping it tightly. I don't get what's going on with her—if she won't talk to me about it, how the fuck am I supposed to fix it?

All these questions are swirling around in my head all night and into the morning when I head into the gym for my pre-game workout.

"Ford! Wake up, man. I asked if you're finished on the rowing machine?" Knox kicks the machine impatiently, and I whip my head up to look at him.

"Hey!" I bark, glaring at him. "Don't be an asshole. You'll know when I'm done because I'll get up and walk the fuck away." I shout the last part and the usual noises of the gym quiet down as all the guys stop their workouts to look at our altercation.

"Ford, can I have a word?" Bugs calls from somewhere behind me. I rise up off the rowing machine, getting right up in Knox's face, a cocky grin spreading over it.

"Punk," I huff under my breath, shoving past him and stalking toward Bugs, who's climbing off the treadmill.

We walk to the water machine, and he hands me a cup of ice cold water which I down so quickly it gives me a headache.

"You wanna talk about it?" he asks. "It's not like you to lose your shit, especially with Knox."

I pour myself another water but sip it this time. "I'm sorry, man. I've got a lot on my mind."

"Is everything okay with Danny?" Bugs puts a reassuring hand on my shoulder.

"Yes, the kid's amazing." I chuckle. "He just rolls with the punches. Nothing seems to faze him. I wish I was half as together as he is."

"So what's up with you? Is it Trixie?"

I look over at him quickly. "Has she said something to you?"

Bugs shakes his head. "No, I haven't spoken to her since the gala. You guys seemed solid that night. Did something happen?"

I scoff and shake my head. "I wish I fucking knew. She ran out the morning after the gala, and she's been distant ever since. Do you think she's having second thoughts about being with me?"

"Did you ask her?" Bugs asks.

"I mean, not outright," I admit. "I asked if she was okay, and she just blamed work stress."

"Then maybe that's it, man. You could be freaking

out about nothing. Did you tell her you're worried?"

I shake my head.

"Maybe you should." Bugs slaps my bicep. "It's obviously on your mind, and you don't need the distraction, especially tonight. The Vikings'll be out for blood so we all have to be completely focused."

"I know. I'll bench this until after the game and talk to Trixie tonight."

"Good. Now finish up your workout because Coach has an extra long briefing today before drills." Bugs gets back on the treadmill, and I wander over to the mats to stretch out next to Thor, trying to push my worries about Trixie to the back of my mind so I can stay focused on the game ahead.

The smell of sweat and determination fill the locker room as Coach Casey gives us his pre-game pep talk. He has a special kind of hatred for the Vikings, but he's never explained why. There is a rumor that their coach, who came up through the NHL at the same time as him, had tried to interfere in his relationship with the now Mrs. Casey. But no one can seem to uncover the truth.

"This is the most important game of the season," Coach barks, pacing back and forth across the rubber flooring. "You know all eyes in the league will be on us. The critics love to analyze every mistake and penalty, so play hard, play fast, but keep it clean."

"Yes, Coach," we all yell in unison, banging our sticks against the benches.

"They will play dirty. They will try to get into your head and make you retaliate, but you are a better team and better men, so keep your shit together and win this game. Start the season with a victory, and I know we can go all the way."

By the time Coach finishes his speech, we're on our feet, and the loud shouts and whoops echo around the locker room. I grab Nate, who sits next to me, and we pummel our fists against each other's chests and knock our helmets together.

"Let's go! Second line, make the first shift count." Coach Casey claps his hands together as we file out of the locker room, Bugs and Matt at the mouth of the tunnel, slapping us all on the back as we pass them, leaping onto the ice as the MC introduces us.

My heartbeat soars when it's my turn, and the adrenaline fills my muscles with rocket fuel as I speed skate around the rink, flicking my eyes to the family section where I see Danny up on his seat, holding the latest sign he made with Annie today. I chuckle when I read what it says: "Kick the Vikings back to the Middle Ages." I know he's been studying the actual Vikings at school so I'm glad he's learning something. I also catch sight of Trixie, and I breathe a sigh of relief when I notice she's wearing my jersey, and she gives me a little wave and smile.

I leap over the boards and take my seat, squirting water into my mouth from my bottle and feel more settled than I have for the last seventy-two hours. I guess it was all in my head—she really was just busy with work. Perhaps my own insecurities let my imagination run away with me. But it's definitely something we need to talk about. I can't keep freaking out every time she goes quiet or has to work late, especially when she has to spend more time in L.A. setting up her new office.

"Let's go!" Bugs yells next to me, and I notice the second line are on the ice, and the puck has dropped. Shit, I need to stop zoning the fuck out and pay attention.

I watch as we win the puck and battle begins.

And what a battle it is. As Coach predicted, the Vikings play dirty from the get go, incurring a two minute penalty for tripping in the first few seconds of the period, allowing the first line to come on for the Power Play. This is my specialty, and all the guys know to get the puck to me so I can try for a goal.

We sprint down the rink, Matt with the puck at his stick, outskating the Viking who's trying to pick his pocket. When he sees the tiniest of gaps, he flicks his wrist and shoots the puck across the ice to me just as I cruise behind the goal, hoping to sneak the puck into the edge of the net.

But I'm so busy concentrating on the minute gap between the post and the goalie's pads that I don't see two hundred pounds of Viking hurtling toward me.

I feel the impact, like I've been hit by a truck. I feel my body flying through the air, then the crunch as I hit the boards.

Then nothing.

24

Trixie

I want to cry, throw up, and faint all at once.

In my line of work I've seen my fair share of horrible sports injuries, but when someone you care about is involved, it's like the world has stopped turning, and everything comes to a screeching halt.

When the Viking defenseman hits Chris low and hard, he actually takes flight, turning a complete somersault before smashing headfirst into the boards. His helmet flies off and skids across the ice, and he lies motionless in a heap. The crowd erupts into a wave of anger and fury. I see fights breaking out between Viking and Whalers players. Bugs has skated over to protect Chris, and it's then I notice he's not getting up to throw his own punches. His limp lifeless body lies still as players and referees scrap around him.

Suddenly the crowd seems to notice how serious this is, and the rink becomes eerily quiet, just the grunts and shouts of the few players still working out their frustration and Bugs yelling for the medical team.

It's then I also remember that Danny is sitting next to me. I drag my eyes away from the carnage on the ice and look down at him. Beth has already pulled him onto her lap. I notice he's got big fat tears rolling down his face, and he looks utterly terrified.

"It's okay, poppet," I say, trying really hard not to show him how petrified I am. I pull a tissue out of my purse, wipe his tears, and let him blow his nose. "Let's go and see how Uncle Chris is. I'm sure he'll need a hug once they look at the bump on his head."

I stand up and sling my purse across my body, grabbing Danny from Beth's lap.

"He'll be okay," Beth says, but I can see her eyes flicking toward the ice where Chris is being loaded onto a stretcher, still completely out cold.

"I'm going to find Cam and Mila, see if I can get some news." I don't wait for a reply, carrying Danny through the stand and up the steps to the exit. The concourse is empty so we rush toward the locker rooms. I flash my Whalers ID badge at all the security guards to get past.

"Auntie Trixie, is he going to be okay?" Danny asks me quietly, his big green eyes shiny with tears.

I put him back on his feet, realizing I've run all the way to the corridor outside the locker room carrying him. I squat down and cup his face in my hands.

"Accidents like this happen all the time in hockey," I explain. "You've seen Uncle Chris come home with bruises before."

"Uh huh," he hiccups, trying to keep his tears in check.

"Well, this time he got hit a little harder, and the doctors need to check him out to make sure he's okay." I wipe more tears from his face and pull him into a hug. "He'll be fine. He has to be fine."

"Trixie!" I pull away from Danny at the sound of my name and see Cam and Mila running up the corridor.

I stand and hold Danny's hand as he shies behind my legs, reminding me of how he was when he first came to live with Chris.

"Oh honey, I'm so sorry." Cam hugs me, followed by Mila.

"What's happening?" I ask quietly, flicking my eyes to Danny so they know to watch how much they say in front of him.

"Hey Danny, shall we go and get a soda while Auntie Trixie checks on your uncle?" Cam says, stretching out her hand toward him. He hesitates for a moment, but he likes Cam, so he takes her hand.

"We'll be in box four," she says, squeezing my arm. "It's empty tonight, so we'll hang out there and watch some more of the game until you find out how things are. If you need me to take Danny home with us, that's fine. Just let me know."

"Thank you," I squeak, trying not to bawl my eyes out in front of Danny. "I'll see you soon, poppet. Go with Auntie Cam, okay?"

He just nods and disappears down the corridor.

As soon as he's out of earshot, I turn to Mila. "Tell me everything."

Mila smiles kindly but I can see fear in her eyes. "The medical team have looked at him. They've put him in a neck brace, and he's on his way to the hospital because he isn't regaining consciousness."

"Oh my god," I cry, finally allowing the emotion and fear to wash over me. I fall into Mila's arms, and she hugs me tight while I sob hopelessly against her shoulder.

I've been in such a weird place these last few days—freaking out about Blake's threats, wondering if what Chris and I have is real and can go the distance this time. I know he's sensed my mood, and he's asked me several times if things are okay, but I've been a coward and not told him what's playing on my mind.

What if he never wakes up and his last thoughts of us are negative ones? What if I never get a chance to tell him that I'm falling in love with him all over again? Despite my concerns, I know this to be true. I am falling for him, more deeply and fully than I ever did ten years ago. This kind of love is exciting, honest, and forever, and I'll never forgive myself if I don't get to tell him that.

"He'll be okay," Mila whispers, stroking my back. "Our guys are made of tough stuff."

I pull away and nod, swiping the sleeve of my jersey under my nose because I gave Danny my last tissue.

Mila starts ushering me along the corridor. "C'mon, I'm going to drive you to the hospital, okay? I'll message Cam and ask her to keep Danny until we have news." Mila grabs my hand, and we rush off toward the parking lot.

Hospitals suck.

The coffee sucks, the hard plastic chairs in the emergency room suck, and the smell of disinfectant and other less pleasant things suck as well.

I feel like I've been sitting here for hours, but when

I look at my watch, it's only been forty minutes. Mila's never left my side, keeping me topped up with shitty coffee and asking questions whenever a doctor or nurse passes by.

At the moment, they aren't telling us anything. All I've managed to find out is that he's having CT scans and other kinds of tests. The assistant coach is pacing around making phone calls and just when I think things can't get any worse, Blake appears to make this day a complete shit show.

He strides past me and Mila, just giving me a distasteful look before tapping the coach on the shoulder. They talk animatedly for several minutes, Blake's eyes constantly flicking over to me and then they shake hands and he heads over.

"Are you happy?" he sneers, standing in front of me with his hands on his hips.

"Excuse me?" I reply, also standing, despite Mila's attempt to keep me seated.

"You heard me. Are you happy now? Chris has probably suffered a career-ending concussion, all thanks to his mind being occupied with other things."

I look over at the coach, and he lowers his eyes, obviously feeling a little ashamed that he didn't share this information with me even though he's seen how worried I am.

"It was a bad hit and completely the fault of the other player," I reply. "Chris was focused and playing well. He wasn't distracted."

Blake barks out a laugh. "If that's what you have to tell yourself, darling. I know my players, and I've seen a change in him this season. And the only things to change in his life are you and the orphan. You do the math."

Before I can respond, Mila steps between us. "I suggest you go and find somewhere else to sit. This waiting room is for friends and family, and I'm pretty sure Chris doesn't see you as either of those things."

"Whatever," Blake mutters, taking out his phone and tapping away at the screen, finding a seat around the corner so he's out of sight.

"Thank you." I hug Mila close, and we go back to sitting on the sucky plastic chairs, waiting for news.

It's another hour before a doctor in blue scrubs comes out and speaks to the coach, who listens to her for several minutes and then points toward me.

"Ms. Cavendish?" the doctor says as she approaches. "I understand you're Mr. Ford's girlfriend."

I quickly stand and begin wringing my hands nervously. "Yes, I am. How is he? I heard he has a really bad concussion…"

The doctor holds her hand up to halt my verbal diarrhea. "Firstly, my name is Dr. Andrews, and I've been treating Mr. Ford. Shall we sit?"

Shit, that can't be good. But at least she hasn't taken me into a private room, so it can't be that bad, right?

We sit and she continues, "Mr. Ford was still slipping in and out of consciousness when he arrived, so first we did a CT scan and found a small bleed on his brain."

I make a weird noise. It sounds a bit like an animal in distress, and I feel Mila grab my hand and squeeze it tightly.

"The good news is, it's small and doesn't seem to

be worsening," the doctor continues. "We've checked for spinal injuries, and so far all those tests have come back clear."

"Thank god," I sigh. "Is he awake now?"

"We've put him into an induced coma because there was significant swelling of the brain, so the safest thing to do is to give it a chance to decrease before we wake him up," Dr. Andrews explains quietly.

I can't help the tears falling down my cheeks, and I put my hands over my face, feeling completely terrified. "Will he wake up?" I ask, my voice muffled.

"We're going to keep him under for twelve hours and then reduce the sedation and see if he wakes up on his own. I can take you to see him if you'd like, but I must warn you that we had to intubate him. It will look scary, but it's just to help him breathe."

I suck in my breath. I love medical dramas, and I know that intubation is not a good sign. But Dr. Andrews seems to know what she's doing, so after giving Mila a long hug goodbye, I allow her to lead me through a maze of cubicles and nurses stations until we reach a private room in the ICU. I can already see Chris laying in a bed through the window, all hooked up to machines, a white bandage on his head that has a bloom of red over his left eye.

"Let him know you're here, hold his hand, and speak to him."

"But he's unconscious," I reply.

"He still might be able to hear you," Dr. Andrews says kindly. "And it might comfort you too. Please stay as long as you want. I can have a cot brought in if you'd like to lay down."

"Thank you," I sniffle, moving carefully around the bed and pulling up a slightly more comfortable chair. I'm scared to touch him in case I pull out an important wire, but slowly I reach out and stroke the back of his hand. His skin there is warm and soft, a smattering of light hair on his knuckles.

Suddenly, I'm overcome with emotion. I grab his hand and bend down so I can feel it against my wet cheek, kissing each of his knuckles, turning it over so I can kiss his rough palm. My quiet sobs fill the room, and I allow it all to come out, all my fear of losing him before we really get a chance to start over.

I must cry myself to sleep because the next thing I know, a big comforting hand is on my back, and I whip my head up, blinking at all the people standing in the room.

"What?" I ask, confused for a second, seeing familiar faces, but not being able to process what's going on.

"We came down here as soon as we finished kicking the Vikings' ass," Bugs says. It's his hand on my back. "That fucker who took Ford down has a two game suspension and a price on his head the next time we play them."

"Fuck yeah," Nate growls. Judging by the state of his face, he got into it with Vikings. I know that he will have made it his mission to cause this guy as much pain as is legally possible.

"We spoke to the doc, and she seems to think once the swelling goes down, he'll come out of this with a hell of a headache but no lasting damage," Thor says, a pained smile on his face.

"He'll be fine."

"Ford is the toughest of all of us."

"He's a fighter. This won't stop him for long."

The guys all say their encouraging statements, but to me it just sounds like the lies you tell a terrified child to soften the blow of bad news.

Suddenly, I think about Danny and I jump up. "Where's Danny? Who has him? Is he okay?"

Bugs puts his hands on my shoulders. "He's fine. Cam took him back to Ford's place so he has his own stuff around him. Beth and Mila are going to take over so Cam can get home for SJ. We've got him covered. The girls have told him Ford is having a long sleep to make his head feel better, and that's all he knows for now. We won't tell him more until there is more to say, okay?"

All I can do is nod, and I sink back into the chair.

"How are you?" Matt asks. "Can we get you anything? I'm happy to go to your place and pack you a bag."

I look over at him and all the guys, touched by how kind and thoughtful these big tough men are.

"No, that's alright. You don't have to do that." I hang my head so they can't see that more tears are leaking out of my eyes, dripping onto my jersey.

"Well if you change your mind, you have all our numbers. Call anyone one of us, and we'll get what you need," Knox says, and when I finally look up, I notice he seems the most shaken of all the guys. I know he and Chris have a strong bond.

"Thank you."

The door opens, and Dr. Andrews squeezes herself into the crowded room. "Okay everyone, I let you in here as a favor, but it's time for everyone except Trixie to clear out. Chris needs quiet and rest."

"Sure thing, doc," Bugs replies. "You have my number. Please call me any hour if you need to." He starts to usher the guys out, but none of them leave without patting Chris on the arm and hugging me.

When they've all left, the room feels bigger than before, and I leave to find a vending machine while Dr. Andrews checks Chris's status.

I return loaded with chips and soda but just leave them on the table because the thought of eating them makes me want to puke. While I was gone, someone brought in a cot, so I drag it up next to Chris's bed and lay down, still holding his hand as exhaustion finally washes over me, and I drift off into a fitful sleep.

I wake up some time later to the sound of Dr. Andrews talking to a nurse. I sit up and quickly try to tame my crazy bed hair and wipe the drool from my chin.

"Is everything okay?" I ask sleepily.

"His vitals are looking really strong. We've slowly started decreasing the sedation, and we're going to see how he does and then try to extubate him. Perhaps you'd like to take a walk and freshen up while we do that."

I get the sense this is a command not a request, so I struggle off the cot, grab my purse, and head off to find a bathroom so I can at least wash my face and assess the damage of sleeping in my clothes all night.

When I return from the bathroom, I see Coach Casey standing outside Chris's room, looking at him through the window.

"It's always hard to see one of my guys get injured," he says in a quiet voice when I stand next to him.

"These men are like family to me." He turns to look at me, and I can see his eyes are rimmed with red. "How are you, Trixie?"

I'm a bit lost for words at his candid confession so I just shake my head and lower my eyes. I feel his hand rest gently on my shoulder, and I look up at him.

"Can I tell you something?" he asks.

I nod and suddenly think he's going to tell me the same thing Blake did—that this accident is somehow my fault.

"I've known Chris a long time, and since you and Danny came into his life, I've seen a real change in him." Coach fixes me with a steely look. "He's been the happiest I've ever known him, and I think that's all down to you and the kid."

Oh god, now I'm crying again—big heaving sobs that become muffled when Coach pulls me into a comforting hug which seems to last for hours.

Once I'm done crying, he hands me a tissue and a card with his cell phone number on it with strict instructions to call him if I need anything.

I know he's one of the most respected coaches in the NHL, and now I can see why.

When he leaves, I go back into Chris's room and take up my seat next to him, holding his hand and talking about all sorts of crap that I hope he doesn't hear.

Dr. Andrews enters the room quietly and explains that they are keeping the sedation light, but they aren't ready to extubate him yet

"But he'll be okay?" I ask.

"All the signs are looking positive, but he still needs rest so don't expect him to fully wake up right away," she explains.

I thank her again, return to my seat, and continue to wait for him to return to me.

During the next few hours, most of the team make an appearance to check on us. It's overwhelming how well loved Chris is, and by the time it gets dark again, I'm dizzy with the amount of people I've spoken to and the number of hugs I've received.

In between the visits, I manage to speak to Danny on the phone, and I can tell by the quiver in his voice that he's trying to be brave. But just like me, he isn't doing a convincing job of it. I do my best to reassure him, but I can tell he is terrified.

I know the feeling.

Finally, when visiting hours end, Dr. Andrews comes in to carry out some checks and announces that she's happy to extubate him. Like before, I leave the room to give them space to work and head to the hospital restaurant. I get a plate of fries that I just push around until they're cold, and then I head back to the ICU. I settle down and study Chris's face now that the scary tubing is gone—the laughter lines around his eyes that don't fade even when he's at rest, the dent in his nose from when it was broken during his last season in college, the horrible bruise on his cheekbone.

"I've loved this face for so many years," I whisper, gently stroking his cheek. "But it's so much more than that. I love your soul and your heart, how open you've been letting Danny into your life. You didn't hesitate no matter how scared you were. As heartbroken as I was ten years ago, I now know it wasn't the right time for us. We had to go away and find out who we are so we can be better together."

I hang my head and kiss Chris's hand, smoothing my cheek against it.

"I had no idea you were so sentimental, Sugar."

I jerk my head up, convinced I'm hallucinating from exhaustion. But when I see Chris peering down at me through half-closed eyes, I know I'm not imagining it.

"You're awake?" I cry, standing up and slapping the on-call button to summon the nurse.

"You keep yelling like that, and I might have to go to sleep again," he rasps, his voice croaky. "I've got a hell of a headache."

"Oh baby, I'm so happy you're awake," I sob, leaning down to kiss him all over his face.

"Easy, easy," he chuckles, just as Dr. Andrews walks in.

"Well, it's nice to see you awake, Mr. Ford," she says, looking at the monitors still attached to him. "How do you feel?"

"Chris. Call me Chris," he replies weakly. "My head hurts like a bitch, and I could do with some water."

"That's to be expected. We're going to do a few tests while you're awake, and then we'll get you some ice chips and let you rest," Dr. Andrews says.

"I'll go and make some calls." I excuse myself, and once I'm out in the corridor, I slide down the wall and hug my knees, softly sobbing with relief. We're not out of the woods yet, but he's awake and seems to be his old cocky self. I can't put into words how happy I am.

I wipe my eyes and take a deep breath. I need to pull my shit together and let everyone know he's awake, especially Danny. I can't even imagine how worried he is—the fear on his face when Chris was lying unconscious on the ice was heartbreaking.

So I get up off the floor and move to the waiting area so I can make my calls, trying Bugs first so I can double check who's looking after Danny. I'm in full lady boss mode now, making calls and organizing people, setting up a phone tree to spread the news that Chris is awake.

It helps me to push aside the fear that he could deteriorate at any minute, and I could still lose him. I need to close my feelings down for now and take care of Danny and take care of business. This is not the time to become a tearful train wreck—my boys need me.

25

Chris

"**I**s there anything else we can get you?" Thor asks, putting two enormous grocery bags on the counter. Lana immediately starts unpacking Tupperware containers full of home-cooked goodies, loading my embarrassingly empty fridge.

"No, man. Thank you both though," I croak, shifting slightly on the couch, my head throbbing with the movement. "At least we won't starve while I'm recovering."

"If you ever need me to come over and cook for you guys, just let me know," Lana offers, snuggling up to her boyfriend, his thick arm draped over her shoulder.

"Thank you," Trixie says, returning from the bedroom with a comforter which she places over my legs. She's being so sweet and caring, but I'm getting a bit tired of being treated like a fucking invalid.

I was released from the hospital yesterday after a few days of observations and tests, and the doctor finally gave me the all clear to go home. But I was told that I'd need more recovery time and more tests before I'm cleared to work out, let alone get back on the ice.

It's frustrating, but I know I need to let myself heal. I still feel dizzy and unsteady when I get up, and the throbbing in my temple is still painful.

As Trixie fusses around, plumping the pillow behind me and getting me some water to take my painkillers, I think back to what I heard her say as I was waking up. At first I was confused about what the fuck was going on—last thing I remember was starting the Power Play and then everything is blank. But to hear Trixie talk about her love for me drew me out of the depths. I was determined to make my way back to her, and the look of relief on her face was priceless. In that moment, I knew what I needed to do. It was time to stop fucking about and tell this incredible woman how I feel about her.

But before that, I need to tell her the truth about what Dr. Andrews revealed to me at the hospital.

"I love that everyone is so worried about you, but it's nice to just have the place to ourselves for a moment." Trixie sighs after saying goodbye to Matt, Mila, Beth, and Nate who came over to visit. The guys have been amazing, dropping by with care packages and food to make sure we have everything we need while I recover.

Annie has also been a dream. She moved in while I was still in the hospital so Danny could have some consistency, and she's taken such good care of him. She's still sleeping in my office because she insists that Trixie needs to spend her time looking after me and not running Danny to and from school and his clubs and activities. I'm so thankful for all the amazing people I have in my life.

"Come and sit with me, baby," I say, patting the space on the couch next to me. We've got an hour before Danny and Annie come home, and I need to talk to her about something really important while we have a minute to ourselves.

"But I need to…" she begins, but I hold my hand up.

"Sugar, I need to talk to you. Come and sit down."

I can tell from the look on her face that she's knows I'm not fucking around, so she puts down the laundry she's started folding and comes to sit next to me, tucking her legs up under her. I sigh when she starts to stroke my hair. My eyes close, and I let my shoulders relax—she has a magic touch when it comes to putting me at ease.

But now isn't the time—we have a serious conversation to have.

"How are you feeling, love?" she asks, feeling my forehead with the back of her fingers to see if I'm feverish.

"I feel okay." I take her hand away from my head and press her palm against my chest so she can feel my heartbeat. "I need to talk to you about something."

Trixie's cheeks pink up, and she drops her gaze from mine. "I know what you're going to say," she whispers. "It's about what I said to you in the hospital, isn't it? All that lovey-dovey bollocks I was saying because I was terrified you weren't going to wake up."

"God, I love it when you ramble because you're nervous. It's completely adorable." I lean forward and kiss her lips. "Even though we do need to talk about that, that's not the topic I had in mind."

"Oh." Trixie visibly swallows hard, and I can tell she's desperately trying not to freak out.

"So when Dr. Andrews was giving me a final work up, she said that the injury I suffered could take many months to fully heal," I explain quietly, feeling the same stab of frustration and disappointment I had back in the hospital.

"Well, we knew that. There's no way the Whalers medical team will clear you to even work out for at least a few weeks."

"But there's more." I lower my eyes and pick at some invisible lint on the comforter. "She said this could be a career ending concussion, and that even if I recover and play again, one more serious head injury could be catastrophic."

Fuck me. I still can't believe the words coming out of my mouth. I've been so lucky and had a blessed career with very few serious injuries. Unlike lots of players, I still have all my teeth, and I only had one concussion back in college when I broke my nose. Other than the wear and tear of being a hockey player in my thirties, I'm in good shape. So this diagnosis has come at me like a puck to the heart.

I look up at Trixie, and tears are rolling down her beautiful face. She knows how much hockey means to me, and the prospect of never playing professionally again is earth-shattering.

"Oh love," she whispers, leaning in to wrap her arms carefully around my neck, burying her face there, the feeling of her tears slick on my skin. "I can't believe it. What are you going to do?"

I sigh, deep and heavy. "I wish I knew how to answer that question. If this had happened last season, I would have worked my ass off to recover and get back on the ice, despite the risks. But now…"

Trixie lifts her head and looks at me. "Danny."

I nod and press my lips to hers, taking comfort in her before I say the next part.

"I can't risk making him an orphan for the second time in his life." The mere thought of leaving that little guy alone in the world makes my nose sting with emotion, and tears fill my eyes. "He needs me here, and he needs me fit and healthy. If I take one more serious hit, I could end up a fucking vegetable."

"Is that what Dr. Andrews said?"

I chuckle. "She said it in fancier, medical terms than that, but that's what she was getting at."

"I'm so sorry. I can't imagine how you're feeling." She leans in and kisses my face all over. "What are you going to do?"

"I think I need to get my head around it first, no pun intended." I smile because what the fuck else am I going to do? "Then I guess I need to talk to Blake."

I notice the change in Trixie's body language at the mention of his name, and I know it's more than her usual dislike of my agent.

"Okay, I know you don't like Blake, but he's my agent. I have to run this by him."

She sighs. "I don't trust him to do what's right for you. He seems so focused on you being part of a Stanley Cup winning team, he might not advise you for the best."

"I know he's an asshole, but I don't think he's so

focused he'd put my life at risk."

"He'd better not," Trixie growls under her breath, and I'm now convinced something else has gone down between them, but now isn't the time to unpack that.

I take her face in my hands and look deeply into her navy blue eyes. "I'm not an idiot. I know what's best for my health and my family. So if Blake does advise me badly, I don't have to take it. I'm my own man, and I make my own decisions."

I see the look of relief on her face, and she nods to show me she agrees with what I've said.

Before we can talk anymore, the front door opens and Danny comes charging in, throwing his school bag down and kicking off his sneakers before diving onto the couch between me and Trixie.

"Hey buddy, I said be careful," Annie calls while she closes the front door and hangs up her coat. "Uncle Chris has hurt his head. You need to be gentle."

"Sorry." Danny reaches up to stroke the side of my head. "Are you feeling better?"

"I am now you're home." I kiss the top of Danny's head. "How come you're back so early? Don't you have soccer today?"

"The coach is ill, so they canceled," Annie explains, busying herself in the kitchen, making Danny a snack. "We went to the park, but he was getting hungry so we came home."

"Well I'm glad you're home. I missed you," I say, tickling Danny under the arms so he squirms and squeals between us.

"Help me, Auntie Trixie," he cries, but she just joins in, and together we tickle him until he wriggles free and runs off toward his room.

"You made me have to pee," he shouts, and the three of us crack up laughing.

But suddenly the exertion of the tickling and laughing have made my head pound like a bitch so I close my eyes and drift off to sleep, the comforting noises of my family around me.

I wake up sometime later to the smell of Lana's lasagna being heated up, and my stomach rumbles and my head throbs. Trixie is busy in the kitchen, but she's put my next dose of painkillers by my glass of water, so I gulp them down and throw the comforter off. I've been sitting on my ass all day, and it's completely alien to me. So I carefully rise up off the couch, check that I'm not overcome by a dizzy spell, and then make my way to the kitchen, propping myself up against the counter.

Trixie notices me and looks concerned. "Are you okay?"

"I'm good, Sugar," I reply, smiling. "I just needed to get up for a while. All this sitting down is making me a little crazy."

"If you're sure." She smiles back and doesn't press me. "Are you hungry? I'm heating up lasagna for us."

"I am, actually." I look around. "Where's the kid?"

"Annie's putting him to bed. You slept for a long time." Trixie opens the oven to check the pasta and then gets back to cutting up tomatoes and cucumber for the salad.

"Yeah, I must've needed it. I'm just gonna go and say goodnight to him." I push away from the counter and walk carefully down to Danny's room where the door is slightly ajar.

"I know you're scared, buddy," I hear Annie say softly. "But he's okay. He just needs some time to get better."

I hear a wet sniffle, and I know that Danny is crying, so I push the door open. They both look up at me, Danny quickly wiping his eyes.

"Trixie is heating up some lasagna," I say to Annie. "Why don't you go and fix yourself a plate and I'll finish up here?"

She smiles and nods, leaning down to kiss Danny and whisper something in his ear. As she walks past me, she squeezes my arm, and I'm yet again thankful she and Danny have such a close bond.

"You ready for a story?" I ask, picking up *Where the Wild Things Are*, which is his favorite book at the moment.

Danny shakes his head. "Are you gonna die?"

Fuck me, this kid just cuts right to the chase. I lower myself down onto the edge of his bed and wonder how the hell I'm going to tackle this.

"That's a hard question to answer, buddy," I begin. "I mean, everyone dies, and I will eventually, but if you're asking if I'm going to die soon, I'll say that I really hope not."

"What about your head?" he asks, maintaining eye contact so I can't shy away from his questions.

I sigh. I need to be honest with him. He deserves that. "The doctor told me that my brain got hurt badly in the accident, but it will get better eventually."

"So you can skate again?"

And there's the killer question. "I don't think so. The doctor said if I have another hit to the head, it could be even worse next time, and I'm not prepared to take the risk."

Wow, I guess I've just made the decision I've been agonizing over.

"What do you mean?" Danny asks innocently.

I reach out and pull Danny onto my lap. "You are the most important thing in my life, you know that, right?"

He nods and I continue.

"I want to be around for all your important moments—when you go to high school, when you go on your first date, and play your first varsity basketball game, when you go to college and get married and have babies of your own. Whatever you want for your life, I'm going to do my best to be there. But if I go on playing hockey, that might not happen, and I refuse to miss a thing."

Danny puts his little arms around my neck, and we hug for a really long time, so long that Trixie gently knocks on the door to tell me dinner is ready.

"Okay, buddy, get into bed and snuggle down." I gingerly stand up and pull his comforter over him. "I love you."

"I love you, too," he replies. "And I love you, Auntie Trixie."

"I love you too, poppet," she says in a thick, emotional voice.

I kiss Danny on the cheek and turn out his lamp, kissing Trixie as we walk arm and arm back to the kitchen.

"That was a really hard conversation to have," I say quietly before we reach the kitchen. "He asked me if

I was gonna die."

Trixie gasps and halts our progress. "What did you say?"

"I told him I would eventually, but if I carry on playing hockey, it might be sooner." I swallow hard and look her square in the eyes. "I told him I won't play hockey again. I can't miss out on what he's going to do with his life. I refuse to."

"I guess you've made your decision." She nods and pulls me into a hug.

"I can't just think about myself anymore. I have to consider what's best for him."

Trixie pulls away and looks down at her feet. "Oh."

I put my fingers under her chin and lift it so she's looking at me. "But I also have to consider what's best for us. I heard what you said to me in the hospital."

Trixie blushes. "Oh," she repeats.

"I can't risk losing you again, Sugar. I lost you once because I was pigheaded and stupid, but I know what I want. I want you and Danny and I want us to be a family. If I play hockey again, I'm putting that in jeopardy, and I won't do it."

"You want us to be a family?" she asks, her chin wobbling.

I cup her face in my hands and kiss her lips. "I can't think of anything I want more. That is if you'll have us. I love you, baby."

"Oh god, I love you so much."

Trixie throws her arms around my neck and kisses me with so much passion, she almost knocks me off my feet. I kiss her back and hold my beautiful woman to me, knowing that now I have her, I have no intention of letting her go.

26

Trixie

Who would have thought life could change so much in a few months? If I look back to the summer, I can't believe how different my life is now.

Back then all I could worry about was business, business, business, and of course, avoiding Chris Ford.

But look at my life now.

I'm standing in the huge living room of our house in the same gated community where Bugs and Cam live, decorating our wonderful Christmas tree with strings of lights.

"Keep them coming, poppet," I say as Danny continues to thread the lights through his hands as I wind them around the branches of the Norwegian spruce. "This is going to look amazing when Uncle Chris gets home."

"He said to wait until he's home so we can put the star on together," he replies as we get to the end of that string of lights.

Danny and Chris have already put up so many lights and decorations on the outside of our house that it looks like a Christmas grotto.

Our house.

Wow, I still get a little thrill when I say that.

Once Chris and I declared our love, everything happened all at once. He worked hard to recover from his head injury and then had a conversation with Blake which didn't go well. I didn't want to interfere so I stayed out of sight while he was in the apartment, but from the raised voices, I could tell Chris was firing him.

"How did it go?" I asked, coming out of the bedroom once I heard the front door slam.

"Well, I don't need an agent anymore, so I guess it's no big loss." Chris shrugged and I hugged him tight. As much of a shit as Blake became, I knew Chris had once considered him a friend.

After that tough conversation, there were plenty more to have. Chris had to take a meeting with Don, the General Manager, Coach Casey, and Bugs to let them know that he wished to be medically retired. As Chris had no representation, I asked Kristen to sit in on the meeting, and according to everyone, she killed it. She negotiated that Chris be put on the injured list for the rest of the season so he would have time to see how his recovery went. I knew he'd made up his mind to retire, but at least this way he got to have an income while he recovered.

The Whalers were amazing, and even though it was heartbreaking when Chris called all his teammates over to tell them his decision, I could see the relief on his face. These men are his brothers, his best friends, and when they played together, it formed a bond like no other. And I knew Chris was worried that their friendship wouldn't be the same once he was off the team.

But when he was cleared to workout again, he went back to the Whalers gym, and I could see the spark return to his eyes. Even though he still couldn't skate, he made it his mission to mentor the younger guys on the team, and Coach even asked if he'd consider a coaching role once he felt fully recovered.

In the meantime, we looked at moving in together. Following a visit from the social worker assigned to Danny, we thought that the apartment wasn't the best environment for an energetic, growing boy. So one day I came over to find the pair of them looking at real estate listings on the laptop, talking about which houses had a good yard for a dog and which ones had a pool.

"Come and look, Auntie Trixie," Danny called, patting the couch cushion next to him. "This one has a good room to be your office."

"My office?" I asked, slightly confused.

Chris put his arm along the back of the couch so he could stroke the back of my neck, making me all shivery. "What the kid is trying to ask is, will you move in with us?"

I didn't even have to think about it for a second. "Yes!" I cried, pulling them both into my arms, kissing their faces and feeling so happy I could burst.

So we looked at what felt like hundreds of houses, and none of them felt right. That was until Bugs told us there was a house for sale in his gated community, and I immediately said no.

"Why not, Sugar?" Chris asked as we lay in bed, gently caressing each other.

"You've seen Bugs' house. There's no way we need

somewhere that big," I whispered, feeling my nipples harden as he tweaked them.

"Bugs said it's much more modest than his place. We should at least take a look." He dipped his head and nuzzled my boobs, slipping his fingers between my legs. "And think about it. When we want to go on a hot date, we can take the kid over to their place for some free babysitting." His fingers slid inside me, and I knew it was hopeless to resist.

"Okay, okay, we'll take a look." I sighed, giving into the pleasure his fingers were giving me.

I'm glad I listened. The house was beautiful, with four bedrooms and four baths, lots of rooms downstairs so Chris and I could have our own offices, but it still had an open-floor plan living room and kitchen which gave it a homey feel. For Danny, there was a big yard with a pool and a little half basketball court where he could run off all his energy.

Chris and I made an offer before the end of the tour, and once it was accepted, we put our places on the market because I insisted on contributing the proceeds of my sale to the cost of the house. It took much persuading, but Chris eventually gave in because he knew how important it was to me that it was *our* home, together.

And now, here we are, the week before Christmas, decorating our first Christmas tree. Even though most of our rooms are still packed away in boxes, we both wanted Danny to have an amazing Christmas.

"Hey party people, I'm home," Chris calls as he slams the front door and shakes the rain off his coat. "I hope that star isn't up yet."

"No, Uncle Chris. We waited like you told us. But look at all the lights!" Danny cries, running up to Chris and hugging his legs.

"Great job, Sugar." Chris pulls me close and kisses me deeply, which he does every time he comes home.

"Stop kissing. I want to put the star up," Danny whines next to us, and we part, giggling.

"Dude, when you get older, you'll understand that kissing the woman you love is the first thing you do when you see her," Chris replies, tickling him under the arms.

"Urgh, gross. I'm never kissing girls," Danny says in a disgusted voice. "Now lift me up so I can put the star on."

"Okay, okay, bossy boots." Chris lifts Danny up so he can reach the top of the tree where he places the star, and we all stand there and look at it for a moment.

Our first Christmas as a family—and Danny's first Christmas without his mum.

As if he read my mind, Chris retrieves his bag from the counter and takes out a small box. My heart misses a beat. This is something we wanted to do for Danny, but neither of us is sure how he'll react.

"Come and sit down, buddy," he says. "We have some special ornaments to go on the tree."

Danny and I join Chris on the couch, and he opens the box he's holding, lifting the tissue paper up so we can see what's inside. Chris lifts the first ornament out, and it's a beautiful clear bauble filled with silver glitter with the word "Trixie" written on the outside in swirly calligraphy. He hands it to me and kisses me.

"You wanna hang yours on the tree?" he asks. I take

it and hang it on one of the branches at the front.

Next, Chris pulls out another clear bauble, this one filled with little hockey sticks and pucks, with Chris's name emblazoned on it.

"Oh cool," Danny gasps, looking inside the ornament, shaking it so he can see the little glittering bits inside.

"Go and hang it up."

Danny leaps up and hangs it on the branch next to mine, and I start to feel a bit emotional about what's going to happen next.

"Do I get one?" he asks, returning to the couch, looking expectantly at the box.

"You do, but there's another one we wanna show you first." Chris looks unsure as he lifts the next bauble out of the box. This one is also clear but contains little white angels and has "Momma" scribed on the glass.

Danny looks at it for the longest time and doesn't say anything, and I fear we've messed up.

"We want your momma to be part of our family, buddy," Chris finally says. "No one will ever replace her, and I know this must be hard for you, not having her around. But now, every Christmas, we can have her here with us. Is that okay?"

Danny just sniffs, nods, and smiles sadly, taking the ornament carefully from Chris and placing the bauble on a branch a little bit away from ours. Finally, he gets his own, filled with little basketballs, and he hangs that between his mum's and ours, joining us all together as a family.

Afterward, we sit for a long time, just looking at the tree, lost in our own thoughts.

Over the years, Christmas has just become a day to catch up on work. I never put up a tree or celebrated. I'd have a bottle of wine and watch *Bridget Jones' Diary*, hating myself for being such a cliché. Occasionally, I'd go to Bugs' but usually I was happy just to be alone.

But now I have a family to celebrate with—a man I've loved for most of my adult life and a child I want to protect and love for as long as I'm able.

I might just be the luckiest girl in the world.

EPILOGUE

Danny

18 months later

I've got a secret, and I feel like I might burst if I don't tell someone.

Uncle Chris told me about the surprise for Auntie Trixie, and I was so excited I couldn't wait for it to happen. But it feels like I've had to wait forever. Every time I see Auntie Trixie, I want to tell her about it, and I'm so worried I'll blurt it out that I've kind of stopped talking to her.

I think she thinks I don't like her anymore—I heard her asking Uncle Chris if she's upset me, and I feel bad that she worries about that. Hopefully when she sees the surprise today, she'll know why I've been so quiet.

"How's that tie coming along, buddy?" Uncle Chris asks, poking his head around the door to Uncle Thor's spare room.

"I don't think it's right." I sigh, turning away from

the mirror so he can see the weird knot I've made. He comes into the room, and I see that his matching tie is really neat. I huff out a breath and pull my knot apart. "I can't do it like yours."

Uncle Chris chuckles kindly and kneels in front of me, quickly tying it and turning me around so I can see what I look like in the mirror. We look cool in our matching navy blue suits, light blue shirts, and patterned ties. It was so much fun going to Uncle Chris's tailor and getting measured for my suit, although it did hurt when I got stuck with a pin.

"Perfection," he says, squeezing my shoulders and turning me back around to face him, his kind green eyes crinkled at the corners as he smiles broadly. "Now, I know I've asked you this a hundred times, but you're sure you're cool with this."

I close my eyes and think really hard, my tongue poking out the corner of my mouth—I think about how happy Uncle Chris and Auntie Trixie have been since his scary accident, how much she loves us both, and how happy I feel now we're all together in our house. I open my eyes, thinking about my momma, and my chest hurts a little bit. I still miss her every day, but I know she'd want me to be happy, and being with Uncle Chris and Auntie Trixie makes me really happy.

"I really, really want us to be a family," I say quietly, and Uncle Chris pulls me into a tight hug.

"I love you, buddy," he says in a weird voice that sounds like he's about to cry.

"I love you, too."

He lets me go and kisses the top of my head. "C'mon, we need to get to Darlene's before Trixie does, or we'll ruin the surprise."

We go with Uncle Thor and his girlfriend Lana down to the parking garage in our old building. We had to get ready here so Auntie Trixie wouldn't know what we were up to. I'm so excited to ride in Uncle Thor's great big SUV, and now that I'm a bit taller, I don't need my booster seat, so he lets me ride up front with him.

"You guys ready for this?" Uncle Thor asks in his deep loud voice.

"We sure are," Uncle Chris says from the back seat. "I still can't believe we've managed to keep it a secret from Trixie. That woman is like a bloodhound when it comes to secrets."

"I've been so scared I'll tell her that I haven't really talked to her," I admit quietly.

Uncle Thor laughs so loudly I have to cover my ears, and he reaches over and ruffles my hair.

"You've done a great job, little man," he says. "Just one more important job to do and it'll all be over."

As he says those words, I pat my pocket for what feels like the millionth time, feeling the little black velvet box is still there. I still can't believe Uncle Chris trusted me with this job, and it makes my heart beat so fast when I think about what would happen if I lost the box.

The ride to Darlene's restaurant seems to take forever, and the closer we get, the more nervous I get. I quickly look over my shoulder and notice that Uncle Chris looks really nervous too. He keeps playing with his tie. He told me Auntie Trixie could get really mad when she sees what we planned.

I really hope she likes the surprise.

"Okay everyone, the driver just texted me. They're three blocks away, so everyone get in your places." Auntie Cam claps her hands to get everyone's attention, and they slowly start to move into the back room. Darlene's son, Kenny, and I have been hanging out while the grown ups fuss about their outfits and get drinks. He's older than me, but he likes hockey and basketball too so we have a lot to talk about.

He high fives me and then walks through to the back room with the others while I stay in the front of the restaurant with Uncle Chris, who looks like he's about to barf.

I reach out and hold his hand. "It'll be okay."

He looks down at me and smiles, just as the door to the restaurant opens and Auntie Trixie walks in.

Wow, she looks like a princess. She's done her hair in a twisty knot with little curls around her face. The light blue dress we left for her to wear is lacy, and when I look up at Uncle Chris, he has that expression on his face he gets when he sees her looking extra pretty.

"Hello there," she says, smiling but looking a little confused. "How are my favorite men in the world?" She leans down to kiss my cheek, and I feel the sticky lipstick she wears leave a mark there, but I don't wipe it off like I usually do. Next she leans up and kisses Uncle Chris on the lips, and I get shy and look away.

Once they stop kissing, she asks, "So what's going on? Why is there no one else here? And why are we dressed up all fancy for Sunday lunch?"

The nervous squiggles in my stomach leap into my

throat as Uncle Chris looks at me and nods, giving me the signal to carry out our plan. Together, we drop to one knee. Uncle Chris takes one of Auntie Trixie's hands, and I take the other. She looks really confused now, but as she looks between us, I think she starts to get it.

Uncle Chris speaks first. "Beatrix Cavendish, you are the most amazing woman I've ever met. I knew it all those years ago, but I let my pride and ambition come between us."

"Chris, what the bloody hell are you doing?" she asks, her eyes getting all shiny as she looks between us for an answer.

"You'll see in a minute, Sugar." Uncle Chris laughs. "I just need to get this right."

"Okay," she breathes, squaring her shoulders. "Continue, please."

Uncle Chris takes a deep breath and carries on with the speech we've been working on for weeks. "Like I said, I think… Sorry buddy. *We* think you're the best person in the world, and we love you so much. We wanted to ask you a question."

A big fat tear rolls down Auntie Trixie's cheek, and she can only nod.

Now it's my turn to speak, so I clear my throat because my mouth is really dry. "We wanted to ask you if you'd spend forever with us." I reach into my pocket and pull out the little black velvet box and open it.

"Oh my god!" Auntie Trixie claps her hand over her mouth, and her eyes flash between me, Uncle Chris, and the rings in the box—one is big and thick for him and the other is thin and covered in little diamonds for her.

"What we're asking is, will you marry us and make this family official?" Uncle Chris takes the box from me and takes out the ring that's meant for her. "Just so you have all the information, if you say yes, we can get married right here, right now. All our closest friends are in the next room ready to celebrate with us. But if you don't want to do it now, we can do it any time, any place you want. We just want us to be a family, and I want us to spend forever together."

I do a fist pump in my head because I knew this was the part he was most nervous about. But he did a great job, and I can tell by the tears rolling down her cheeks and the big smile on her face that it's going well.

"You two are very, very naughty for springing this on me, and we'll be having words about that once we get home," she says, trying to look mad, but she can't seem to stop smiling. "But right now, I want to go in there and get married."

Uncle Chris leaps up and grabs her in a big hug, kissing her so hard I feel my cheeks heat up, but this time, I don't look away because they're both so happy.

Suddenly, a big thick arm shoots out and a hand grabs my collar, pulling me into their hug where it's warm and familiar, and I let the love wash over me. This is my family, and for the first time in a really long time, I feel completely safe.

Trixie

I'm getting married. How the bloody hell did this happen without me having a clue?

I mean, at first I'm a little bit pissed off that I had no input into my own wedding, but when I realize Cam and Mila have planned it, I know it will be spectacular.

And it is.

As we enter the back room of the restaurant, it takes my breath away—the room is full of candles in mason jars, ivory roses and blue forget-me-nots which perfectly match the color of the dresses all the women are wearing. All our closest friends fill the room, and as Otis Redding's soulful voice fills the air, Cam hands me a beautiful bouquet, and Bugs pins ivory roses to Chris and Danny's lapels.

"You ready for this, Sugar?" Chris asks, taking my hand in his.

"I've been ready for this for the last eleven years," I reply, smiling so hard my cheeks hurt.

We follow Danny toward the gorgeous flower arch at the back of the room, and I suddenly wonder who the hell is going to perform the ceremony. But as we reach it, Coach Casey steps forward, and I can't help but laugh out loud.

How completely perfect.

As Chris and I face each other and Cam quickly takes my bouquet so we can hold hands, I realize this is it—I'm finally getting the family I've always wanted.

Coach Casey begins to speak, and I look down at Danny. My little poppet has become so special to me that I couldn't feel anymore like his mum if I'd given birth to him myself. It's been a difficult time, I'm not going to lie. There have been times when he's struggled and pushed back against me and Chris, but every time we break down another piece of his barrier, we get a little bit closer.

It didn't come the conventional way and it wasn't easy, but little Beatrix Cavendish, whose mum didn't love her, has finally got the family she's always wanted.

Chris

"To the newlyweds!" Thor stands, raising his glass of champagne. "This is the weirdest wedding I've ever been to, but the love between these two is clear to see. So congratulations, Chris and Trixie! We love you guys."

Everyone stands up and raises their glasses and I look over at my wife—fucking hell, my wife of exactly thirty minutes, and I lean over and kiss her beautiful lips, feeling so blissfully happy I can't even put it into words.

This was a huge risk. Trixie could've easily dug her heels in and refused to marry me today, but I'm so pleased she appreciated the romance of the moment and went with it.

Everything went perfectly—the girls buying Trixie's dress and matching their own to the color I know she loves, the guys getting their matching suits, the keg of Trixie's favorite bitter finally arriving from the U.K., and Darlene's magnificent soul food wedding meal. I couldn't have asked for more.

Once the meal is over, the guys clear away all the tables, and we set up the room for music and dancing. Trixie and I have our first dance to Al Green, swaying and pressing our bodies together in a way that makes even a room full of hockey players blush.

We then cut the glorious three tiered red velvet and

cream cheese wedding cake, Trixie and I grabbing a handful each and spreading it all over each other's faces. Then I grab Danny and give him the same treatment, all of us laughing and licking frosting off our fingers.

"You know how much I love you, Mr. Ford?" Trixie whispers in my ear as she sits on my lap, sipping a frothy pint of bitter which leaves enticing white foam on her top lip.

I lean forward and kiss her, licking the foam from her lip. "How much, Sugar?"

"So much, I can't even believe how lucky we are," she says breathlessly, my hand sliding down her back so I can get a handful of her juicy ass.

"We're pretty fucking lucky, aren't we?" I chuckle. "I can't wait to get you on a plane to Italy so we can start our honeymoon."

Trixie leans back and smiles. "Italy? Really? What about Danny? He has school…"

"He's gonna have a little vacation with Uncle Bugs and Auntie Cam," I say. "So you and me can eat pasta and look at lots of ancient shit and fuck as loudly as we want."

Trixie giggles and buries her face in my neck. "I can't wait."

The End

Playlist

Check out my playlist, full of songs to help tell Trixie and Ford's story

https://open.spotify.com/playlist/5uzBqxB1V0fOd-tZ0zU5SlE?si=69240362f3f3499c

Coming Soon

Get ready to read the final installment for the Seattle Whalers Series!

All For Her—Seattle Whalers Book 7

Can the bad boy of ice hockey ever change his ways, or will his career go up in flames?

Benjamin Knox has always had a taste for trouble. From his tough start in life to his meteoric rise to fame as the hot-headed, young winger for the Seattle Whalers, he just can't stay out of the glare of the media or the beds of sexy puck bunnies.

Knox is on his last warning, so when he wakes up in a jail cell after another wild night, he finally has to face the wrath of his Coach and the disappointment of his teammates.

But Coach Casey has more than his wayward winger to worry about. His niece, Imogen, has come to stay in Seattle. He remembers a sweet, shy girl who was a child figure skating star.

So when a young woman he hardly recognizes

turns up at his door, angry at her parent's divorce and covered in more tattoos than most of his players, he's got no clue how to handle her.

Imogen and Knox have no idea they are on a collision course toward each other, so stand back and enjoy the fireworks.

Book Club Questions

1. What part of the book did you enjoy the most?

2. What part of the book do you think could be improved?

3. Who were your favorite characters? Which characters would you like to see get their own book?

4. Which character gave you the strongest emotional response (either good or bad)?

5. If you were making a movie of this book, who would play the lead characters (They don't have to be actors)?

6. Share a favorite quote from the book. Why did this quote stand out?

7. What did you think of the book's length? Too long or too short? Are there any parts you wanted to be developed more?

8. What songs does this book make you think of?

9. If you had a chance to ask me anything about the book or being an author, what would it be?

10. Which characters would you like to invite to a dinner party and why?

11. How realistic were the hockey scenes? Is there any way I can improve these?

12. Did you like the slow burn, or do you prefer insta-love?

Author Bio

Emily began reading romance novels in 2019 and became instantly hooked. She was inspired to write her own during the 2020 lockdown and first self-published it on Wattpad. With the help of Instagram, she gained a loyal following and eventually secured a publishing contract with 4 Horsemen Publications. Emily is a recent but enthusiastic follower of the Dallas Stars and in particular the delicious Tyler Seguin. She loves an espresso martini, dirty-talking alpha heroes with tattoos, and a lazy Sunday breakfast.

https://www.facebook.com/emily.bunney.927/

https://twitter.com/emilybunneyaut1

https://www.instagram.com/emilybunneyauthor/

http://www.emilybunney.com/

More books from Emily Bunney

All or Nothing

All the Way

All Night Long: Novella

All She Needs

Having it All

All at Once

Discover more at
4HorsemenPublications.com

10% off using HORSEMEN10